WHISPERS ON THE WIND

ISBN: 978-1-908200-54-9

Belvedere Publishing
Mirador
Wearne Lane
Langport
Somerset
TA10 9HB

WHISPERS ON THE WIND

BY

ELIZABETH REVILL

Author's Acknowledgements

This book is dedicated to all those who have supported and encouraged me, especially my husband, Andrew Spear who puts up with my constant tap, tapping away on my laptop at all hours and has helped me with many farming facts.

To Jim Moore who gave me an invaluable insight to farming practices in the thirties. It was after chatting with Jim that I had the inspiration for the character of Ernie Trubshawe.

To my lovely Dad, who has aided me with the all the Welsh names, colloquialisms and their spellings. I have been reliant on my father for lots of interesting, local, historical facts and the accuracy of the geography of the area.

To my dear friend, Hayley Raistrick-Episcopis, who has continually encouraged and willed me on to succeed.

To Lee Levinson, award winning New York Producer, who has always believed in me and after reading, Whispers on the Wind urged me to write it as a screenplay.

Michael Rolfe with whom I worked many times at the BBC and who saw the merit in this story as did Stephanie Rogers who has been an inspiring mentor and whose wise advice I always listen to.

And not least, thanks to Sarah Luddington and her team at Belvedere who made this possible. Thank you one and all and here's to the next...

...Shadows on the Moon, coming soon!

Terms and colloquialisms used in

Whispers on the Wind

ach y fe:	you dirty thing.
bach:	male term of endearment - dear.
blas:	flavoursome, tasty.
cariad:	term of endearment – my love, little one.
cawl:	Welsh stew/ broth.
chopsy:	mouthy, cheeky.
cwtsh:	snuggle, cuddle.
Duw:	God.
Dadcu:	Grandfather.
esgyrn Dafydd:	bones of David - an exclamation.
fach:	female term of endearment - dear.
fy merch 'i:	term of endearment - little lady.
iechy dwriaeth:	an exclamation.
Jawch:	an exclamation like crikey.
jib:	an unpleasant expression on the face.
Mam-gu:	Grandmother.
paid:	don't - stop it.
potch.:	soaking wet.
rhwyn dy garu du:	I love you.
tschwps:	a lot, cried the rain.
Wuss:	friend, mate, pal - local to the region not what it means today.

HENDRE

THE OLD HOME

Chapter One

A shriek of agony pierced the chill morning air.

Hendre Farm was in an isolated spot, nestled deep in the Dulais Valley; surrounded by lush green woodland and a patchwork quilt of fields; some loamy brown, others with a sprinkling of yellowing green as the first shoots of spring pierced the rich, soil carpet.

Sobs could be heard, carried on the breeze, from an upstairs-latticed window.

"Push, Miri. Push!" The midwife, Morfa Davies puffed as she mopped the sweat-laden brow of Miri Llewellyn. She comfortingly stroked those hands raw and enflamed from tugging on the twisted bed sheet strung around the head of the brass bedstead.

Miri's face was contorted with pain as she struggled to bear down when the next contraction came. She grunted and groaned with the effort, her wet hair sticking in strands to her flushed, tired face. Her exhausted body flopped back on the flock mattress where the starched white sheets, once crisp and fresh were now damp, crumpled and had rucked underneath her, exposing the mattress ticking and buttons, which embedded themselves at different points in the flesh on her back.

"You should have had this baby hours ago... no, days ago," Morfa muttered anxiously to herself.

Downstairs, Brynley Llewellyn sat at the scrubbed pine table in his shirtsleeves, the dregs of a bottle of whisky in front of him. He rubbed his bristly chin with his calloused hands as he heard the screams coming from upstairs.

Carrie, his youngest, was standing silently at his elbow, a terrible fear showing in her eyes. She eventually interrupted his anguish with her crystal clear voice, "Mam will be all right, won't she, Dad?"

Bryn turned to his daughter, her sweet open face clouded with worry and her eyes shining with tears ready to overflow and run down her cheeks.

He fondly brushed back the silky tresses of Titian hair, smiled and with more confidence than he felt, spoke in measured tones, "Of course, Carrie fach. Hasn't John gone with old Tom for Dr. Rees? As soon as they're back everything will be all right, you'll see."

Another cry split the bird song outside. Carrie snuggled into her father's strong, weather browned arms. Relieved at the warmth of human contact, the tears that had been locked inside Bryn Llewellyn rushed to escape and he gave a whimpering animal yelp as he held on tightly to his daughter.

Trixie, the soft tempered, black and white collie rose up from her slumbers in front of the kitchen range with its black leaded grate; padded off the multi-coloured rag mat across to her master and thrust her chin down on his knee attempting to offer her own form of comfort.

There was a clatter on the cobbled yard outside as the battered farm cart, driven with uncharacteristic fury by old Tom, rattled to a stop.

Old Tom, sprightly for his sixty-eight years, hopped down from the cart. With him was Dr. Ieuan Rees, half spectacles perched on the end of his nose, clutching his Gladstone, doctor's bag and young John Llewellyn, tall for his thirteen years with a dark mop of unruly hair.

Dr. Rees stooped as he crossed the threshold into the farm. Even inside he was unable to rise to his full height and his shoulders remained bent.

He opened the pine door to the stairs and without a word to anyone ran up the winding staircase and along the passage to where he was needed.

"Mam will be all right now, Dad," offered John, "You'll see."

Bryn managed a strained smile and put his hand out to his son. Father and children huddled together and waited.

Upstairs Dr. Rees had scrubbed his hands and arms with water from the freshly refilled ewer. He spoke in hushed tones to Morfa, "She's only four fingers dilated, that's the problem. The baby's travelled so far and can't get any further. If we're not careful we'll lose them both. Hold on to her tight, I'm going to have to cut."

Morfa braced herself. She forced Miri's blood stained legs apart and held on tightly for all she was worth. Dr. Rees inserted his hand almost half way up to his elbow and the perineum tore like tissue paper. Miri rent the air with a pitiful wail as she felt a scalding burning where the doctor cut.

Dr. Rees grasped the infant by the crown and pulled. There was a strange sucking sound and the baby slipped out of his mother's body onto the birth stained sheets.

"My God, what have you given birth to?" uttered the midwife before she could stop herself. Miri in one last effort pushed up on her arms and looked at the child she had brought into the world.

She saw the sweetest angel face, in spite of the mess of blood and membranes. She saw the tiny little quiff of hair that curled on his forehead just like Bryn's. She heard his lusty cry and then she looked down and saw his abdomen and passed out in sorrow and weariness.

The baby was perfect in every way, but the roof of his stomach had not formed. Everything could be seen working inside him.

"What's happened?" questioned Morfa who had never seen anything like it in fifty years of midwifery.

"I'm not sure. I don't know if the placenta was adherent and has pulled away the stomach wall or of it didn't form in the womb."

"What shall I do?"

"Clean him up, wrap him and place him with her. But, we'll have to let him go. There's nothing I can do for him. We must look to saving Miri."

Once more the doctor inserted his hand and dragged away the remaining pieces of placenta, as he did so there was a rush of dark red blood. "Quick! Towels, we need to stem the flow."

Morfa packed three together and thrust them between Miri's legs. "She's already lost a lot of blood."

"She's haemorrhaging badly," agreed Dr. Rees.

Miri's eyes flickered open. Her face white and drained,

she whispered, "Can I see him?"

Morfa placed the little one, now swathed in cloth to hide the abnormality, into Miri's arms. Miri smiled down lovingly on the innocent face that was a perfect replica of Bryn's.

"He's beautiful," she murmured.

Dr. Rees bent over her and said gently, "He won't survive, Miri. I'm sorry, there's nothing I can do to help him." A moment later he thoughtlessly added, "I've not seen anything like it before. When he's gone can I take him away for study?"

"Pickle my baby in a bottle for people to stare? No! He'll have a decent Christian burial. The hours he has left, he'll have at my breast, in my arms and will die with dignity and love," she rasped angrily.

As Miri Llewellyn spoke those words her body shuddered and she died.

Morfa stared long and hard at the doctor, "You'll not take the child. I shall see her wishes will be carried out."

Little Gerwyn Llewellyn lived for three hours. He was placed in the coffin in his mother's arms and they were buried together.

Chapter Two

Bryn Llewellyn stood on Bull Rock and gazed down the hillside of bracken and heather into the murky depths of the rushing water of the Black River. He took off his Sunday best chapel hat, and ripped off the black armband worn over the sleeve of his sombre suit and uttered a cry so terrible that it echoed through the wooded valley and beyond.

In his grief he slumped down onto the mossy stone and cried. When the tears finally stopped he looked out over the valley and the land he loved and had played in as a boy, and he remembered. He remembered the games of soldiers on the mountain track, the dares of the village boys on the bridge above the river and the stories from his childhood. He thought of the day his father's prize bull had crashed through the undergrowth and had stood here, in this same spot, surveying all around him when startled by, some said, a slithering adder, he lost his footing on the slippery surface from so much rain the night before and tumbled down the mountain side, breaking his neck, to die in the swirling, swollen river below.

Bryn thought then of following the path of that bull. His life held nothing for him without Miri. But he thought of his children and with eyes reddened from weeping, he replaced his armband and hat, and made his way back along the rutted mountain track to Hendre, the old home, where the funeral party was still in progress.

He trudged along the pot-holed lane and into the yard where the strains of melodic Welsh voices were raised in harmony. The beauteous simplicity of this act struck deep in his heart and he too joined the bass voices in a rendition of 'Guide me o'er thy great Jehovah.'

The women folk hushed, in black widows' weeds scuttled between the kitchen and parlour, bearing trays of sandwich squares, scones and Welsh cakes hot from the griddle. The women retired to the kitchen and scullery to sip their tea from Miri's best china whilst the men drank the spirits and beer in the parlour.

By nine o' clock that night, after the female members of the family had cleared away, they cajoled their men folk to gather themselves and leave. Brynley had drunk himself into a stupor and was slouched in a fireside chair, his chin on his chest, dribbling in time to his snores, soaking the front of his shirt and waistcoat wetter than a baby's bib.

John looked at his sister, whose innocent eyes stared with compassion at her drunken father, "Help me to get Dad to bed. He can sleep here by the fire if you get the clothes."

Dutifully, Carrie ran to the linen closet and took out some blankets. She fetched the pillow from her parent's room and suppressed a tear as she caught sight of her face in Mam's dressing table mirror with its silver vanity set that was always displayed with pride, next to the little used powder and puff. She took the bedding to John, strong capable John, who looked more mature than she had ever seen him.

"Fetch me Dad's pyjamas. Then you go to bed. I'll do the rest."

Carrie did as she was told. John prepared his father for bed, not knowing that Brynley would never sleep upstairs again.

After John built up the fire, he mounted the steps to bed.

Carrie called to him from the little box room that was her bedroom, "John..."

He pushed up the latch on the pine door and peered in, "What is it, cariad?"

"Please John, I don't want to sleep alone tonight. Can I come in with you? I won't wriggle, promise!"

John smiled at his little sister, "All right then, just this once. Come on."

She scrambled gratefully out of her bed and hopped on the cold linoleum.

"Make sure you settle on the left, I can't sleep on the right," he called after her as she dashed into his room.

That night as they huddled together in the feather bed, John too, was glad of his sister's company. He thought over the day. His aunts, cousins and Mam-gu fussing over them and he remembered Aunt Annie's words, "There's dark days ahead for you. You go careful now," and he wondered what she meant.

Chapter Three

Three months had passed since Miri was buried, in the family plot in St. Margaret's Cemetery, Crynant.

The children had watched in sorrow as their father became more reliant on the bottle to help him sleep. He was starting to drink in the daytime and Hendre was suffering. John was working long and hard to keep the farm going. He had missed so much schooling now that the village schoolmistress had given up asking Carrie about her brother's continued absence. He would soon be finishing in education anyway.

It was too much for old Tom who lived in the worker's cottage next to the barn. He was too aged to shoulder the responsibility of Hendre and he couldn't cope with the swinging moods of the master. Although he felt he was betraying the children's and family trust he decided to see the month out and go to live with his recently widowed sister in Cilfrew. He promised on the day he left, "I'm not deserting you. I've worked here for fifty-four years with your Dadcu, when he was alive and then your Da. I'll come and visit. If there's any real trouble you know where to find me."

It was with deep sadness that Carrie watched the old man who had been her friend; pack his belongings into his sister's cart, which trundled across the yard and down the track to the mountain road.

Brynley had his good days, of course. It wasn't all doom and gloom and although Hendre would sometimes ring with laughter, all too soon the shadows from the past would raise their spectre heads and drain the warmth from his eyes and the love from his heart.

Carrie had put herself wholeheartedly into her schooling. She wanted something better for herself than to be a farmer's wife or to be saddled with children living in a mining community, which seemed to be the only other option for girls in this part of Wales.

Carrie had other ideas, ideas above her station her Aunt Annie said. Carrie looked down on those in service, another suggestion that had been given for her future, which she had immediately quashed.

Carrie wanted to run her own farm. Hendre was big enough and when the time came she would demand her right as if she were a boy and not the youngest daughter. If not, then she would use her education, become a teacher and move away.

Carrie kept her thoughts to herself as she saw her father stagger across the doorway and slump into the rocker by the range while she kneaded dough, for bread making. He belched loudly and wiped those once strong, hard working hands across his mouth. He belched again bringing with the foul smelling air a spurt of yellow vomit that reached across the table and splashed on her hands.

"I'm sorry, fy merch 'i," he muttered seeing the look on her face. He tried to rise from the rocker and fell sideways into the hot coals burning on the range. Carrie rushed to him. The smell of burning flesh was strong in her nostrils and she struggled to pull him out of the fire.

Even in his numbed alcoholic state Brynley cried out with the searing pain in his face. He flailed his arms knocking Carrie sideways and she struck her head on the corner of the table and passed out. Brynley managed to rise. He stumbled to his feet and blundered out of the kitchen where he fell, his hair aflame and his skin blistering in red, raw bubbles where the flesh sizzled and melted in shreds.

Trixie bounded into the yard and started nuzzling her master, giving little whining yelps. She loped into the house and finding Carrie lying motionless on the slate floor ran like a champion to the fields where John was hoeing the thistles and docks from the crop of corn.

Trixie barked and danced around him, leaping up dementedly and wagging her tail fit to bust. She'd run on a few yards and then lollop back, whining and barking.

Eventually, John threw down his fork and spike and started to follow the dog. She gave a yelp of excitement and tore down the field to the gate where she stopped and waited, calling to him with little whimpering sounds deep in her throat.

"What's the matter, old girl? You want me to follow eh?" Suddenly John realised that this manic behaviour was for a reason and that there was something wrong at Hendre.

He rushed after the dog as if the furies from Hell were on his tail. He scrambled up the hillside. The pennant sandstone crumbled under his feet falling in showers through the heather. His hands were torn and bleeding after scrabbling through the scree. By the time he reached the yard his breathing was hard and heavy. He saw his father on the stones and made haste to his side.

John turned him over and recoiled in horror when he saw the hideous mess of scorched flesh that had once been the left side of Bryn's face.

He dashed into the house and found Carrie, unconscious on the flagstones, her hands still white with flour and a livid purple bruise surrounding some dried blood on a cut on her temple.

"Oh God. Oh no. Noooo!" The cry he made was reminiscent of that made by his father when he had stood on Bull Rock after seeing Miri interred. John cried out as if he'd fallen into the pits of Hell itself.

Tearing the faded, tapestry cushion, made by their Mam, from off the rocker, he gently lifted Carrie's head and rested it on the pillow for support. He grabbed the plum, fringed velveteen table cover lying over the back of the chair and used it for a blanket. Now that Carrie was looking more comfortable John looked wildly around him and his eyes lit on some outdoor clothes. He took an armful of old coats from the hallstand and ran back to his father to alleviate Bryn's discomfort.

Once his father was attended to, he spoke sharply to the dog, "Now Trix, you stay. Stay with Dad while I get help." John ran to the barn, harnessed Senator to the cart and crashed out into the yard and with the same urgency he felt when his mother was in difficulties with her labour he urged the horse on, into the village and the doctor's house.

Chapter Four

Dr. Rees treated Brynley's burns as best he could. There was no doubt that he was blinded in one eye. One side of his face was so badly burned that he would be scarred for life. A Janus face, Dr. Rees called it; one side normal, the other the face of a monster.

"You'll have to get assistance, John. Your father will need careful nursing. Carrie can't do it all. And you'll need help with the farm. It's too much for you."

"What about Dad?"

"He'll survive... If you can get the money together, he might be able to go to London, see one of the doctors there.

Some of them did wonders with the mustard gas burn cases in the war. He could have his face rebuilt. It's something to think about."

"Will he ever look normal again?"

"He'll never look the same, but they could improve his appearance somewhat... But let's get back to my first question. Whom could you call on?"

"Mam-gu wouldn't manage, but maybe one of my Aunties could."

"And the farm?"

"I would ask old Tom but it's hard work for him. I'll have to see. Anyway, it'll soon be time to buy in workers from the hostels in Neath, for the picking."

"If Tom can't come, maybe you could advertise. See what your Dad says when he's feeling a bit better. Also," Dr. Rees' tone became more serious, "More importantly, you've got to try and stop him drinking. If he doesn't cease, he'll soon be joining your mother in St. Margaret's."

Dr. Rees saw the look of consternation on John's face and said quietly, "They're harsh words, wuss. But they needed saying."

John nodded dumbly and then remembered the doctor's fee. "I'll just get the jar." The family kept a kitty for all emergencies in an old stone flour jar in the scullery. "How much do we owe you?"

"Nothing this time, John. You've had more than your fare share of troubles. Let's call this a visit of goodwill. Who knows, if I hadn't been delayed two days at Seven Sisters when your mother needed me, we may have saved her."

John acknowledged the doctor with his thanks and saw him out of the house.

Carrie came running out, her cut cleaned and dressed. Her Titian hair was a wild tangle of fire in the sunlight. She looked more grown up than someone approaching her twelfth birthday. August the fourteenth was only two weeks away. It was unlikely that they could have any proper celebrations but John knew he'd do something for her on that day. He felt a surge of love for his sister. She was someone very special.

"John?" Dr. Rees turned as he picked up the reins of the horse and looked at the two children, "It might be an idea if your family joined the village health scheme for the miners. If times get any tougher it will mean peace of mind for you all, in case of illness."

"Thanks, Doctor. I'll talk to Dad when he's feeling up to it," replied John.

Aunt Annie arrived early that evening. Her suitcase was packed to overflowing and she carried with her a large brocade bag full of wool and knitting needles with the beginnings of some shapeless voluminous garment that no doubt was intended for Uncle Dai or one of her teenage boys.

She was a plump woman with a merry, cherubic face and rosy apple cheeks. Her straight, iron-grey hair was parted in the middle and drawn back into a bun. As soon as she walked into the house she clicked her tongue disapprovingly. She set to scrubbing and cleaning; removing the dirt and dust that had accumulated in the corners, which Carrie had missed during in the last three months.

Soon the kitchen and scullery smelt of carbolic and disinfectant. The pots and pans were shining and there was a basket full of freshly washed and mangled laundry ready to put on the line early the next morning. Finally, the parlour was transformed into a sick room for Brynley. Carrie was soothingly comforted by the presence of this strict but warm natured aunt.

Annie took Miri and Brynley's bedroom for her own but when she saw the anxious look on Carrie's face she thought to ask, "Do you mind me sleeping here? I need a bit of space, a big Bessie Bunter like me."

Carrie laughed, "Course not, Aunty... It's just no one's been in here to sleep since Mam died."

"Well, I'll not disturb too much. But, I'll need to air the bed. You can come and help me, now."

Annie noticed Carrie looking at the silver vanity set that her mother had been so proud of. It was now looking dull and tarnished.

"First thing we'll do, is give these a good rub," she pointed to the brush and mirror, "Then you keep them in your room. Your mother would have wanted you to have them. They're more use to you than to an old woman like me."

Annie's face broke into a dimpled grin and when she did her whole expression radiated such warmth and love that Carrie felt a sudden rush of emotion. She ran into her aunt's cosy arms and wept. She eased the burden in her heart by letting her tears flow.

"That's right," soothed Aunty Annie. "You cwtsh up to me now. Come on. Cry the rain. You'll feel better. You've hidden your sorrow for too long. Eleven is a tender age to become a little house mother."

"Nearly twelve," sniffed Carrie, glad of the warmth of those soft arms.

"So it is. And we must do something about that. There, there. It's nothing to be ashamed of. When my dad went, God rest his soul, I cried tshwps."

For the next six weeks the house was filled with the smell of baking. Carrie and John were happy.

Aunt Annie fussed and clucked over Bryn like a broody hen, changing his dressings with never a complaint and never altering her expression.

Bryn was in extreme pain much of the time and needed

large draughts of laudanum to help him sleep and to counteract the searing hurt that throbbed without respite.

He hadn't seen his altered looks. Annie had carefully removed the mirror from the hall on Dr. Rees' advice, and replaced it with a small table and the aspidistra from the landing. It was too early to remove the dressing and the doctor was afraid of Brynley's reaction to his reflection in his unstable state. Dr. Rees knew that the removal of the bandages had to be done delicately and Brynley should be properly prepared for what he would see.

John was still trying to work the farm alone. Come September he'd buy in help from the potato pickers at the hostel in Neath, and he knew for the price of a good fry up he could rely on aid from the villagers. All the local farmers would pull together for the harvest as they did every year, each helping one another.

Brynley's flesh was slowly healing but he was coming to realise that one side of his face would always be a hideous Halloween mask whilst the other would be recognisable as Bryn. He knew this but he had not yet accepted it, nor had he seen his face without the bandages.

He buried his fears for the future in a brave show of laughter in front of the children. He made jokes about his problem judging distances, now that he only had the sight in one eye. He would encourage merriment at suppertime, with his inability to spearfish a potato and instead spurting the seeds of a stabbed tomato across his plate.

In secret, he drank. He hid it well during the day but by the time the sun had set and the children were in bed Brynley was left with his own brooding thoughts. He would become morose and uncommunicative. Annie searched to discover his secret hoard but all she ever found were empty bottles.

Annie tried to talk to him when the children were asleep or out of the house, "You ought to be ashamed of yourself, Brynley Llewellyn! Yes, you've lost Miri. But it's the children you should be thinking of now. They need their father. They need you, not some drunken sot with his lips stuck round a bottle drinking himself into the grave."

Bryn would bury his face in his hands and cry like a baby, promising to change. But his hand continued to tremble and he continued to drink.

Chapter Five

Two days before Carrie's birthday Annie insisted that John should go across to Bronallt where Megan Thomas, Carrie's best friend, lived and invite her to the birthday tea.

John had been planning his own surprise for his sister. Whilst he watched the sheep at Maes-yr-onnen, the meadow of the ash tree; with his whittling knife, he had carved a small, wooden man that swung on a trapeze. Tucked away on a corner of a bench in his workshop stood the gaily-coloured little chap just waiting for a coat of varnish to add the finishing touch.

Annie had been busy with her needle. She had taken one of Miri's dresses, of rich green silk and had cut it down. With the threads from the sewing box she pinned, tucked and sewed, decorating the front with smocking and pretty jasmine rose buds. It would perfectly complement Carrie's fiery Titian hair.

Brynley roused himself sufficiently to ask Annie to bring Miri's wooden and ivory jewellery box from the bedroom. He forced himself to look through the few trinkets and precious items that Miri had loved and worn. He selected a delicate pink cameo locket on a gold chain. The cameo opened to reveal pictures of Mam-gu and Dadcu Lloyd, Miri's parents, who were both long gone. His shaking hands removed the pictures. And with Annie's help, he replaced the empty spaces with a miniature picture of Miri and a cutting of her chestnut red hair taken from a plait she'd had cut in her teens, now residing in tissue paper in the drawer under her wardrobe. Wiping a tear from his eye he wrapped the gift and gave it to Annie to keep safely until Carrie's special day.

Annie had made a rich fruit cake covered it with a thick coating of almond paste and frosty white icing. The lettering of Carrie's name and age had been done with care and love. It waited in the cool of the pantry under a fine gauze umbrella. Everything was set for a happy day. Even Trixie was to wear a brightly coloured satin bow on her collar.

"You can't catch me," squealed Carrie as she ran up the path putting as much distance as she could between herself and her best friend, Megan Thomas.

The bubble of laughter burst through the door and into the kitchen where Annie was buttering the bread. Bryn, still with the bandages swathing his face was sitting in the rocker, gazing into the coals of the fire as if they held some secret that would be yielded up to him if he stared at them for long enough. Trixie lifted her head that had been resting on Bryn's thigh and turned her soft brown eyes on the girls.

"Afternoon, Mr. Llewellyn," giggled Megan.

Brynley stirred from the pictures in the fire and managed a half smile for Megan Thomas with her freckled face and hair the colour of conkers.

"Hello, Megan. Nice to see you. How's your Mam?"

"Fine thank you, sir."

"Keeping herself busy with her horses, I'll be bound?"

"Cobalt's in foal, due any time now. Mam thinks that with the Arab sire she may have a winner, given a few years."

"Going into breeding in a big way now is she?"

"Not in a big way. Just a sideline really. Dada says it keeps her out of his hair so he's building her a new stable block and she's got some bigwig coming down from London to have a look at Rainfall a week Saturday. After her win on the flat at Chester he may be interested in buying her."

"Well, I wish her well. Remember me to her, won't you?" Brynley continued to no one in particular, "At school together we were. Chopsy little madam then. Proper tomboy. Could fight as well as any of the boys. Many's the time she'd send Raymond Griffiths home crying, and look at him now. No one would dare to part his hair on the wrong side."

Carrie smiled and gestured Megan to sit, then settled herself at her father's feet. It wasn't often Bryn talked of the past but when he did, she loved to listen. The stories, the fun he'd had. He always made his life sound more interesting than any book she'd ever read. One day, she promised herself, she would write it all down, everything she'd been told.

Brynley talked on and the warmth that emanated from him embraced the trio in the kitchen. They listened with obvious enjoyment to tales of his boyhood scrapes and courting days.

"I remember once when I was your age and we were on a Sunday school outing at Pendine Sands, Pembrokeshire near Carmarthen, it was. And they had horses on the beach. Now your Mam," he nodded at Megan, "Could out ride any farmer's boy even then. Me? I was never that good. Didn't get on so well with the creatures, but I was always willing to have a go. I was better at swimming and climbing. Anyway, they had horses on the sands and Nancy Meredith, as she was then, issued a challenge that she'd race any one of us on horseback along the sands around a big rock at the far end of the beach and back. Egged on by all the boys and acting braver than I felt, I took up her offer. She picked a perky little grey and I had a fine roan. We mounted, kicked our heels and were away like grease lightning. Neck and neck we were; stride for stride; I really thought I might beat her when the man with the horses gave a shrill whistle. The horses stopped dead in their tracks, turned round and galloped back to their master. Your mother stayed elegantly in place like a top class jockey. Me? I slid round the under the horse's neck and was hanging on for dear life only to tumble down on the sand and into a freshly laid dung pile as the horse catapulted me off when he stopped. Oh yes, your mother had the last laugh that day."

Everyone chuckled together but the mood was broken by the arrival of John, in from the fields, grubby and hot.

Annie ordered him to wash and shooed the girls into the sitting room where the table was laid for tea with ginger pop and dandelion wine. There on the settee were Carrie's gifts waiting to be unwrapped.

Carrie was as excited as if she had never had a birthday before. Everyone watched as she opened her presents. So thrilled was she with her dress that she had to try it on immediately. She twirled and swirled around the room. Bryn said she looked like a little princess. John had never seen his sister more beautiful. He felt an overwhelming feeling of pride grow in his heart as he watched her dance.

Carrie loved the little wooden toy John had made her and giggled infectiously as the figure swung on his trapeze.

When she opened her father's present, no words would come. She hugged him tightly and Bryn with quiet dignity fastened the cameo around her neck.

"It's yours now, cariad, just as Mam would have wanted."

That evening Hendre was a happy home, full of chatter and laughter. Brynley didn't take a drink and Annie thought that maybe at last, her brother had seen sense that he was going to be a proper father to the children. She hoped that she would soon be getting on with her own life and back to her own family. But it was not to be.

Chapter Six

Seven days had passed since Carrie's birthday and Brynley had returned to his drinking although he was trying to keep it well hidden by making an effort to stay sober during the day.

Dr. Rees had been attempting to prepare Bryn for what he would see once the bandages were removed. The family were to expect the doctor at ten o' clock that morning.

Clutching the mahogany hand mirror from the hallstand, Bryn sat silently in the rocker in the kitchen, from eight o'clock, waiting.

Dr. Rees' arrival was heralded by the barking of Trixie who leapt and danced in the yard outside. Annie dried her dimpled hands and went to greet him. Bryn sat in the still rocker, mirror in his hand.

John had gone out to the fields after taking Carrie over to Megan's where she was to spend the day.

Dr. Rees stooped as he stepped into the kitchen. "Well Bryn, today's the day. Remember what I said. Although the flesh has healed it will be tender for some time. The scar tissue will look and feel strange to the touch. That side of your face will not be pleasant to look on, but if you have the money you can get expert treatment in London to improve your appearance."

Bryn grunted in the chair, "I know what you're saying, Doctor. I'm prepared. Let me see what I have to live with."

Annie, who had changed the dressings, knew what to expect. She moved behind the rocker and rested her hands on Bryn's shoulder, "Courage, Brynley. You'll not like what you'll see."

Dr. Rees carefully removed the bandages, gauze and lint covering the left side of Bryn's face. As the last piece came away Bryn slowly raised the mirror.

He stared at his reflection with his one good eye for what seemed an eternity. No one spoke. Finally, Brynley broke the silence, "Well, the village won't be stuck for casting the ogre in the Christmas play this year," and one half of his face smiled whilst the other rippled in a painful, angry grimace.

Dr. Rees cleared his throat uncomfortably. "I'll leave some more laudanum to aid sleep and ease the pain. And try not to drink too much. I know the whisky bottle calls but it doesn't help you know."

Bryn hunched his shoulders defensively, "I know, but after Miri... well, I went to pieces. I'm on the mend now. Annie'll see to it I'm kept on the straight and narrow."

"Annie won't always be with you. She has her own home and family to go to. You're going to have to help yourself."

The doctor replaced his hat and started for the door. Brynley didn't move.

"I'll send my account."

"No need. I'll settle it now. Annie the jar."

Annie respectfully obliged. The money passed hands and Dr. Rees left.

Brynley rose. The mirror he'd been holding crashed to the floor shattering on impact into numerous glass shards. The rocker, now empty, swung crazily on the slate.

"I can't let the children see me this way," said Bryn quietly.

"They'll get used to it," soothed Annie.

"NO!" His voice was sharp and strong. "I'm going to the workshop. I'll make a covering for this side of my face. I don't want my own kin to be sickened as I am sickened when I see this... this Janus face."

Annie didn't stop him. Maybe it was for the best. Maybe he'd start looking after the farm again.

She busied herself, clearing the broken glass and glanced at the calendar, August twenty-first. Was it really seven weeks she'd been living at Hendre? Dai had been patient but she knew it would soon be time to go. She had her own life to live and with harvest time nearly upon them she would be needed on her own farm. Annie decided that she would stay another week. If there were any more problems her sister Netta could take her turn. But in her heart she hoped that wouldn't be necessary. Netta could be hard and although Annie didn't know it she could be cruel too.

Evening came. John had returned from the fields. He'd washed and changed and taken the cart over to Bronallt to collect Carrie. Annie had the meal prepared and the smell of game pie filled the kitchen. She hadn't seen Brynley since he'd disappeared into the workshop.

As the grandfather clock in the hall was striking seven, the door to the kitchen swung open and filled with Bryn's bulk. He stood there a moment blocking the evening sun, his form casting shadows in the room. His face resembled that of an actor from a Greek tragedy. He was wearing a half mask whittled and moulded to cover the offending side of his face. It was constructed from a light soft wood that had been fashioned so that the livid, scarred flesh was hidden and only revealed his good side.

Annie gasped as she stared at her brother. The mask cut his brow in half, travelled down his nose hiding the fire nibbled nostrils, left his mouth clear and resumed its path down his chin fitting snugly into his jaw bone.

"Well, what do you think?" he asked.

Annie went to her brother and held him. "Your children love you anyway, but if it makes you feel better then it's worth it."

"At least I won't frighten the visitors."

"That's true," Annie laughed.

"What's for supper? I'm starved," Bryn growled.

Annie's dimpled face grinned; he was starting to sound like his old self again. Maybe all would be well after all.

The family sat around the supper table that night and there was a lightness in the air that hadn't been present since Carrie's birthday.

Discussion was animated and Bryn agreed that it would be worth joining the village health scheme as Dr. Rees had suggested. They would make enquiries the next day; then proceed to Neath to book in workers for the potato picking. The crop was ready early this year.

It was in hushed tones that Brynley next spoke as he

made a vow, "Fetch me the Bible, cariad." Carrie brought in the heavy tome with its gold clasps and Brynley laid his hand on it and swore, "By all that's Holy I'll not drink like I have, no strong spirits. Hendre and you... You are what's important."

With love in their hearts the Llewellyn family rested more easily in their beds that night.

Chapter Seven

Carrie stood at the window and watched the dawn breaking. The sky flooded with dusty pink fire that bled over the hills, washing the clouds red as the slowly rising sun awakened the life in the land. The first whistle of the blackbird would soon be echoed by the sparrows, thrushes, linnets and larks.

She loved this time of the morning when the lush green grass glistened with dew and she longed to run barefoot in the meadow with the wind in her hair and freedom in her heart.

Silently, she crept from her room, still in her calico nightgown; stealthily crossed the landing and tiptoed down the stairs.

She inched through the hall and passed the open door of the parlour where Brynley was asleep and snoring. His head was buried in the pillow and his cosmetic mask was dangling over the back of the chair. She was tempted to sneak in, to look and see what had been so carefully hidden from her but the morning was calling to her.

Gently she turned the brass knob on the door to the kitchen where Trixie lifted her eyes to see which family member was up so early and the dog whined softly in her throat.

Carrie moved silently through the kitchen like the shadow of a thief, into the scullery and glasshouse. She skipped out into the yard where she ran ooch ouching on the stones followed closely by Trixie.

She hurried down the path to the meadow whilst the sun was still rising and the moon was still visible. She kicked up her heels and ran barefoot through the moist grass.

She felt the springy wetness wriggle up between her toes. The blades tickled and licked her feet. It was sheer ecstasy. Dog and girl gambolled and danced until her laughter joined the bird song growing around her.

Finally, when the sun had risen to colour the meadow

with rays of golden light and its beauteous glory had eclipsed the moon from the sky Carrie stifled a yawn and sped back to the farm, Trixie at her heels.

She quietly retraced her steps and flopped on top of the bed; her feet soiled from the earth and her nightdress grass stained. She tossed her whirlwind of curls, and giggled before snuggling back under the covers to sleep until the clatter of cups could be heard downstairs.

Hendre was alive that morning, bursting with chatter and song. Annie's soprano voice rang out above the noise of the washing up. Brynley was whistling as he harnessed Senator to the cart and John, more confident than ever, was talking to his father, man to man. Carrie? She sat and giggled deliciously, happy that the heart of Hendre pulsed once more.

The Llewellyn family gathered themselves together and piled in the cart leaving Trixie to watch over the home. Once they had left the boundaries of Hendre, it was seven miles to the village.

Brynley stopped off at Gareth Williams' cottage. The family waited in the cart. Senator shifted his feet as he waited, eager to be off, gently rocking the wagon.

A quarter of an hour later Brynley emerged shaking Gareth warmly by the hand. "It's all arranged then. Once a month I'll pay my dues. A small price to pay for peace of mind. John can collect the papers when he's through this way again."

The Llewellyns had joined the village miners' health scheme.

The cart was soon trundling on its way through the cobbled streets, past the butchers and the dairy. Senator stopped outside the grocery store, and it was Annie's turn to take charge. She consulted her list and John and Brynley loaded the cart with an assortment of boxes, packets and tins. Carrie came out sucking a mint, holding a ha'peth worth of sweets, the bag full to the brim.

"Right, we'll be on our way. Call on Dai at T'yn-y-wyn and arrange a day for the reaping. Then off to Neath to book our pickers."

The cart rolled on out of the village of Crynant and

stopped at the outlying farms on route to his sister's farm known as T'yn-y-wyn where Brynley gathered promises of help from dawn to night at Hendre for Wednesday.

At T'yn-y-wyn Annie was greeted rapturously by Dai who could hardly contain his delight and emotion at seeing Annie. She dropped off a box of her things and said that they could expect her home by the weekend.

Dai fairly waltzed round the yard with her. The two brothers-in-law hugged and they ate a hearty lunch together before the Llewellyns continued on their way to Neath and the hostels.

They arrived at Castle Street and Brynley stepped down, avoiding the curious looks of passers-by, who stared at his partially masked face. He entered the hostel through the heavy oak door and into the entrance hall where Virgil Hughes sat with his register.

"Afternoon, Virgil."

"Hello, boyo. What's happened to you?"

"Oh, I had a bit of an accident with the fire. Not a pretty sight, best kept covered."

"Right you are." He didn't pry further.

"I'll be wanting some help at Hendre, two weeks Saturday. Four pickers, the work could take two days. The cart will pick them up at seven."

"Fine, leave it to me." Virgil made a note in his book Brynley nodded and left.

"Well, girls," said Brynley as he mounted the cart, "I'll let you have two hours to go round the town. I've other business to attend to. John and I will meet you here at four-thirty."

Annie and Carrie beamed at each other. Carrie put her hand in Annie's and they headed straight for the market.

Chapter Eight

"Duw Duw, I think we've walked our feet off," laughed Annie as they returned to the wagon to meet John and Brynley. "They're singing a song..."

"All out of tune," finished Carrie who knew her Aunt's expressions better than anyone.

"Well, what have you been up to then?" asked Brynley as the cart's wheels began to turn.

"We went round the market. I bought some cloth, lace and other bits and bobs."

"She's going to make me a dress for best," added Carrie.

"Well, there were some bargains on the draper's stall."

"And we had faggots and peas after. Then we walked round the town. Some of the shops were real posh. Aunty Annie tried to buy a new hat but we were laughing so much we had to leave."

"They would have thrown us out else. Everything I put on my head, Carrie giggled. She wouldn't stop, and then she set me off. Face like a fiddle the assistant had. You should have seen her jib."

"So you didn't get a hat?"

"No, no hat."

"She tried on one and it looked just like a pork pie."

"Like a pig had sat on it, you said."

"Oh yes," chortled Carrie, "There was this one, that looked as if a lady in a carriage should be wearing it and waving at the crowds. It had this big feather, except when Aunty turned to show me, the end of the feather went straight up my nose. I started laughing and the frowsty old assistant whisked it away thinking we were going to damage it." Carrie started to chuckle, "Anyone would think it was all me in that shop, but if you'd have seen the faces Aunty pulled when she was trying them on, you'd have roared."

"Yes, well perhaps I'm a little guilty as well," agreed Annie. She turned to her brother, "Did you complete your business?"

"I've put an advertisement in the paper for a farm worker. Hendre's too much for me on my own and I can't expect John to shoulder all the responsibility."

"I don't mind, Dad."

"Nevertheless, we do need help. We'll see what replies we get and pick the best. Maybe you'll be able to get back to some of your schooling next term."

And so the chatter continued until they reached Hendre.

Wednesday was the day for reaping. All the local farmers would be turning up at the farm, just as Brynley and John would return the favour when they were summoned.

Carrie was woken by a loud squealing from the glasshouse downstairs. Curiously, she trotted down the stairs to see what was making the commotion.

A huge castrated boar was being dragged up the steps with its feet tied. It was screaming with fright, as if it knew what was to come.

Carrie turned and ran back up the stairs into her room. She covered her ears with the pillow and started to sing at the top of her voice to drown out the creature's terrified cries.

Carrie loved life on the farm, but this was one thing she couldn't reconcile herself to. She knew if she had any hope of running part of the farm herself one day, she would have to get used to it. But, she felt in her heart that there must be some other, more humane way of killing an animal than by cutting its throat.

Carrie's voice trembled as she sang. She sang for the pig, she sang for herself and a stray tear escaped her eye, which she brushed away with annoyance.

There was a knock on her door and John walked in. He knew his sister well enough. "It's over now, cariad. You can come down. We'll need help with the salting."

"I'm sorry, John. I feel so sorry for the beast. I hate killing any animal. Even though it's to feed us with."

John put his arms around his young sister and felt a bond of love so strong it unnerved him. "Come, Carrie. Let's go down. There's the pork to cure and potatoes to peel. Annie'll be needing your help."

The farmers arrived in their droves. By ten o' clock there were eighteen extra pairs of hands ready to work in the fields. The excited chatter outside was infectious. The spirit to toil was bubbling to begin. The motley collection traipsed their way up to the corn fields where the reaping would start, followed by sheafing and stacking until ten o' clock that night with nothing in between but water and a few hunks of bread.

Carrie and Annie busied themselves. After taking what they needed, the hog was cut into strips salted and stored in a chest at the back of the barn. Scrubbed trestle tables were put in the yard and long wooden benches taken from the barn and dusted off. The placings were set for twenty-four. The cider barrels were left in the shade; an array of mugs and tankards lay out alongside.

There was a mountain of potatoes to peel, to cut into chunks and left to soak in lightly salted water.

Carrie went off with a basket into the meadow to gather mushrooms, big, flat, field mushrooms with delicate pinky beige gills. Trixie accompanied her, dashing around in circles having what Carrie called, 'a mad half hour'.

Carrie returned to find her Aunt in floods of tears. "Whatever's the matter?" she asked anxiously.

Annie hid the knife she'd been using to strip and cut the onions. She moved away from the sink and pretended to hide her face in her pinny.

"Aunty Annie?"

"No, it's too terrible. Too terrible."

"What?"

"Your father told me... he said..." she stuttered, "That I've got to buy the hat with the feather in Neath," and then she roared with laughter at the surprised look on Carrie's face. "There, there, Carrie fach. Peeling onions I was," and she laughed again, this time Carrie joined in with her.

At ten that evening the workers returned. Tired and hungry, their sweat stained faces smeared with dirt. They were greeted by the smell of bacon, sausages, and spit roasted pork. Chunks of fried potatoes were served up in pans with onions golden and gleaming and tasty fried mushrooms, all washed down with mugs of cool cider.

There was quiet while they filled their bellies. All that could be heard was the scraping of the knives and forks on the enamel plates. The men tore into the hunks of bread mopping up the juices from the meat. There was nothing like a good feed after a hard day's work. Food seemed to have more blas then.

When Annie appeared carrying five plates of hot apple and blackberry tart with cream fresh from the dairy, it was no surprise. Every farm had an orchard and it was almost always the guaranteed dessert.

But then, the chatter began, the laughter, the stories with everything seeming funnier because of their weariness and cider consumption. Finally, fed and contented they collected themselves together and started back to their homes; fare-well pleasantries were exchanged until the next gathering, which was to be at Bronallt that Friday.

Annie and Carrie set to clearing away the debris. Trix was in for a feast with the bones. There was little else left.

Brynley filled a jug with water from the big, black kettle boiling on the range. He took it into the parlour to wash in privacy. The dust from the fields had settled under his mask, irritating and burning his tender flesh.

He stripped himself down and removed the grime from his arms and torso. The water clouded with the dirt and he went to empty the bowl outside, then returned to the kitchen to refill his jug. As he turned from the range with the huge iron kettle in his hand, Carrie stepped into the kitchen.

The scream was terrible to hear, but not more terrible than the cold grip of shame and fear that overflowed in Bryn Llewellyn's heart.

The sight of Carrie's horror stricken expression would torment him at night and live with him through all his days. Her look of revulsion at the hideous, lumpy, purple flesh and the gaping socket housing a creamy opaque ball of aqueous jelly, destroyed in him that noble spark of manhood by which he judged all things. That judgement was now sullied.

Too late Carrie realised what she had done. Her tiredness had not prepared her for a shock such as this and she had reacted without thinking.

She ran to her father, apologising and hugging him. She wept, soaking his stomach and chest with her tears.

Annie tried hard to soothe them both and although Bryn said it was all right, and that he understood; Annie saw the look of pain in his good eye. She knew the damage had been done, damage that might never heal.

Chapter Nine

The house was still and silent except for the ponderous tick of the grandfather clock that sliced time away with every swing of its pendulum. It chimed out the hour, one... two... three... Carrie stole from her bed. She hopped on the cold oilcloth until she reached the fluffy sheepskin rug in front of the window. She drew back her patchwork curtains and looked out on the yard that shone silver in the moonlight, and to the fields beyond.

There was something mysterious about the moonbeams bathing everything in its frosty, satin sheen. The leaves of the pear tree that stood by the gate shimmered like glass in the moon's icy glow.

An owl swooped low over the barn and flew across to the woods on its nightly hunt. A grasshopper chirruped frenziedly in the grass outside calling for a mate to come and dance.

Carrie turned and looked around her room where the ribbons of moonlight filtered in. Everything was so different at night. The sock on the floor became a deadly snake; the coat on the hook a devilish intruder and problems in the darkest hours loomed larger and more insurmountable.

Carrie knew she had upset her father. She hadn't meant to. It was the shock of seeing him like that, without warning. But his face...

Carrie shuddered with disgust as she thought of her father's once handsome face, now disfigured, and she felt alone, so alone.

With hardly a sound she moved to her door and lifted the latch. She stepped lightly along the passage to her brother's room, opened the door, and tiptoed in.

She stood for what seemed an eternity, watching him sleep. His breathing was deep and even; his lips turned up in a half smile. She wondered what he was dreaming about.

She crept closer to the side of his bed. John stirred in his slumbers and turned onto his side. Something nudged him to consciousness, his eyelids fluttered open and his gaze came to rest on Carrie's sweet face. He pushed himself up on one elbow, slowly coming to, "What's the matter, cariad?"

"Oh, John, I can't sleep. I keep thinking about what I did to Dada. I feel terrible. My head's going round and round. I don't think he'll ever forgive me."

John pushed back the blankets and invited her into his bed. She scrambled in gratefully and snuggled down under the warm covers. John gently stroked her fragrant, silky hair and safe in John's caress she fell into a longed for sleep.

John remained awake for a while, his rest disturbed. He hoped Carrie's fears were unfounded but he suspected this inner strength his father had discovered wasn't permanent.

On the surface things continued to improve at Hendre. Bryn appeared to observe his oath and have his drinking under control although there were occasional lapses, usually on reaping days when he allowed himself nothing stronger than a few draughts of cider but no one took him to task for that.

The discomfort between father and daughter following the sighting of Bryn's injuries was gradually diminishing.

Friday came. Brynley and John set off for Bronallt to help in the harvesting and partake in the fry up that would follow, prepared by Nancy Thomas.

Carrie remained at Hendre with Annie and helped her to pack her belongings. She did this reluctantly and with sorrow. She had grown close to Annie who had mothered and comforted her since Bryn's accident.

"Now, don't worry, gal. Everything will be all right. I have to go home. Dai and the boys need me. If things go wrong Netta will come and stay."

"I don't want Aunty Netta. I want you."

"Netta's not that bad. She seems hard on the surface but her heart's in the right place. But if it gets too tough you can always come to stay with me at T'yn-y-wyn."

"Oh, Aunty Annie! I don't want you to go," Carrie cried, rushing into those plump warm arms.

"I shall miss you too, cariad, you know that. Besides if there's any real need, I'll be back."

John and Bryn returned late that night in sweat toiled shirts and with dirt warm hands.

Bryn's oath not to touch strong drink was intact, but in the company of his fellow workers and friends this was one occasion that he had allowed himself to become merry on cider. John didn't mind. It seemed a just reward for all their hard work. Bryn sang out as he stepped into the glasshouse, through the scullery and into the kitchen.

Annie was sitting in the rocker, needles clacking away at some amorphic garment destined for her husband. She looked up at her brother. "Not so loud! You'll wake Carrie. She's not long gone to bed."

Brynley put his fingers to his lips and giggled tipsily, "Ssh - mustn't wake the baby." He weaved his way to the fireside chair and started to take off his boots, breaking out into laughter when he had difficulty and got into a muddle with the laces.

"You'll need a good wash. I've left the kettle, and a pan of water boiling on the range. It should be enough to wash away the day's grime."

"Thank you, Aunty Annie," smiled John.

"I've also left a bit of supper in case you wanted it."

"No thanks, not for me. I'm full with the fry up."

"And I'm full from the cider," added Bryn.

"You need a bit of bread to soak up the liquor. Come on, you'll have less of a head in the morning if you nibble something now."

"Stop fussing woman. You're worse than Mam."

"Dad!"

"Oh all right - all right. Anything for a bit of peace."

Bryn gave a lopsided grin, flopped back in his chair, his mask askew. His head began to nod and he started to snore.

"We'll have no more sense from him tonight. Go on, John, you have a wash and get to bed. I'll see to Bryn."

John picked up the steaming kettle from the range to fill his basin, stopped and turned, "Aunty Annie? Do you have to go?"

"Oh, John bach; I'd like to stay, but I'm needed at home.

It should be better for you now at Hendre but if it isn't, you know where to find me."

"Thanks."

"No thanks needed. I'll come and visit."

"Please."

Annie sighed and put down her knitting. She grunted as she pulled herself out of the rocker. She took the kettle from his hand and replaced it on the range; then she wrapped her ample arms around him. He didn't pull away, but nestled into her motherly warmth.

"I miss Mam something terrible," John confessed in the shelter of Annie's soothing embrace.

"Course you do, John bach."

"Will it ever get any better?"

"The loss you feel will always be there, but it will get easier, you'll see."

"I still think sometimes that Mam's there. I forget she's gone, then I remember and it hurts twice as bad."

"I know. I know. Now you get washed and into bed."

John lightly brushed his lips against Annie's apple dumpling cheek and taking the kettle to fill his bowl he moved towards the stairs.

"I'll bring this down when I've finished. Good night."

"Good night, John bach. Sleep well."

John mounted the twisting stairs to his room whilst Annie attended to Bryn.

Bleary eyed and dehydrated from an excess of cider the night before, Bryn, bristly chinned, attacked his breakfast with surprising vigour. Annie poured him a second cup of tea.

"Well, Bryn bach. I shall be off after lunch. Are you sure you can cope? I can always send for Netta."

"No, no. It's time we stood on our own feet. We'll manage. I'm better now, or at least as good as I'll ever be. We'll be fine."

Bryn stopped chasing the bread around his plate and looked at his sister. "And thank you. You've brought laughter and warmth back to Hendre. I'll not forget it, nor will the children."

Annie's eyes filled with tears and she choked back the lump that was rising in her throat. It wasn't often that Bryn gave thanks for anything.

Bryn put down his knife and fork and covered his sister's dimpled fist with his hands, "Thank you, fy merch 'i."

Annie pulled back her hand and removed his egg stained plate from in front of him muttering gruffly, "Never mind that old nonsense. It's family duty." But, secretly she was pleased and Bryn knew that.

At three-thirty that afternoon, Dai's cart rattled into the yard. Trixie disorientated by the hustle and bustle of goods being bundled into the cart retreated to her favourite spot by the water butt at the side of the house opposite the pigsties where she went into a frenzy of barking.

All activity stopped as a man dusty from tramping the roads turned into the yard.

He was tall, powerfully built and dressed all in black like a preacher, carrying a sleeping roll and a black Gladstone bag. He wore a hat with a broad brim that shadowed his eyes. His skin was tanned gypsy brown.

He stopped at the cart and smiled, his pearly white teeth glinting like a film star in the sunlight.

"Excuse me. I'm looking for Brynley Llewellyn. Is this Hendre?"

Annie turned from the cart and looked deep into the stranger's eyes. "This is Hendre. Brynley's my brother. Can I help?"

"I don't know. I've come in answer to the advert that appeared in the Neath paper."

Annie paused slightly then Dai spoke, "Here's Brynley now."

The newcomer turned and faced the semi-masked man emerging from the farmhouse with Annie's brocade knitting bag.

"That's the last of it now, Annie fach. All gone..." He stopped mid sentence when he saw the visitor in the yard.

"Brynley Llewellyn?"

"Yes?"

"Jacky Ebron. I've come about the job."

"Come in, come in. We'll discuss it in a minute. Carrie!" He shouted to his young daughter to usher the man into the house.

Annie frowned as she saw the man's expression when his eyes lit on Carrie. She watched him as he followed her indoors and a feeling of cold disquiet crept through her.

Chapter Ten

Jacky Ebron proved to be a quick and willing worker. He had a calm, easy manner and a keen sense of humour that made the children warm to him.

After a day's work in the fields Jacky would take a drink, which a reformed Bryn would staunchly refuse, and they would have a game of cards. Sometimes the children would play too; "Top of the Bus" was their favourite.

Squeals of delight would accompany the hands that Carrie won, subtly aided by Jacky. He enjoyed hearing her laugh and would watch her face closely as if bewitched by her impish expression.

It was when the evening shadows lengthened into night that Carrie's tremulous fears returned. More and more frequently she would seek the comfort and safety of her brother's bed and John would tolerate the intrusion even though he had to suffer the covers being kicked off and her constant fidgeting throughout the night. The bond between brother and sister was growing stronger with the passing of each day.

Jacky took over old Tom's cottage and there he discovered the remnants of Bryn's secret hoard of liquor. The cottage had been locked since old Tom had left and no one had thought to look there for the stash. Bryn let Jacky keep the remaining bottles of spirits that had been surreptitiously transported in from the village.

Bryn swore that there was no way he was walking the way of 'Father Booze' again, and even a cider at a farm fry up, for him, was to be outlawed.

Jacky observed Bryn's reactions when drink was present. He noticed the rolling of the eyes, the quickening of breath and he stored the facts away for the time when he could use them.

It was surprising for a man, but Jacky Ebron had the cottage looking as spic and span as any house proud woman.

His possessions grew. The dwelling was fast becoming a real home.

Jacky and Bryn spent more and more time together and the farm flourished in spite of the difficult times.

The general strike in support of the mineworkers had collapsed two years previously in May nineteen twenty-six but its effects had been far reaching extending into the years that followed. The golden era of the twenties boom was fast fading showing it had been a period of false hope and security. But there were pluses. All women over the age of twenty-one had been given the right to vote, alongside the men. This was something that Carrie cheered loudly in her heart.

A year passed. Jacky was now almost a part of the family and had replaced old Tom in the affections of Carrie. John who originally accepted Jacky as whole-heartedly as Carrie was beginning to have reservations. He tried to push these to the back of his mind when Jacky's wit and charm came to the fore. But, he kept his thoughts to himself and said nothing.

There was a maggot of wriggling doubt that nibbled away at his conscious mind. John felt guilty that he should have such misgivings about someone as hard working and charming as Jacky. This questioning seed had been planted by Annie who had warned John several times not to put his complete trust in the man. He, too, had seen the way Jacky looked at Carrie and he had felt a tingling twinge of jealousy.

Jacky sat, one evening, around the old oak table and talked about the disaster that had beset his family and forced him to walk from Merthyr to Neath in search of work. He'd been prepared to keep right on travelling, right on, even to London if need be, to add his voice to the growing chorus of complaints, caused by the hardship unemployment had brought. Thankfully, he had gained employment at Hendre and he promised to continue working loyally for Bryn to safeguard his job.

Carrie listened soulfully, her enormous wide eyes further widening in sympathy as he told his story. This captive audience did not go unnoticed by Jacky and he played it, as a seasoned professional would perform the climax of a play. Carrie was initially drawn to this man who shared his secrets and his life history.

Jacky bided his time. He allowed his eyes to run over her budding body. Time enough he told himself. Time enough.

Following the Wall Street Crash in America in the October of nineteen twenty-nine, the depression was to affect every country that had received economic aid from the USA. Britain was badly hit especially in the industrial north and in Wales. All the old industries were cutting back. Millions were unemployed. It seemed no one was unaffected; the miners, ship builders, iron and steel workers, and those from the cotton mills. No one had the money to import British goods and many countries had learnt how to manufacture their own cotton clothes and build ships.

Even farmers, famous for their self-sufficiency were struggling. All the jobless had to look forward to was the dole. But at least this was better than twenty years ago.

Jacky Ebron looked at the life around him and as he gradually managed to erode the doubts in John's mind, a strong trust grew up between him and the Llewellyn family. Now, he decided it was time to stake his claim.

Chapter Eleven

"You can do it, wuss. To tell you the truth I'm finding it harder and harder to face the stares of outsiders at market. I've selected a lovely ewe, healthy and strong with twin lambs. You should get a reasonable price for them, in spite of the times."

"Aw come on, Bryn. Aren't you being over sensitive? You're a familiar figure at market. Well respected too."

"Maybe so, maybe so."

"And you drive a good bargain. Will I get such a good price as you?"

"Certainly, you are just as capable."

"You flatter me."

"Flattery be damned. You know what you're doing and I trust you. You're practically family now, been here well over a year."

"Well, if you're sure I'll do you justice, I'd be honoured."

"Take John with you, if you like, or Carrie."

There was a barely imperceptible pause, "Not this time Bryn. I'd feel self-conscious with their eyes on me. Next time p'raps."

"Right you are."

Jacky had neatly manipulated Bryn's decision and was to have free rein at market. He kept his face expressionless, but inside he rejoiced. The first step was underway. A good sale, further trust and he could start feathering his own nest. He would need security. He was convinced that things were going to get tougher.

The next part of his shameful scheme would be more difficult. He would have to persuade Bryn to take a celebratory drink with him on his return from market. Jacky would make sure there was something to celebrate and then his plan would be well on its way to completion. For Jacky Ebron the final glittering prize at the end of his machinations would be the daughter herself, Carrie. But, for the time being he was content, a slow smile slid across his face. Part one had been put into operation.

Jacky arrived back at Hendre late that night, dusty, foot-sore and tired. His eyes glinted wickedly as he walked through the yard clutching his bottle of liquor.

"Bryn, Bryn," he called excitedly as he strode up the glasshouse steps.

"I can't believe it, wuss. Look!"

Jacky burst into the kitchen and emptied the contents of a leather drawstring pouch. Five gold sovereigns chinked onto the table.

Bryn's face registered surprise as he counted the coins. "That's better than I dreamed. How did you do it?"

"Oh, the old Ebron charm," smiled Jacky. He went to the dresser and took two glasses. He filled them up with a malt whisky and passed one to Bryn.

"To celebrate."

"No, Jacky lad. I took an oath. No strong drink."

"Aw, come on. One won't hurt. Just this once. No one will know. You know I don't like drinking alone."

"Much as I'd like to oblige, I can't." Bryn was firm on this.

"What about an ale then? That doesn't qualify as strong drink."

Bryn hesitated fractionally before answering, "No, even though I'd enjoy it. No."

"Right. I'll not press you further. But, you must have something. A cup of tea or cocoa?"

"Sounds dreadfully bland after what's on offer, but tea it is."

Jacky laughed as he put the heavy iron kettle onto the range and started chattering. "You know a few more sales like that, and if I were you, I'd be tempted to settle some money into one of those insurance schemes."

"Dead money, Jacky boy. I've always put profit back into the farm."

"And so you should. I just think a little bit put by in these difficult times would be a wise thing to do."

"I'll think about it. Now, where's that tea?"

"Coming up. The water's not quite boiling yet." Jacky downed his drink in one gulp and left the other glass in front of Bryn.

"I think I'll join you in a cuppa, thirsty work the market".

The kettle started to bubble. Jacky prepared the pot and soon the aroma of freshly brewed tea was mingling with the smell of whisky in the snug kitchen.

Before Jacky turned away from the range, he deftly took a small bottle from his pocket, containing a clear liquid and slipped some into the pot. Then he poured two steaming hot cups of tea. He picked up the whisky tumbler and emptied a proportion into one of the vessels.

The two men laughingly toasted each other. Bryn took a huge swallow and hastily put his cup down as if he'd been stung, as the scotch spirit warmed his throat.

"You've given me the wrong cup, wuss!"

"Have I? Sorry, Bryn. I must have yours. Here let me get you another."

Jacky tipped away the rest of the remaining liquid in Bryn's cup and gave him a fresh one apologising profusely. "Didn't mean to, wuss. So sorry." He pointedly drained the rest of the scotch into his own tea.

Bryn took another sip, "This doesn't seem quite right either."

"That's cause you've had a taste of the liquor, or maybe the smell's still on the rim. Mine's the one with the whisky. Smell." He thrust his cup right under Bryn's nose. "See!"

"All right, all right. Anyone can make a mistake." Bryn forced a smile. His taste buds were warming. His mouth was suddenly dry. He took another swig of his tea and licked his lips. His eyes glittered dangerously, his pupils dilated and he felt a buzz inside his head, a buzz that lessened with each mouthful of tea until he felt really good.

Jacky smiled. He recognised the symptoms. He hadn't been sure until now, but the tiny beads of sweat that broke out on Bryn's forehead and upper lip confirmed his suspicions. He pressed Bryn to a second cup and the tremor that had started to manifest itself slowly began to diminish.

Bryn guffawed and flicked a sovereign to Jacky, "Here you are. Call this a bonus for a good sale. I've still made a profit."

Jacky's easy smile appeared and he touched his forelock in a one-fingered salute to Bryn, as a mock gesture of thanks. He tucked the gold coin he'd added to the price of the sale back in his waistcoat pocket. He wasn't to suffer a loss after all.

"Let's have another cup then, Jacky boy."

The teapot was emptied that night and Jacky ensured that it was thoroughly rinsed before retiring.

He helped a very merry Bryn into his bed and like the pretender to the throne swaggered his way out of the house and back to his cottage.

Chapter Twelve

"I don't understand it, Aunty Annie. Dad doesn't seem to be drinking. I've not found any bottles anywhere, empty or full. But, his eyes in the morning are bloodshot and he stinks of booze."

"Well, he must be getting it somewhere."

"He swears he's not touched a drop."

John was voicing his concerns to Annie on a surprise visit to T'yn-y-wyn.

"He seems sincere enough that he's not on the bottle. Jacky says he hasn't seen him take a drink."

"Jacky! I wouldn't trust that man as far as I could throw him."

"He's not that bad. Although, I must admit I went through a period of being a little jealous of him, him fitting in so well with everyone and all. But, I reckon he's a good enough bloke. Hard working too."

"Yes? Well, you're entitled to think what you like but I feel there's something that doesn't sit right with him. Call it a gut instinct. I'd have more faith in a hungry ferret down a burrow to fetch a rabbit. Oh, I know he's all charm and good humour, but try as he might he'll not win me round. Remember John, first impressions are almost always right."

Annie listened to all John had to say and she was worried.

Jacky had been with the family nearly two years now. Bryn was entrusting more and more of the running of the farm to him; taking his advice, giving him the responsibility of deals at market. Some of the prices that goods and livestock fetched at market were less than expected. Jacky was siphoning off two and six here and five shillings there, building up a tidy little nest egg for himself.

He'd cunningly persuaded Bryn to take out insurance. Dummy documents were served with the help of a corrupt

Neath lawyer and phoney receipts were issued. The premiums were then pocketed by Jacky.

Bryn was becoming more and more dependent on Jacky. His will was being sapped and numbed by the regular cuppas laced with vodka and pressed into his hands. Bryn, too, was aware that his mind was becoming addled but so reliant was he on this elixir that he refused to hear a word said against Jacky.

Annie had no facts just suspicions. She was concerned. It was then that she ordered the pony and cart to be harnessed. She and John went off to Crynant village to Mam-gu's and Netta's. It was time one of her sisters helped out.

Annie couldn't leave T'yn-y-wyn for the present as she had her own difficulties to deal with, difficulties she'd not burdened her relatives with. Netta would have to do her part until such a time as she, Annie, could get away. Netta was still single and could be more easily spared. Their mother could manage well enough without her.

Netta complained loudly, in her contritely, over patient way but finally agreed to pack a few things and return to Hendre where she had not set foot since she and her mother had moved out of the family home after her father's death.

Netta was convinced that this charmer whom she had heard much about, but had never met, would not fool her. Primed by Annie she was to keep a close eye on the affairs of the house and report back. At least that was the plan.

Chapter Thirteen

Netta was a tall woman, slender like a willow, full bosomed with rounded hips. At thirty-three, she was Annie's youngest sister. She had a wide forehead and high cheekbones. But for her complexion she would have been considered a handsome woman. Her skin was pitted with old chicken pox scars where the rash had been bad and had tormented her itching fingers to scratch.

Her glossy, black hair matched her diamond bright, navy-blue eyes. Her mouth was wide, the bottom lip fuller than the top giving her a somewhat petulant appearance set over a dimpled chin.

She had never married. She had once been engaged to a local boy who had died tragically in a mining accident when she was just twenty-three. After this loss Netta changed. She became very bitter and resigned herself to looking after her mother when her father died. She gave up her job at the millinery shop in Neath. Her world narrowed and with it she hardened.

Netta stood framed in the kitchen doorway, a dark monolith blocking the sun. She stepped further into the room and the light behind her, refracted in rays, darting forth like a scene from a biblical picture.

"Well, well. I can see that Hendre needs a woman's touch," said Netta as she lightly ran her gloved fingers along the dresser shelf.

"Carrie does her best," muttered Bryn defensively.

"She's just a child. She needs help. It's a good job I'm here for a while." Her voice was brittle and dry as if she'd sucked on a lemon.

She moved further into the room bringing with her an icy blast of air as the black silk of her skirt rustled and the heels of her black button boots tapped on the slate floor.

She moved to the range, warmed her hands and lifted the kettle to boil on the fire.

"My luggage is in the cart outside. If someone can bring it in," she gestured grandly.

Bryn dutifully went out to the yard to collect her things, whilst Netta surveyed all around her with a critical eye. The dust and the yellowing patches in the corner didn't go unnoticed.

She gently teased off the fingers of her gloves and tossed them on the table, smoothed her hands down her skirt and set her mouth in a hard line. There was a slight sound behind her.

"Put the bags by the table. We'll take them upstairs in a minute." Hearing no reply she turned around and came face to face with Jacky.

Netta started in surprise and moistened her lips. Her voice instantly softened to a warmer, fuller tone. Her hand moved involuntarily to her throat and her cheeks flushed with colour behind her defensive make-up.

"I'm so sorry. I thought you were Bryn."

Bryn appeared behind Jacky carrying a vanity case and a hat-box.

"I'm the one who should apologise." Jacky Ebron's eyes lingered over her. He liked what he saw. Their gaze locked together causing Netta to blush even more. Something touched a corner of her frozen heart and the ice maiden started to melt.

Bryn broke the awkward silence that had grown up in the room.

"Netta, this is Jacky. Jacky Ebron, my right hand man. Jacky, this is Netta my youngest sister."

"You never told me you had such a charming creature for a relative." He took Netta's hand and pressed his lips into the back of it whilst looking deep into her eyes and unnerving her still further.

She withdrew her hand as if she had been burnt and modestly lowered her eyes. Her heart felt as if it was working overtime whilst a thousand red-hot needles probed electrically in her lower belly awakening desires that had been imprisoned for many forgotten years.

Bryn put the trappings on the table and adjusted his mask.

"Come on then, let's have a cuppa first. Jacky'll take your things up and then we can get back to work. How long are you stopping?"

"Long enough to make sure you're managing properly. Then Gwenny or Annie will take a turn. We'll all do our share until Carrie can manage all the housework."

"Very kind of you, I'm sure, but we're coping all right."

"Don't say that wuss," broke in Jacky, "Let's keep her here a while. I could do with some decent cooking and feminine company. Besides she brightens up the place."

Jacky was rewarded with another rush of colour to Netta's cheeks.

She presented no obstacles to his desires. In fact, he suspected she might even help him.

Chapter Fourteen

Netta took the main bedroom for her own and like a vulture picking over the bones of the dead she helped herself to Miri's things.

At first, no one noticed. Netta was careful to pack away items she wanted to keep, but as the days went on she grew more careless about wearing pieces of Miri's jewellery.

Carrie was the first to notice her mother's sapphire brooch adorning the neck of Netta's starched crisp blouse and she whispered to John, "See! She's got our Mam's brooch that Mam-gu Lloyd gave her when I was born. She's no right to that. It was promised to me on my sixteenth birthday."

"Hush now, cariad. I'll see to this."

John waited until Carrie had taken the mushroom basket to the meadow and his father was with Jacky in the barn. He chose his moment wisely. Netta was singing in the kitchen, something she was doing more and more now that Jacky's silver tongued flattery was having its effect.

"Aunty Netta?"

"Yes, John?"

"Why are you wearing my mother's brooch?"

If she was flustered she didn't show it. She turned coolly to him, "Trinkets are no use to a dead woman. Besides your father said I could have something of your mother's to remember her by. I've chosen this."

"That brooch was our grandmother's and promised to Carrie on her sixteenth birthday. It's been in the family years. Dad would never have agreed for you to take that."

"Oh, he didn't. I took it myself. I didn't think anyone would mind. He should have said there were things I shouldn't touch. I wasn't to know," she snapped defensively.

"No one's saying you can't have a memento," John sighed, "Just ask first."

"Are you accusing me of something more?" Her mouth

shut like a rat-trap and she turned away, her lips set in a grim line.

"No, really, I'm just saying, ask; that's all."

Netta sniffed imperiously, unfastened the pin and slapped it into his hand. The open brooch came down with such force that the pin pierced the flesh on John's palm. A trickle of blood seeped out as he withdrew the pin. A glint of pleasure registered in those dark eyes as she saw him flinch.

"So sorry, bach," she uttered mechanically, "I didn't mean to hurt you." But John knew by her expression that she did.

Mealtimes at Hendre were changing from a gentle family gathering into a platform for Jacky. He indulged Netta with a full peacock display and constant words of admiration. She coquettishly teased with her eyes, her words and her demeanour. Bryn laughed at what he thought was innocent flirting, but the children were becoming more subdued and more than a little anxious. They were uncomfortable with the developing relationship between Netta and Jacky.

Money was tight now. There was a constant flood of enquiries from strangers arriving in the village and visiting surrounding farms looking for employment. The country was in the grip of an economic depression. Prices were rising and goods were few and far between. Yet Jacky never seemed to be short of a bob or two.

John watched closely when they played cards in the evening. More and more the bets were placed with money and not matchsticks or buttons, which they used when the children joined in the game. John and Carrie would look at each other and at night Carrie would creep into John's room and they would discuss what they were going to do in the future.

"When Hendre's ours," Carrie would say, "We'll run it together. Build it up to be the biggest farm around. Then, when you marry we'll divide it up and I can have my own farm to run."

Carrie often fell asleep telling her dreams to John and the pillow, while he stroked her hair.

"Tickle my back, John," murmured Carrie sleepily, "It

makes me have nice dreams."

"As long as the nice dreams don't involve you riding horses. Got a kick like a stallion you have. You twisted right round in bed last night and ended up with your foot in my mouth."

Carrie giggled as she remembered the incident, her mirth threatening to explode into an uncontrollable fit of laughter when they heard a sound outside the door.

John tensed and touched his finger to his lips. Carrie slid down under the covers and waited.

They heard the click of the latch on Netta's door and low voices whispered from the room behind.

John slipped out of bed and tiptoed on the oilcloth, the cold nipping his toes. He gingerly opened the door, and careful not to make any noise he peeped out.

The grandfather clock was chiming out the hour. John counted, two, two o'clock. He eased his way across the landing hearing the rumbling snores coming from downstairs and he moved to the narrow band of light that showed underneath Netta's door and listened.

There was a clink of glasses and the sound of liquor being poured. He heard Netta giggle in an absurd way more suited to a sixteen year old than a grown woman in her thirties. There was a rustling of silk petticoats and a smacking of lips. John fastened his eye to the hinged side of the door where the wood had warped and light escaped. He could see into the room and the bed.

Netta lay back on the bed in her bodice, her petticoats above her waist. John caught his breath as he saw the thick mat of black pubic hair that curved in a gentle mound. Her legs were open and she was gently fingering herself with little stroking movements, moistening her fingers with her mouth at regular intervals. Using her other hand she thrust her middle finger inside her and squirmed in pleasure.

Jacky was sitting naked in the chair, watching Netta with a drink in one hand. His excitement was growing and he rose rubbing himself until a few drops of his love milk glistened and dripped. He put his drink on the bedside table after pouring some of the liquid on Netta's belly. It ran down her womanhood in rivulets and he leaned across, teasing his body over hers and lapped at the moisture with his tongue, probing her most secret parts. Then, he sat astride her; his hand movements working on himself getting faster and faster, before he finally grasped Netta's hands and pinned them above her head. He pushed into her making grunting animal noises.

Netta's head was thrashing from side to side in a frenzy of ecstasy. Jacky's body thrusted rhythmically against hers and culminated in a final throbbing spasm of pleasure. His body now slippery with sweat flopped to Netta's side as he still spurted out hot semen. He groaned and taking Netta's face in his hands gave her a long lingering kiss.

John stole away from the door and crept back into his bed. Carrie was sleeping soundly. He was both disturbed and excited by what he had seen and he found himself exploring his own body with inquisitive hands and feeling the intense fire that spread through his groin, he lifted back the covers and gazed on his sister's innocent budding body. The rosebud nipples like twin peaks pushing against her night-dress, her developing adolescent hips and he manipulated his own maleness until he was relieved by a flooding surge of melting delight that made his eyes flutter and roll, and his limbs lock.

Carrie stirred and murmured softly in her sleep. John froze guiltily. He lay there for a moment damp with sweat but felt so heartily ashamed he quietly left the bed and went to his sister's empty room where he sobbed himself to sleep.

Chapter Fifteen

Christmas was fast approaching. Lack of money didn't seem to curb people's optimism. Most believed that things would improve in nineteen thirty-one. However, the newspapers were full of debate. Although old industries, which had once made Britain the workshop of the world were dying, they were fast being replaced by new ones in car and radio manufacturing, chemicals and rayon. But their growth rate initially was slow.

Europe was seeing the rise to power of fascist dictators who promised the people simple solutions to their countries problems, and anxious for a way out of the depression, ordinary folk were looking for political solutions and listening to promises that seemed to provide an answer to their prayers.

The supper table was a mixture of chatter and clatter interspersed with pauses whilst the family satisfied their hunger. Today was special to Carrie. Aunty Annie and Dai had come for the day to drop off their modest gifts. The family were sharing in a feast that would be seen on few tables around the country.

Annie glanced up from her food and watched the faces of those around her chatting animatedly about Herr Hitler who was promising the electorate an economic miracle in four years, if they would give him their support.

The stolen looks that passed between Netta and Jacky Ebron were carefully noted, as was the slightly slurred speech of her brother, Bryn. What she was not prepared to see was young John gazing at Carrie with such a burning in his eyes that she nearly choked on a chunk of lamb in the richly nourishing Welsh stew, known as cawl that steamed in a big pot on the table.

Dai slapped her hard on her back until the offending piece of meat flew out from her mouth.

"Duw, Duw, I'm sorry," she rasped huskily, taking a mouthful of cider to soothe her roughened throat. She took another look at John who was this time laughing innocently at something Dai had said and she wondered if she had imagined it. Then she spoke. The table became hushed as she banged on the cloth with her dessertspoon and everyone realised that she had something important to say.

"You must have guessed by now that there's more to this visit than just a social call." She looked at her husband, Dai, he was a big man, weather browned and hearty with an irrepressible twinkle in his eye. His mouth always looked as if there was a promise of a smile just waiting to dance across his face. But at this moment he looked more serious than Carrie had ever remembered seeing him, except at her mother's funeral.

Dai nodded across to Annie and she continued, "As you know my eldest boy, Thomas lost his job at the pit six months ago when the colliery closed and David who's been helping out on the farm has nothing to look forward to when he finishes school next year."

"Surely, he'll come into the farm, won't he?" slurred Bryn.

"He would have done, if we had a farm to run."

"What do you mean, Aunty?" said Carrie her face full of concern. She knew she was about to be told something very serious and her mouth suddenly went dry. She took a gulp of lemonade and listened.

"Well, the farm has been struggling for a long time now. We don't seem to have the luck of the Llewellyn's for growing great. Even if the government give the farmers the money they're promising and get this idea of a milk marketing board off the debating table and into practice, it will be too late for us." She paused and took another sip of her drink. Her hand was shaking with the embarrassment of what she was trying to say.

"Now, I know you'd have offered help if you'd known what dire straits we were in, but I'm proud, like Mam and like you, Brynley." Brynley nodded even in his slightly hazy state he understood what his sister was trying to say.

"Anyway, there was money outstanding on the farm that we couldn't pay, with the boys not working an' all. We even had to let George go. He's been with us since we started."

"Come to the point, Annie fach. There's no need to mince words," prompted Dai.

"Well, we've sold the farm, paid off our debts and with the remainder we're emigrating to a new life in Australia. There are plenty of opportunities out there. We might have another farm or try our hand at gold mining. People say there are fortunes to be made."

No one spoke, a lump was rising in Annie's throat and she had to wait a minute before she could trust herself to speak.

"So, we're leaving on February the fifth. Our passage is booked. That will give us time to spend our last Christmas here and tidy up all our odds and ends."

There was a silence, broken by Annie blowing loudly into a large clean rag that Dai had passed her. She beamed round at the assembled company, her eyes unnaturally bright, "Well, aren't you going to wish us well?"

Carrie pushed her chair away from the table and ran out of the room, tears streaming down her face in a wet, but silent protest. Annie bit her lip in concern and made to follow Carrie but Dai stopped her. There was an awkward silence until John looked up from his bowl, his appetite lost.

"Course we do, Aunty. We wish you all the luck in the world."

"Yes, an exciting adventure it will be," added Netta.

"And never mind Christmas at home. You'll spend it with us, a proper family one like the old days. Mam is going to Gwenny's, so there's nothing to stop you," said Bryn, suddenly sober.

But the only one to realise the full implications of Annie's announcement was Jacky who glanced slyly at Netta. He now knew there would be no one to stop him in his scheme of things and he smiled secretly to himself.

Chapter Sixteen

"Got to make this Christmas special, cariad."

"Yes, I know. For Aunty Annie. I wish she didn't have to go, Dad."

"You've grown very close to her." It was a statement not a question.

Carrie and her father were going out on the hillside to look for a suitable tree to dig up and take home to decorate.

Brynley whistled shrilly and Trixie came bounding into the yard and padded after them.

Bryn was unusually bright this crisp, fresh morning and seemed to be in full control of his speech. His hand still shook a little but he was looking better than he had for a long time.

They walked through the yard and down the mountain track, past Maes-yr-onnen, through a five bar gate, across a field where the ground had been cow hoof turned.

"It will be a sad day for us all when they leave."

Carrie nodded in agreement as her hair with its green satin ribbon blew in the breeze. They started to climb steeply towards Gelli Galed, a dilapidated property on the side of the hill.

"Dad, why do they call the old house 'Hard Living'?"

"Because it was. Farming on a hillside is not easy. Ploughing can be a nightmare. Our farm started its life here many generations ago. It was a difficult time but with good management and hard work it grew in prosperity, spreading the tendrils of success, reaching right out into the valley below." Brynley stopped to draw breath, Trixie waited at his feet and Carrie listened eagerly for what she might learn of her beginnings.

"Dadcu Llewellyn remembers Hendre being built. He was just a boy then, but even he was amazed at the thickness of the cob and stone walls. Houses were built to last then."

Bryn went silent. All that could be heard were his breathing and the pounding of his feet on the rutted track to the derelict house. Carrie pressed him.

"Go on, Dad, tell me about it"

"You've heard it before, you could probably tell the story better than me."

"Please, Dada," she pleaded with her voice, her eyes and her hands.

"Now, how can I resist the prettiest girl in the valley?" Brynley laughed when he saw her earnestly solemn face. "All right." And he launched into a routine that he had performed many times before.

"Hendre was lovingly built by Dadcu's grampy. To his specifications. None of the modern rubbish for him. No. This is where his idea of a glasshouse had come, instead of an ordinary washhouse. All the utilities could be there. A sink fashioned round the pump. A glass roof to trap the sun's heat in the summer. Shelves for his exotic plants and vegetables. He even had an indoor line for the washing in case it rained."

"And what about the winter?" Carrie prompted.

"In the winter they would need to warm it with an oil stove to stop the cold fingers of frost from prising under the door and into the scullery. Mam-gu would make a bolster for the threshold to stop the chill poking its way into the kitchen and pinching the toes of the children."

"Say about the vests."

"We had to wear our vests long and tucked in tight with no gaps or a clip round the ear we'd get and a dose of castor oil."

Carrie loved the next part of the story.

"I remember when Annie dressed up as an eastern dancer after reading a book about Lawrence of Arabia. She pinched the velveteen cover from off the table and tied it around her middle. And draped a shawl around her head. She borrowed Mam's treasured silk square from her drawer and covered half her face and started wiggling up and down the hall. Mam caught her. She was given such a scolding and a big dose of castor oil. Anyway, Mam went out back, to get the coal and Dad came in. He saw Annie disappearing up the stairs in her costume and went after her. She had another good hiding for acting like a shameless hussy and another dose of castor oil. If she did! She was up all night with the squits and bellyache for a week. But did she leave it there? No, not Annie. She laced an apple tart with a heavy helping of the same and Mam and Dad were so bad they left the newspaper squares to chill on the frosty shelves of the glass-house for a week."

Carrie giggled delightedly at the thought of her plump Aunty Annie as some sort of exotic dancer and chuckled even more at the idea of her grandparents' discomfort and sore bottoms.

By the time Bryn had finished his tale they had reached the old house, now in bad need of repair, and stepped up on-to the wooden veranda.

"We ought to fix this place up," said Carrie, "When things get better we might be able to let it. That would bring some money in. We don't use the land around this house. It's a waste."

Bryn nodded at her wise words and adjusted his mask. The tapes that secured it were frayed and needed replacing. Carrie watched him solemnly.

"Will you always have to wear that, Dad?"

"Looks like it. I can't see me taking any trip to London to see some fancy surgeon no matter what Dr. Rees says. I doubt they could do much for me anyhow."

"You never know. If they could and you hadn't even found out about it, you'd regret it forever."

It was the first time Carrie had broached the subject of the mask since the night when she'd faced her father without it.

Bryn leaned against the rickety balustrade and looked down the hillside. "You know, I worry, cariad."

Bryn's tone had changed and Carrie sensed that he was taking her into his confidence, "Something's happening to me. I've not taken a drink since my vow but I wake most mornings and my mind is fuddled as if a lead curtain has been drawn around my head and the inside stuffed with cot-ton wool. My hands shake and tremble like some gin sodden priest serving communion wine." He stopped, momentarily searching for the right explanation. "I think I have some terrible disease." He put up his hands to silence the words he knew she would say, "No, let me finish please. I'm going down to the village on Friday to see Dr. Rees. Maybe he can tell me what's happening to me."

Carrie didn't know what to say. She went up to her father and put her arms around his waist and comfort hugged him tightly. Brynley swallowed hard.

"Come on, let's get round the back and see if we can find a spruce or a fir that will favour our house.

They stepped off the ancient porch, moved down a weed strewn path, and through a rotten gate, hanging off its hinges into the old apple orchard now overgrown with docks and thistles. Trix ran around, her nose exploring every corner with a feverish delight.

The ground was ridged and hard where the night's frost had caked the surface solid like iron.

At the back of the orchard was a small clump of trees, holly, fir, spruce and even a few Christmas trees that had been replanted after previous yuletide seasons that were now grown tall and spreading.

"What about this one, Dad?" Carrie pointed to a magnificent specimen, a needle proud pine that was a rich mix of greens from the base to the tip.

"It's splendid I grant you, but it's a bit big to stand in the house and it would be a shame to cut it down. It's too big to dig up. I fear I'd damage the roots."

Carrie nodded in assent. "Here's one!" she exclaimed loudly.

Tucked behind the larger tree was a smaller bushy one about five feet in height.

"That's better. It will fit into a pot. Look a treat in the corner of the sitting room by the settle."

Bryn tried to pierce the ground with his shovel. It bounced back as if striking rock.

"Oh Da, we'll never be able to dig it up. The ground's like stone."

Bryn wiped a fleck of earth from the good side of his

face. The fraying tape of his mask snapped and it slipped down his raw cheek revealing the livid, lumpy skin.

Carrie caught her breath. Tenderly, she put up her hand to her father's face and stroked the numb and withered flesh.

"Oh Dad, I'm so sorry."

She had no need to say anymore. Dropping his spade he held his daughter tight and she buried her face in his chest.

"Rhwyn dy garu du, Dada."

The demonstration of affection was too much for Bryn and a tear squeezed out from his good eye and rolled down his cheek splashing onto her wild curls and glistened like a dewdrop on a fine spun silk web.

"Oh cariad, why have things gone so horribly wrong? First your mother, then... this..." he gestured with his free hand to his face, "and now..." he tailed off.

"What, Dada?" Carrie turned up her face and looked at him. Bryn could see in her expression, Miri's concerned eyes, and Miri's soft velvet lips that were drawn back in a wondering half smile.

Trixie could sense the surging emotion passing between the two. She sat beside them listening, her head cocked first one side then the other, her ears pricked and with a low rumbling in her throat as if she was trying to talk.

Bryn swallowed hard, "Duw, you're so like your mother, fy merch 'i."

Carrie beamed at him even more. She loved to be reminded of her resemblance to her mother.

She took the mask with its frayed tape and pulling the ribbon from her hair threaded it through the holes at the side and handed it back to her father. Gratefully, he retied it around his head and ran his hand over her wild hair.

"Well, we've got to think how we're going to get this home. We won't dig it up that's for certain."

"We'll have to cut it, Dad."

"I hate doing that. I'd rather have it roots and all. Let it live on after the celebrations. Goes against the grain just to chop it down."

"Can't we put some water on it? Drench it to soften the ground?"

"Not with a frost. It wouldn't work. It's not like making mud pies. I need a pickaxe and I didn't think to bring one with me."

"Are there any tools left around Gelli Galed?"

"It's possible. Let's look."

Father and daughter retraced their steps to the house and the old workshop. There was an ease between them that hadn't been felt for a long time. A fresh understanding had started to blossom.

They lifted the rusted latch to the workshop and the door creaked open. A rat with half a tail scuttled out from the dark and into the freedom of the light. Bryn propped the door open with an old iron shoe last that lay forgotten on the workbench and as the light filtered in, the disturbed dust could be seen as a swirling, cloudy haze.

Carrie gave a shout. Under a broken ladder-back chair was a pickaxe head. A further search around revealed the handle. Brynley hammered the handle into place and returned to the selected evergreen. He began to pound the frozen ground, gradually breaking up the soil. Carrie clapped her hands in delight.

Bryn spurred on by the encouragement struck the stubborn, unyielding earth some more before stopping and wiping the sweat from his cheek with the back of his hand.

"Carrie?"

"Yes, Dad?"

"What do you think of Jacky?"

"He's all right."

"You're not that keen are you?"

"Oh, he's well enough. I used to like him a lot. He's so wrapped up in Netta now, he doesn't seem quite the same." Carrie didn't reveal her real reasons for her change of heart, "Why?"

"I don't know. I'm starting to wonder. If only I can keep my brain clear. I need to start looking into the farm's affairs."

Bryn didn't explain further. He resumed the pounding, a grunt accompanying each hit until the surface earth was thoroughly broken up and he could winkle the tangled roots free.

With the release of the tree Carrie and Bryn made their way back to Hendre. Trixie bounding her way in front.

As they reached the ramshackle wooden gate, the first flakes of snow came drifting aimlessly down.

Hendre was going to have a white Christmas.

Chapter Seventeen

A white crystalline coverlet of snow stretched as far as the eye could see. The trees laden with their icy burden bowed under the weight.

Carrie rubbed at the frosted diamonds on her window-pane and blew her hot breath, steaming like smoke, onto the glass. She shivered, hopped across the cold floor and dived back into her bed, pulling the covers up round her neck. Her nose was cold. She popped her head under the blankets, cupped her hands around her mouth and blew hard trying to generate some heat to the tip of her nose.

Her eyes appeared over the blanket like a Persian princess in a yashmak. She stretched out her arm and felt for her clothes resting on the bedside chair. The tips of her fingers grasped the flannel of her dress and she tugged, bringing the dress and bundle of undies into the bed. The garments felt slightly wet next to her body but slowly warmed in the heat of the bed and eventually lost their damp chill. Carrie manoeuvred, twisted and turned, dressing herself under the covers. She lay there fully clothed for a few minutes longer determinedly putting off the moment of rising. The count down from ten began and on 'one' Carrie finally threw back the covers and dared to brave the acute cold of the morning.

The water in her jug had a thin layer of ice skating on the top. She gasped as the icy splashes showered her face in the semblance of a wash. She rubbed at her hands with a rough towel. The shock of the water had chased away all remnants of sleep and her face tingled. She was alert and awake.

Grabbing her boots, she hastened down the stairs to the kitchen to toast her toes before encasing them for the day.

A wave of warmth welcomed her and the sizzling smell of crisping bacon wafted up her nostrils. She bounced into her seat at the table and poured herself a steaming hot cup of tea, letting her nose hover over the vapour in an attempt to defrost its stubbornly frozen tip.

"That smells good, Aunty."

Netta turned from the range and snapped, "This here's for Jacky. You'll have to wait for yours."

As if on cue, Jacky Ebron swaggered in through the door and sat himself in Bryn's seat at the head of the table. Immediately Netta placed a generous breakfast in front of him.

"There. That'll warm the cockles of your heart," she simpered.

"I don't need this to do that. One look at you and I'm on fire," Jacky laughed.

Netta blushed, took the seat next to him and watched as he began to devour every morsel.

Bryn was the next to come in. He nodded a good morning to Carrie and then said, "You're in my seat, Jacky boy."

"Sorry Bryn, Netta told me to sit here."

Carrie looked up in surprise. She'd heard no such thing and was just about to say so when Netta added.

"My fault, Brynley. I laid his breakfast there. I just didn't think."

"I'll move if you like." said Jacky glibly, continuing to eat with relish.

"No, no. It's all right, as long as he doesn't get my helping too," he joked.

Netta laughed, swept herself up from the table and served Bryn's breakfast. Carrie noticed her father's one egg to Jacky's two and Jacky's extra fried bread, and she frowned.

"Carrie not eating this morning?" Bryn queried as he took a mouthful of tea. He grimaced.

"It's just coming," said Netta in irritation as she returned to the pan on the range.

Carrie was lost in her thoughts and her eyes blurred. She hardly noticed her father pushing his teacup aside and saying something to Netta and Netta removing the cup.

Carrie watched hungrily while her father ate and Jacky finished mopping up the remaining egg yolk with a chunk of bread. She sat patiently; sipping her tea when the door opened and John came in, his hair sticking up in tufts.

"Lost for a comb are you?" Bryn chuckled.

John's answer was to yawn and rub at his sleep filled

eyes. He looked in surprise at the seating around the table and sat opposite Jacky.

Carrie again had to wait, like all girls in Welsh families, whilst John was served before her.

"What time's Aunty Annie coming?"

"They're arriving after lunch and staying till the twenty-ninth. I need you to help me get the beds ready," said Netta pointedly with pursed lips.

"Oh. I was going to decorate the tree with Dada."

"That can wait". Netta's mouth clamped shut. The brittle notes that she had disguised for so long escaped through her tight mouth. She softened her tone as she turned to Jacky, "More tea?"

"Not for me, fy merch 'i. Maybe Bryn would like a cup," he nodded meaningfully.

"No thanks," said Bryn, "Netta made me my own pot. It didn't taste quite right."

"I poured it away and made a fresh one," said Netta hurriedly.

Carrie said nothing but continued to sip her tea and was eventually rewarded with a breakfast, half the size of John's but full of flavour, nevertheless. She promised herself that if she ever had daughters she wouldn't make them wait on the men folk hand and foot. Netta was worse than Mam-gu.

If John ever made a mess, Mam-gu used to make Carrie clear it up. She'd always found that grossly unfair.

Carrie munched a piece of bacon and glanced around the table. Jacky was looking at her, his eyes wandering over her face, exploring her innocence, tarnishing her with his stare.

Netta, too, saw him eyeing Carrie and felt a stab of jealousy strike at her heart. She picked up the teapot. "More tea, Carrie?"

"No thanks, Aunty."

Netta reluctantly replaced the teapot with its newly filled scalding contents that could so easily have spilled out when she poured. She sighed, "Come on. Get that down you. There's work to be done before you go decorating trees."

"It's all right, Netta. I'll give you a hand. Let her prepare for Christmas," smiled Jacky and he gave Carrie a broad wink.

At that point Netta felt like tipping the tea into Jacky's lap. That'd wipe the smile off his face. But the next minute the Ebron charm was working its magic and Netta would have forgiven him anything, even murder.

Chapter Eighteen

The hustle and bustle while preparing Hendre for Christmas was infectious. The old home was full of contentment and companionship. And although Brynley was none too well, he said little about it. The festivities, as far as the rest of the family were concerned, were relatively uninterrupted. Even Netta stopped her griping and joined in the family fun. The house rang with merriment over 'The minister's cat' and other such games.

With the family present, Bryn had not been receiving his regular dose of specialist tea. Christmas Eve, he had suffered enormously. Annie believing he had some sort of ague had confined him to bed. He shook uncontrollably and complained of terrible cramps in his stomach and the pains of Hell in his head.

Annie changed his sweat soaked sheets. She was on the point of sending for Dr. Rees but Brynley stopped her. He gestured her to shut the door on the laughter emanating from the kitchen.

Annie gently closed the door and sat by Bryn's side.

"Don't bother the doctor at Christmas. I'm seeing him next Friday," and he told her of his fears that he had contracted some debilitating illness that was destroying his mind.

"Stuff and nonsense," retorted Annie, "Think back. When was the last time you were ill like this?"

Bryn shook his head in confusion.

"You've got a short memory, Brynley Llewellyn. Head like a sieve, I've always said. When you gave up strong drink was it as bad as this?"

A light gradually dawned in his eye.

"I was only saying to Carrie, my mind was addled like, with drink - but I've not touched a drop since my oath except..." he stopped.

"Except for when?"

"By mistake I drank some of Jacky's tea. It had a tot of whisky in it. That was a good while ago. But come to think of it, that's about when I started getting fuddled in my mind."

"Mmmm," Annie frowned. "I don't trust that charmer. There's something evil under that veneer. I asked Netta to keep an eye on him, but she's not noticed anything. She's said nothing to me."

"I'm not surprised, thick as thieves, those two. At first I thought it was harmless flirting between the two of them but now I think it's something more." Bryn hesitated.

Annie urged him on, "Come on, I can see there's more. You might as well tell me."

"I'm almost ashamed to say it. Master of Hendre and I'm not sure what's going on under my own roof."

"How do you mean?"

"I'm not saying he's fiddling the books, but..."

"Go on."

"It's just I know times are hard, but we don't seem to be faring as well as we should. My fault. I've been letting him take the animals to market."

"Oh Bryn!"

"Now I've got my suspicions I'll make sure one of the children goes with him."

"Not Carrie! I've seen the way he looks at her."

"Now there you're wrong. He's not interested in Carrie. I wasn't going to say this but I think Netta's sharing his bed."

"Netta? Duw, Duw."

"Aaah..." Brynley doubled over in pain as another attack of cramp came. "It's like steel fingers raking away at my guts," groaned Bryn.

"There, there. You rest by here awhile and I'll be in to see you later. You can take your mask off. I won't let anyone in."

Annie left Brynley in the parlour and returned to the celebrations in the kitchen. As she opened the door Jacky was kissing Netta under the mistletoe. It didn't look like it was their first kiss.

Annie closed the door with a flourish. Netta and Jacky

sprang apart. A blush spread from Netta's starched bloused neck to her cheek. Annie cleared her throat. Dai heaved himself out of the carver chair and thrust a glass of sherry into Annie's hand.

"It's a toast we must be making," he said pointedly.

"What for?" said Annie.

"Come on, can't you guess? Netta and Jacky. Netta tell your sister the news."

Netta took a step towards her sister. "I know this is sudden, but I'm not getting any younger. I really thought life was passing me by at home with Mam, and now..."

"Get to the point, Netta," pressed Annie a hint of ice in her voice.

"Jacky's asked me to marry him and I've said, yes." Netta turned her shining eyes to Jacky who with simulated pride placed an arm around her shoulders.

"So we're to be family, Annie fach."

Annie forced a smile to her lips and stuttered her congratulations. "How are you going to manage? Where will you live?"

"I've got a bit put by. Jacky can continue working for Bryn until we've enough to set up on our own, maybe by going half crease. Until then we can live in old Tom's."

"What about Mam?"

"Mam will be all right. Gwenny will keep an eye on her. I'll visit and if need be, once we're settled she can live with us. That won't be a problem."

"I see. You certainly have it all worked out." Annie sipped her sherry. "I wish you well, as long as you're sure you're doing the right thing."

"Course I am. Tell me, have you ever seen me looking so happy? I've not felt like this since before Penry died."

"Do the children know?"

"Not yet. They're out in the snow with your boys. I'm sure they'll be delighted for me. They're very fond of Jacky."

Annie attempted a smile that didn't quite reach her eyes and took a sip of her drink. Dai pumped Jacky warmly by the hand and gave his sister-in-law a hug.

Annie turned and gazed into the range with its tongues of fire licking over the red coals flickering blue, orange and red. The flames leapt and danced like little devils in impish glee and reflected in her deeply troubled eyes.

Carrie breezed in through the door bringing a flurry of snow with her. Her fiery Titian tresses flecked with snow-flakes peeped out from under her fur hood. She gazed around the room at them.

"What's the matter? Why are you all looking like that?"

Jacky swiftly moved across the room to her and lifted her off her feet, "Meet your new uncle, Carrie."

"What?" The rosy bloom on her cheek faded and she turned quite pale, "Uncle you say?"

"Yes, Carrie. Jacky has asked me to marry him."

"Why that's wonderful," she said almost automatically, hoping her voice didn't betray her innermost feelings.

John and his cousins pushed into the room with a stamping of feet and a rubbing of hands. They too heard the news and were instantly delighted.

"Does dad know?" asked John.

"Not yet," said Annie, "Wait till he's feeling a bit better and then I'm sure he'll want to congratulate you both himself."

Annie's mind was working overtime; a million thoughts were racing through her head. She wasn't quite sure how to handle this. Finally, she broke the excited chatter around the happy couple. "When's the wedding?"

"Not yet. We're not rushing things. We've got to be absolutely sure, although I know I won't change my mind," said Jacky. "And anyway, I need to speak to Bryn first."

Annie looked at the assembled company, chattering delightedly, all except for Carrie whose face had grown serious. It seemed there was another family member who shared her concerns. Annie had to act quickly; there was so little time. Soon, she would be leaving the country and then the Llewellyn's fate would be in God's hands.

Chapter Nineteen

All was quiet. The house was still. The celebrations of the day, an excess of food and drink and a liberal helping of excitement had left the household exhausted.

Annie was the only one who rested uneasily in her bed. The day's events were churning over in her mind. She listened to Dai's sonorous snoring next to her, the creaks and rattles of the old house settling itself down to rest in the bitter chill of the night. She heard the grandfather clock announce the time with two strokes and gradually nodded off to sleep.

Carrie woke with a start. She had burning pains in her stomach that knotted and twisted. She was overwhelmed with a searing heat that set her to trembling. Believing she'd eaten too much rich food she stepped from her room and slipped across the landing. Cautiously feeling her way down stairs, she reached for her boots and made a dash for the closet. The moonlight flooded the glasshouse and she felt no need for a candle this bright starry night.

So hot was she, that in spite of the cold, she wanted to strip off her nightgown, liberty bodice, vest and bed jacket. Trusting to the lateness of the hour and the lock on the closet door, she did just that, divesting herself of all her clothes, which then littered the floor.

She even kicked off her boots, leaving only her bed socks as protection from the frosty night air that fingered its way under the door. There she sat enthroned in acute discomfort.

After relieving herself she felt no better, and moved to wipe herself dry with one of the newspaper squares that hung on a nail on the back of the door. To her horror when she removed the paper it was smeared with something dark. Closer inspection revealed that this was blood.

She froze and forced herself to look down the lavatory pan, which was stained red. Rivulets of blood ran between her legs, thick, dark and spreading. She recoiled in horror, wondering what had happened to her and how she may have injured herself. She thrust her liberty bodice between her thighs to contain the steady flow that streamed from her. Suppressing a sob she redressed. The shaking had stopped but now she was over taken with a numb terror. Carefully wiping the seat, she removed the evidence of her shameful secret and flushed away the paper with a bucket of icy water left in the closet. She didn't stop to refill this, as was the family custom after using it, but hurriedly retraced her steps back to her room where she tried to rock herself to sleep, her knees up to her middle clasped firmly into her with both arms.

Carrie believed that something terrible had happened to her. It was God chastening her for all her ill deeds and bad thoughts. She resolved that if the bleeding stopped she would never do anything wrong again.

That night she prayed in earnest to be forgiven for whatever sin she had committed and for the punishment of blood to cease. Eventually she was rewarded with the freedom of sleep.

At four a.m. she awoke. The grandfather clock was chiming out the hour. She felt sticky and damp and thought with embarrassment that she may have wet the bed although she had never done so before.

She eased herself out of bed and carefully lit the oil lamp to look at what had happened. Her nightgown was soiled and the sheets bloody. She didn't know what to do. She took some clean rags that she usually used as handkerchiefs, rolled them into a wad and pressed them between her legs, holding them in place with a pair of knickers. Carrie stripped her bed, and gathering the sheets under her arm she sneaked downstairs to the glasshouse where she scrubbed at the mess in an effort to cleanse the bedding.

This time, Annie's alert ear heard the gentle click of the latch and the soft footfall on the stairs and she waited. When the footsteps did not return, she removed Dai's protective arm from around her middle, stepped out of the warmth of the bed and ventured downstairs in search of the mysterious night-walker.

She found a distraught Carrie scrubbing away at the bedding and offered her a hand. When the washing was complete they took clean linen to remake the bed. Carrie changed her nightgown and Annie sat her in the bedside chair. She placed an arm around her shoulder and drew her into her breast.

"It's nothing to be feared of, Carrie fach. You're becoming a woman. Without a mother to tell you, you weren't to know."

Carrie turned her tear stained face to Annie who launched into an explanation that was a mother's responsibility and with it came a warning.

"Let no man mess with you until you're married or you'll end up like Suzy Evans in the village."

Suzy Evans was a simple soul. She wasn't married but she had four children and rumour had it that she was pregnant again. The gossips in the village couldn't wait for the child to be born so that they would have an opportunity of identifying the father. Each of the rest of her brood bore a strong resemblance to supposedly respectable married men and word had it that this time the village policeman was responsible.

Annie kissed the top of Carrie's head and reassured her. Then in her own inimitable way came up with a phrase to make Carrie laugh. "As Mam-gu always said to me, keep your hand on your fan and you'll be all right. Now, back into bed with you and no more tears. It's all perfectly natural. In the morning I'll show you how to keep a check on the calendar, so you'll know when to expect the next one."

With that Annie tucked Carrie back into bed, smoothed her brow and tenderly kissed her. She turned out the lamp and padded back across the landing towards her room.

Snores rumbled from all directions, and she was just about to lift the latch on her door when she saw a flickering light on the path outside.

Annie moved closer to the landing window and recognised two figures, one holding a lamp, creeping back across the yard to the house. It seemed her sister Netta, was indeed sharing Jacky Ebron's bed.

She watched them kiss; Jacky's hand was exploring Netta's body under her nightdress and finally after a last embrace and giving a furtive look all round they went their separate ways. Annie supposed that with the family present it was safer for them to sleep in the cottage. She sighed deeply and not wishing to confront her sister retreated to her room and Dai's thunderous snores.

Carrie tried to settle and although the griping pains in her stomach had eased and everything had been explained to her, she still felt in need of comfort.

She waited until she heard her Aunty Annie return to her room and lingered a while longer. Netta's footsteps went past her door, Carrie guessed at where she'd been and wondered if her aunt would have a baby like Suzy Evans.

Carrie crept out onto the landing and made for John's door. Reluctantly, he let her into his bed and there she poured her heart out to him. He stroked her back and held her close until she fell asleep.

Annie woke early. She stoked up the fire on the range and set the kettle to boil for tea. Thinking to reassure Carrie after her anxious night, she went to Carrie's room with a cup of tea and was surprised to see her bed empty and cold. She looked out of the window, but there was no life in the yard. Everything was still dark. She stepped out into the passage and watched as the latch on John's door lifted. Carrie emerged, yawning and moved back towards her room. Her Aunt followed.

"Carrie, what are you doing sleeping in your brother's room?"

"I don't often, Aunty," Carrie said defensively, "Only when I can't sleep or I've got a problem. John doesn't like me in there. He says I've got a kick like a mule."

"You're a bit old to go in your brother's bed, especially now, cariad."

But Carrie either didn't understand or want to understand what her Aunt meant. In her innocence, she saw nothing wrong in taking comfort in John's arms.

Annie didn't press further, nor did she want to awaken

the whole house. She gave Carrie her cup of tea and went downstairs to her brother. Bryn would have to be told and he could speak to John himself.

She pushed open the door of the parlour and delivered Bryn's tea before launching into a speech of her concerns and worries about the family, finally adding, "Don't you know what's going on under your own roof? It's not healthy and it's not wise. If you can't see where it's leading you're not fit to be a father. Now, I've said my piece. I'll trust you to speak to John. Let's get on and enjoy the rest of Christmas."

But in her heart Annie knew that wasn't the end of it and she wished she could stay at Hendre to help them through the troubles she was sure would come.

Chapter Twenty

Christmas passed quickly at Hendre. Too quickly for Carrie who was feeling saddened by the approaching departure of Annie. She felt safe with Annie close at hand, and without her, she knew that she indeed, had lost a good friend and confidante.

John had been distant with Carrie for some time and she wondered what she had done to displease him. She hadn't noticed him looking at her in his unguarded moments, his face a confusion of emotions. Overwhelming love burned deeply in his eyes alongside acute shame and disgust. Carrie felt rejected by the one she was closest to and try as she might, she could not warm towards Netta.

Of Jacky Ebron, she was wary. She was careful not to be caught alone with him, for a small voice cried out within her, that the man was not what he appeared to be and his company held some danger for her. She tried to tell herself that this was foolish and had not Annie warned her of her own misgivings, then Carrie might have suppressed those inner warnings and be swept along on the tide of goodwill that appeared to surround the man.

Brynley appeared to be making a recovery from his mysterious illness. He was careful to drink only that which he made himself or had been prepared by Carrie. Tea foisted on him by his sister or Jacky, no matter how big his thirst, remained untouched. The aspidistra in the hall benefited enormously from its little extras and grew bushy and tall.

Carrie had taken to going on long walks up the mountain, and trekking across to Bronallt, always with Trixie loyally following in her wake. The girl and the collie were becoming inseparable. At every opportunity Carrie would try to sneak her upstairs. The dog was a huge source of comfort to her. With Trixie, Carrie shared her innermost secrets and her darkest fears; she talked to her in love, shared and confessed her anger and worries; the dog always seemed to understand her moods and would nuzzle her hand lovingly.

Netta was not so understanding about it. She ranted when the mud from the fields daubed the stairs. She chased the dog out to the barn and tied it up outside during the hardest frosts and she laughed at Carrie's unhappy expression, taking pleasure in the girl's hurt.

Farm business was gradually picking up. Jacky found himself accompanied on most trips, by John, who stayed close to him so that no fiddling could occur. Brynley too, made the occasional trip and although to the stranger he still cut an odd figure in his worn, wooden cosmetic mask; the people who knew him had come to accept the face covering as part of him, neither staring at it nor referring to it.

The weekend before Annie and the family were to set sail, a family get together was organised at Mam-gu's. Relations from across the valley came to say their goodbyes.

Annie took Carrie on one side, "I know times are tough, and that you're feared for the future but both Dai and I have agreed, if you want to come with us and start a new life in Australia then we'd be happy to have you."

"Oh Aunty Annie, I'd love to come with you. You're embarking on such an adventure but my place is with Dada and John. I couldn't leave yet. Maybe in a few years when you're settled and I'm older, then I can make the trip. But for now my life is at Hendre." Carrie hugged her Aunt tightly.

"Go careful now, remember all I've said."

"I'll remember. Netta's not you, but she's not all bad either. I think we'll survive."

Annie's eyes clouded with tears, inside she felt so afraid for her little niece. Fear grabbed at her heart that had no justification other than a woman's intuition and the Celt's inherited feyness and precognition; right now, her mind was screaming warnings of things to come and she started to tell Carrie who raised her hand to stop the onslaught of words and chorused with Annie, "I know. There's dark days ahead."

February the fifth came and went. A new family moved

into T'yn-y-wyn. Carrie felt the lonely desolation of the be-
reaved. For her it was like losing her mother all over again.

A fortnight passed and Brynley seemed to be taking more
control of the farm and of his life.

In private Jacky glowered and swore, his fury at having
his plans thwarted, rankled and he made new schemes to
make himself master of Hendre.

Netta was becoming an encumbrance and he yearned to
taste the sweet young flesh of Carrie's flowering youthfulness. But he knew he had to tread carefully. A period of hard
work and good humour was needed. He'd put too much into
this venture to lose now.

The Ebron charm was magnificent. He flattered, he beguiled and he had Netta hanging onto his every word, making obeisance to his every whim.

John was carried along on the wave of this charm. He put
his previous misgivings aside and put his complete trust in
Jacky, working alongside him with obvious enjoyment.

Only Carrie remained distant. Even Brynley, felt that
maybe he'd misjudged the man. The more Jacky did, the
more Brynley felt Annie had been wrong. Jacky was making
himself indispensable. He was well liked in the village and
at market, and Brynley bludgeoned his remaining doubts
into submission and silence.

Plans were drawn up for a September wedding. Brynley,
by now completely won over, promised to foot the bill.

In April, Hendre received its first letter from Australia.
The news was good. Although life was hard, they were making a living. Muscles like Popeye, Annie said she had now
and as Carrie read her Aunt's words she could imagine Annie's voice and face and she felt sad. She immediately set to,
writing her own letter with all the family news, about Jacky
and Netta, the new family at T'yn-y-Wyn and that Trixie
was in pup.

It was one spring Saturday morning, Carrie, Megan and
Megan's brother Gwynfor, were playing a make believe
game of wartime adventure in the Llewellyn's barn.
Gwynfor was the wounded soldier, Carrie was the nurse and

Megan played the traitorous spy. Fun was being had by all when Carrie had to pretend to make an escape from their secret hideaway to get help. She darted round the side of the barn and tripped lightly along the track towards the round-house, where the grain was stored and ground.

The wind blew her skirts and petticoats above her head and she felt just for an instant that she was being watched. She shook off what she considered to be an absurd feeling and came level with the slatted door. Jacky Ebron stepped out from the shadows. His voice took on an oily quality as he reached up and stroked Carrie's gossamer cheek with the back of his wind-chapped hands. Carrie jumped back as if she had been struck.

"What's the matter, cariad? You looking for me?"

"No!" she shrieked, her cry drowning in the violence of the wind.

"Come now, you mustn't be afraid. You should be nice to your Uncle Jack, after all we're family now."

Carrie lashed out with her hand, and screamed for all she was worth but her words were as whispers on the wind. Jacky raised a hand to his reddening face and laughed.

"I like a filly with spirit, it's more fun taming them." He looked deeply into her eyes and promised huskily, "One day, cariad. One day soon."

Carrie pressed close against the roundhouse door and shuddered. She didn't see the curtains flutter and Netta's face bitter with acrimony. Netta felt a jealous rage snatch at her heart. She believed her niece was at fault. She didn't witness the whole incident and from her vantage point believed that her niece was deliberately enticing her man. She saw the closeness of his body next to Carrie's and whispered words between them. She laid no blame at Jacky's door and made up her mind to wreak her own form of revenge on Carrie. Oh yes, she would make her suffer. Harbouring, murderous thoughts she set her plans against her.

Chapter Twenty-One

"Trixie! Trix!" called Carrie echoing her brother's shouts. "I don't understand it, why doesn't she come? She's never late for supper."

"Maybe her time has come and she's off somewhere quiet to give birth. She was getting very heavy, her dugs were nearly touching the floor," said John.

"Leave it until morning. She'll be back you'll see," added Bryn.

"Aye, your father's right," agreed Jacky. "Look if she doesn't put in an appearance by morning, we'll go looking for her. Right?"

Reluctantly, Carrie put the dog's bowl of meat outside the glasshouse door in the yard, and went in for her own supper.

Netta served up a plateful of meat, potatoes and gravy and added her own condolences to Carrie.

"I'm sure the dog's all right. I don't like her messing up the house but I wouldn't wish her any harm. She'll turn up tomorrow, you'll see. If not, we'll all help you to look for her."

Carrie had to be satisfied with that and the matter was not discussed at dinner again. But Carrie pushed her untouched meal away. Worrying about Trix had taken her appetite away.

"Not going to leave that are you?" said Jacky, and seeing her lacklustre look, he picked up her plate and offered it around.

"Anyone want to share this with me? It's a pity to waste it."

John nodded that he'd have some and between the two of them they finished it off.

Netta was excitedly putting the finishing touches to her wedding plans. She had been shopping to Neath to buy silk for her dress and had finished cutting it out and pinning it. She was going to start sewing it on Miri's treadle machine that evening. Carrie was to wear a dress of lemon silk and Netta was trying to persuade Jacky to get himself fitted with a smart fashionable suit.

"Oh, I've heard enough of all this prattle about the wedding," he said with a wry smile. He turned to Bryn, "Come on wuss, let's you and me have a game of cards."

Bryn laughed in acknowledgement, "I've not got much to play with Jacky bach, not since we've put the deposit down for the reception at the 'Rising Sun'."

"Aw come on! I'll go mad if I hear the words 'bottom drawer' again."

Bryn chuckled good naturedly, and the two men retired to the sitting room for a game of poker.

Carrie helped Netta clear away, then made her excuses and stole up to her room. She lay on the bed thinking and worrying about her beloved Trixie.

She heard the merriment downstairs and the chink of glasses. The sound of the sewing machine whirred up to her and she felt vulnerable and alone.

She missed her dog, which was more of a friend than a pet or worker and decided that as soon as she could, she would venture out to search for her. If indeed Trixie had gone into whelp, anything might have happened. Nature had a habit of going horribly wrong, as she well knew.

By nine-thirty the noise downstairs had subsided. Even the whirr of the sewing machine was only occurring in short, sharp bursts. Carrie took a warm woollen cardigan that had been made for her by Annie and went back downstairs.

"Time you were in bed, my girl," puffed Netta as she struggled with a huge swatch of material under the foot of the sewing machine, pushing it to one side.

"I can't sleep. I'm just going out for a breath of fresh air. A short walk should do wonders."

"Make sure you wrap up warm. I don't want to be accused of not looking after you properly," moaned Netta.

"I'll be all right. John, do you want to come?" Carrie asked her brother, slumped in a chair reading a comic book.

"Aye, do me good to stretch my legs."

They passed by the sitting room where the card game was

still in progress. The frivolity had vanished and both Bryn and Jacky were studying their hands with equal gravity. A bottle of whisky sat in front of Jacky and Carrie noticed her father licking his lips nervously.

"You're not drinking are you, Dad?" she asked anxiously as she passed through the room.

"Jawch, no. Don't worry girl. Just dead set to win that's all." He smiled up at her and she and John went down the glasshouse steps and into the yard.

Brother and sister walked together talking easily for the first time in months. The pale light of the moon shone eerily on the mountain track magically tinting everything it touched. The grey pebbles glinted like opals and the pearlised sheen on the leaves gave the world around Hendre a fantasy look.

John and Carrie continued down to the meadow where she and Trixie had run together. Carrie turned to her brother and squealed. "Come on, John. Let's run through the grass." She kicked off her shoes and leaped over the gate, running for all she was worth, until she felt her heart would burst.

She tumbled over giggling and let her fingers run through the dog, wet-nosed moisture of the dewy grass. Her adolescent breasts heaved up and down with her laughter.

John came galloping up and fell down beside her. He too had kicked off his shoes and was laughing delightedly. He pushed himself up on one elbow and gazed at his sister with her sparkling eyes, so alive and vibrant. At that moment the brightness was eclipsed as a cloud shadowed the moon stealing away its light. In that instant John knew what he had not dared to believe before, that he loved his sister more than was wise or safe. In his heart he promised to protect her from all ill and look after her for as long as he was able.

Roughly he pulled her to her feet. "Come on, cariad. We'd best head back, we don't want the family worrying."

"John?" Carrie's eyes locked onto her brother's, penetrating his very soul, "I'm afraid of Jacky." And she started to tell him about her encounter by the roundhouse.

"He was probably just teasing you," offered John. "You know what he's like. I'm sure if he thought he'd frightened you he'd be really upset."

Carrie smiled wistfully at her brother, she accepted what he was saying but didn't believe it.

Arm in arm they ambled back towards the house. Carrie nestled her head on John's shoulder, which both disturbed and excited him. But he set these strange feelings aside and indulged in a show of brotherly love and hugged her to him.

They passed the slatted gate to the roundhouse. Carrie stopped and pressed her fingers to her lips and listened. John made to speak and she silenced him with a look, urging him to listen too. A strange snuffling sound could be heard coming from under the door. John pushed at the slats. The door rattled open and the crystal light from the sky beamed across the dirt wood floor. Huddled in a corner and in obvious pain was Trixie.

She was struggling to give birth and the sack of animal skin was wriggling half in and half out of her body. John eased the dog's torment by helping her to deliver her pups. Three black glistening bodies broke free from the bag and squeaking with alarm were helped to Trixie's full teats where they suckled contentedly.

Trixie turned her soft brown eyes lovingly on Carrie and weakly licked her hand. It was then that Carrie noticed the deep gash in the dog's stomach as if she had been slashed with a razor or some other instrument. No wonder she had, had difficulty birthing.

Carrie sat with her gently smoothing her head whilst John ran up to the house to fetch a warm box and bedding for mother and pups and some disinfectant to cleanse the wound.

John imagined Trix must have torn her belly on some barbed wire and voiced this to Carrie, but Carrie had her doubts.

Dog and pups were carried back to the house and allowed the warmth of the kitchen. Carrie insisted on sleeping on a makeshift bed alongside them. Carrie was so pleased at finding Trix; she didn't see Bryn's grim expression as he wished her good night.

Chapter Twenty-Two

Carrie sat up all night nursing Trixie. The pups were fighters and appeared to be surviving. Trixie was in a very weakened state and Carrie made sure she was kept warm and properly nourished, feeding her every two hours to replenish the goodness that was going out in her milk.

The marks on the dog's belly were a puzzle. The cut was too regular to be barbed wire and yet Carrie could think of no other explanation.

Carrie was attending to mother and babies when the first rays of the morning sun filtered through the glass on the top half of the door. Trixie whined softly in her throat and licked Carrie's hand in a simple gesture of love, but the whine turned into a deep throated growl when Netta breezed in opening the curtains and setting the kettle on the range. Trixie's hackles rose and she pulled back her lips revealing sharp, white teeth that would tear and rip at the slightest opportunity.

Netta backed away defensively. "What's the matter with the stupid mutt? Surely she doesn't think I'm going to hurt them."

Carrie turned and looked at her Aunt. "Probably not. She's just warning you to keep away from her babies. She's always been protective of any pups she's had."

"She doesn't seem to mind you."

"No, well she's used to me. She knows I love her."

Netta snorted and returned to preparing breakfast. Carrie didn't see the sly smile creep onto Netta's face nor observe the dog constantly watching her; following each of Netta's movements with her eyes.

Jacky arrogantly strode into the kitchen. He put his arms around Netta's slender waist and nuzzled her hair.

"I'm such a lucky man, a place to work, a family and a good woman." He rubbed his hands and full of self importance he sat at the table giving Carrie a broad wink. "Yes,

I'll say I'm lucky. Charming company and I believe luck is with me." He beamed a lopsided, boyish grin at Netta as she put the tea on the table. "I reckon my ship's come in, Netta gal." He didn't explain further but a curious smile passed between the two of them. Carrie watched suspiciously.

John came in to the kitchen and chattered brightly laughing at Jacky's quips, obvious admiration shining from his eyes.

Breakfast was served; Brynley was the last to be seated. He seemed subdued this morning and said little to anyone. Carrie wondered what was wrong and made up her mind to follow her father from the table and talk to him.

John and Jacky left together still laughing and teasing each other. Bryn sat silently in his shirtsleeves, elbows on the table his huge hands fingering the grubby half mask where it met his flesh. Carrie saw in his eye a distant look, a look of deep-seated pain and anxiety. She was just about to ask him what was troubling him when Netta moved closer to the dog's box in an effort to clear the table without disturbing Brynley in his morose state. As she did so she put herself within striking range of Trixie.

There was a growling snarl and snap. With the accuracy of a cobra, Trixie, her hackles risen and fur standing on end had leapt forward and sunk her teeth into Netta's ankle, drawing blood, and leaving jagged flaps of skin that were already turning blue with bruising.

Netta lashed out with her foot and caught the dog in her stomach reopening her wound. Carrie screamed and leapt to the dog's defence catching the swiftly following second kick in her own stomach.

Carrie doubled over in pain and Netta hissed in anger, "Get that bitch of a dog out of here before I put her and her pups in the mincer."

Bryn snapped out of his trance. He seemed to see everything in slow motion. Suddenly, everything became clear and he thundered at Netta, "Leave the dog alone and get yourself out of here, now."

His tone and expression did not warrant arguing with and Netta, nursing her savaged ankle limped wordlessly out of the kitchen.

Bryn knelt down and lifted Carrie to her chair. He gently stroked the dog's velvet head and she whined softly in her throat.

"Are you all right?"

Carried nodded, she was winded but the colour was starting to come back to her cheeks.

"I'll fetch the first aid box. We'll see if we can cover Trix's wound so it will heal."

Brynley went out into the glasshouse to the cupboard by the sink and returned with some lint and sticking plaster.

"If we don't cover it, she'll worry the cut to death and it'll never heal."

"Dad?" Carrie's voice was questioning.

"Yes, fach?"

"Why did Trix do that? It was more than just protecting her babies wasn't it?"

Brynley knew it was, but he didn't answer. His mouth was set in a hard line. He knew his sister and he remembered things from his childhood that he had never told another human being. Perhaps now he should.

Netta made a big fuss over her dog bite and the collie and her pups were relegated to the barn. Netta tried to persuade Jacky that the dog needed shooting but he shook his head in disagreement.

"Everyone's allowed one mistake, and every dog's allowed one bite. Besides she can be forgiven for being temperamental with pups around, she's never hurt anyone before." There was no arguing with this, so Netta sniffed disdainfully and promised herself that at some time she'd have her revenge.

That night it rained, heavy torrential rain that tamped down on the glasshouse like a thousand ball bearings. It was so fierce that Carrie feared the glass would crack; such was the pounding it received. Jacky and Bryn retreated into the parlour to play cards. This was to become a regular evening feature and the consequences were to be disastrous.

Chapter Twenty-Three

Five weeks had passed. Netta's ankle had healed although the tendons and muscle around the ankle were tender. The skin was thin here and it looked like she would bear the marks of that attack forever. Using the stairs was the worst especially coming down them. Netta made the most of every opportunity to bemoan that fact and everyone was heartily sick of hearing about it.

Trix was kept tied up in the barn with her pups. Carrie spent every spare minute with her. The dog's wound had gradually healed and Trixie continued to show complete distrust and fear whenever Netta was in the vicinity. Homes were found for her offspring, a good working dog from a strong family line was always in demand.

One pup was to go to a farm outside Dowlais, another to Tonna, and the third to the new family at T'yn-y-wyn. Carrie said her good-byes to the cuddly bundles as each one was collected. She now hoped to persuade her father to allow Trix back in the house. But she held out little hope for that until Netta was gone from under their roof.

Carrie was maturing early and felt quite capable of looking after her father, John and herself, and she resolved to say so when the opportunity presented itself.

Card games were continuing in earnest and this time the children were excluded from the parlour when they were played. Jacky and Bryn would tuck themselves away, sometimes playing long into the night. Netta would occasionally sit in with them but more often than not she would be preparing for her wedding, scouring and rummaging through Miri's things, taking what she wanted that she felt wouldn't be missed.

The night was bright. Carrie didn't know what had awoken her, she imagined that perhaps the silver moonbeams from the partially open curtains had danced on her face and like a magical nymph weaving a spell had summoned her awake.

She stepped out of her warm bed, drawn to the window and the mystery of the night. She loved looking out at the countryside around Hendre, by moonlight, sunset or dawn. She felt the power of nature and she would always wonder at its eternal beauty and delight in the knowledge that she was privileged to live here. Not for her, the smug acceptance of the surrounding fields and all it had to offer; not for her, complacency or disdainful neglect. She delighted in everything, the song of the birds, and the changing seasons. She loved Hendre and appreciated it all with a fierce passion that was surprising in one so young.

A movement caught her eye. Trix was pulling at her restraining rope, anxious to escape into the night. Carrie looked past the dog to see what had excited her and saw the disappearing figure of her father, a bottle in his hand, blindly stumbling towards the mountain track.

She heard in the dewdrop stillness of the night the honeyed latch on the glasshouse door and saw the shadow of Jacky Ebron stretch and grow in the yard below. As if sensing her presence, he turned and looked up at her window. She stepped back quickly hoping the fluttering curtain would not betray her. She heard the harsh scrape of his boot in the yard and ventured back to her vantage point and saw him swagger to the gate. He stood there a while watching Bryn's disappearing figure and then turned back to his cottage, raising a jubilant hand in a gesture of triumph he punched the sky before he fairly ran across the yard to his home. Although he made no sound, Carrie could almost hear him give a whoop of glee because of the way he moved. She waited until she saw his bedroom light was extinguished and snatching a cardigan from her chair, she determined to follow her father and speak to him.

Brynley sat on Bull Rock staring trance-like at the black swirling waters below. The torrent boiled and churned tossing its spray over the boulders by the bank. The racing river had swollen with the cloud burst earlier in the week and threatened to spill out into the undergrowth drowning the mess of mud and roots.

He took a swig from the bottle, then glared at it in distaste and hurled it from him with a groan of anguish. The bottle seemed to spin through the frosty night air in slow motion. Each turn was like the whirr on a propeller, first the neck, then the base, each catching the satin rays of the moon. It seemed suspended in mid flight, before finally plummeting down to smash in a million pieces on the stones below. The river swallowed the fragments hungrily and appeared to be roaring for more.

Brynley staggered to his feet and swayed unsteadily on the mossy rock now dangerously slippery from the rain. His world was crumbling, falling away like the stones on the mountainside and shattering like the glass in the bottle. All too clearly now, he could see his mistakes. The errors of a lifetime materialised into shapeless horrors that grew crazily in front of him, leering and jeering at his weakness and inefficiency.

Bryn let out a cry from the depths of his soul soon to be damned in Hell and ripped off his hated mask. He stared at the battered face covering and moved to step back and hurl that too into the flooding waters below. He misjudged his footing and stumbled, freeing the mask from his grip as his fingers opened in an attempt to save himself from being catapulted into the inky waters. The mask came to rest, carelessly, atop the bracken a few feet below the rock. He struggled to regain his balance and caught hold of a tree root to stop himself falling head first into that yawning blackness that called out to him. The root came out of the ground like pus popping on a boil and Brynley felt himself tumble out into space. Roots and branches came off in his hand as he desperately grabbed at anything in a last ditch attempt to save himself. His body hit the side of the mountain several times bouncing off like a stuffed tailor's dummy. A deep-throated cry wrenched from his lungs was cut off, as he smashed against the boulders and hit the water below. The river accepted the sacrifice. The bubbling eddy swirled and sucked the body beneath the surface, tugging it downstream with the current and out of sight.

Carrie froze on the mountain track. The hair pricked up on the back of her neck and she shivered involuntarily as she heard that cry; long, loud and agonised. She stumbled into a run, her breathing coming in short sharp gasps as she strained to reach the source of the sound. The mud squelched over her feet. The brambles, like fingers of malevolent spirits tore and clasped at her clothes. She was openly sobbing now, salt tears stinging her eyes and in a frenzied burst of speed, she reached the path that led to Bull Rock.

She saw the broken twigs, flattened bracken and her father's booted foot prints in the soft mud and she paused.

Carrie scrambled down to Bull Rock and from its dizzy heights she gazed down at the devil's bowl beneath. She caught her breath when she saw, lying just out of reach, her father's weathered mask. Carrie carefully picked her way down trying not to dislodge the surface earth and stones. She struggled to find secure footholds and bracing herself under the overhang of the rock itself, reached out with her hand. For one moment it seemed as if the mask was to be lost forever in an avalanche of pennant sandstone threatening to cascade down the mountainside. Grunting with exertion she stretched as far as she dared and her fingertips touched the ribbon tape. She teased her fingers out a fraction more and managed to grasp it firmly and pull it up to her. Carrie edged her way carefully back onto the rock and sat there a few minutes, her shoulders heaving with emotion and the effort of retrieving the mask.

She sat for what seemed like an hour but was in fact only a few minutes. In her numbed state she could not think what to do. A cool breeze probed its way through her nightgown and cardigan setting her teeth to chatter and her body shivering.

That cry! She would remember that cry, all her days, a cry of sadness and loss. Carrie pulled herself up onto her feet and peered out into the night, looking down the cliff side and into the river. She heard the rushing water; she saw the foaming river but she did not see Bryn. Clutching his mask to her chest she retraced her steps to Hendre. She ran to the barn and buried her face in the black collie's fur sobbing until her tears ran dry. Then, she untied the dog and in a funereal walk, she shambled back to the house and roused her brother.

Chapter Twenty-Four

The hushed tones in the chapel whispered into silence as the minister stepped forward. He laid his hand on the coffin and addressed the assembled congregation. His gaze lingered on the figures and faces in the front pews.

Netta straight laced, iron backed, in burnished black bodice and skirt; dry-eyed and veiled, clinging stiffly on the arm of Jacky, in his sombre Sunday best; his broad brimmed hat held loosely in his hand. John, uncomfortable in an ill-fitting suit, too tight and too short, fingered his collar awkwardly, his eyes downcast. Carrie, in her dark school serge, stared sadly in front of her, her eyes wide and distracted.

Reverend Richards launched into a litany of praise regarding the life of Brynley Llewellyn, his life cut short at the age of forty-two years.

The words echoed around the hewn stone walls of the chapel, full to bursting point whilst before Carrie's eyes sped a montage of events kaliedoscoping into each other. Memories of happy times with her father collided with the horrors. Images of her father's cruelly disfigured face, choosing a tree for Christmas, sitting at his feet and hearing him talk, and the shocking discovery of his body wedged between two rocks at a bend on the river overhung by willow and lime.

The voice of Reverend Richards seemed far away. He appeared to be talking through a fog. Carrie's head was like marshmallow; her eyelids were heavy. She felt as if she was floating on a sea of darkness. She wavered and the blackness lapped around her ankles, reaching up her legs to her knees, eventually suffocating her mind. The ground rushed up to meet her as she crumpled down to the quarry-tiled floor oblivious of all around her.

Strong arms lifted her up and carried her into the vestry while the funeral service continued. Carrie lay quietly. It took a few minutes for her to come round. She opened her eyes and met the concerned gaze of her brother, and Gwynfor

Thomas, Megan's brother who was eyeing her anxiously.

"Well, it's just you and me now, cariad." murmured John.

"What happened?" she said dazedly.

"You fainted," John said simply. "It's the strain. All the worry, and then losing Dad like that."

All Carrie's fears came flooding back to her. "What's going to become of us, John?" Her eyes stared wide with alarm.

"Don't worry, cariad. We'll be fine. We've got Hendre and I'm old enough and capable enough to run it. Dad will have seen us all right. I'm sure he was paying into an insurance scheme. We'll find out tomorrow when we go into Neath for the reading of the will."

John placed an arm around his sister's shoulders and hugged her to him. She tilted her chin and looked into his eyes. Dear John. What would she do without him?

Gwynfor asked, "Anything I can get you, Carrie? Glass of water or something?"

She nodded dumbly and Gwynfor lumbered to his feet to search out a glass.

Gwynfor stood six feet one in his stockinged feet. He reminded Carrie of a big bear. A gentle giant that best befitted the pages of a storybook. A strong young man who had secretly mapped out his life and had set his heart on winning beautiful Carrie's affections when they were both older. It was his ambition to combine Hendre and Bronallt and make the biggest farm in the region.

The service ended. Brynley's coffin was borne out by the pallbearers and so began the slow processional, winding march to St. Margaret's. The men of the village sang from their hearts. Their melodic voices merged in harmony stirred intense emotions from the depths of the soul.

Mam-gu set up a keening and a weeping that she should lose her only son. Gwenny's consoling arms enfolded and comforted her mother, whilst Netta remained stiffly at Jacky's side.

After the funeral party Hendre remained hushed and quiet. The walls of the house creaked as the night air grew cooler, settling the rooms to sleep.

Carrie lay and listened to the sounds around her. She wondered what the future held believing her dream of running the farm was coming true, but it was not in the way she wished.

"No! I don't believe it. I won't believe it!" Carrie cried despairingly in the office of Phillips, Pugsley and Pugh, Solicitors at Law.

Barn owled Mr. Phillips in his heavy framed spectacles peered gravely across the desk.

"I'm afraid it's true." He stood up and strutted around like a little turkey cock. "The papers were drawn up by the firm only a week ago." He resumed his seat, a flush rising to his already ruddy complexion and wisely looked back at her. "They're all signed. Perfectly legitimate."

"So what you're saying is that Hendre is not ours?" questioned John.

"That's right. Under the terms of the new will, you and Carrie keep Gelli Galed and the surrounding hundred and fifty acres." Eyebrows raised, he looked quizzically at the two youngsters.

"What's happened to Hendre?" wailed a shocked Carrie. "And the other 250 acres, stock and cattle?"

Jacky Ebron rubbed a hand over his mouth trying to disguise his pleasure. "Well, John lad, Carrie, I'm the new owner. Netta and I will be running the farm. Of course, we are not turning you out. You are welcome to stay and live with us as long as you like. Between us we will fix up Gelli Galed and when the time's right, we'll help you move. Go and wait in the cart. I'll be out in a minute." Jacky Ebron nodded to the door, and the children, their dreams shattered, started down the old worn steps walking like automatons to Senator and the waiting cart.

Jacky lingered, to pay Mr. Phillips his fat fee. Clasping Hendre's deeds to his chest, he smiled brightly. "Better than expected Phillips boy, better than expected."

"You'll not turn them out?"

"I'll not turn them out... yet," said Jacky and he set his mind to working and his silver tongue to talking; to placate, soothe and numb the children's hurt. He was confident that he would win them round, perhaps too confident.

Carrie was silent on the journey home. She cuddled into John, her face expressionless. The wind had dried her tears leaving her face salt streaked and red.

John, too, was stony faced. His heart was heavy and he said little.

Trix pulled on her rope outside the barn when she heard the wagon rattle into the yard. She set up a frenzied barking that flustered the chickens and ducks. There was a clucking and a quacking and a flurry of feathers.

Netta came out to greet them and growled at Jacky, "She's got to go." She nodded at the dog, "Now Hendre is ours, that bitch must go."

Jacky saw the flicker of alarm in Carrie's eyes and soothed, "Now, now. I know the animal's angered you, but she's Carrie's. Poor dab. It's all she's got now; love her. She's lost everything. Let her keep the dog." He spoke as if he had nothing to do with the disaster that had beset the children. "When the time's right, they'll all be at Gelli Galed. You won't be worried when they're there. Come on, Netta, for me."

Netta softened her expression and smiled up at him. She was a slave to his desires. "I suppose I can cope for a little while then."

Carrie and John, heads and eyes downcast, mournfully shambled into the house. Carrie had never felt so alone. Once through the door, she pounded up the stairs, flung open the door of her room, which she slammed shut behind her. She threw herself on the bed and wept for everything she'd lost. She lifted her eyes, swollen and red in supplication to the Lord.

"Oh, God. What are you doing to us? What have we done to deserve this? Mam always said you were a kind forgiving God. I'll not believe it and I'll not believe in you if these wrongs are not righted." She continued to pray hard in her heart and the tears continued to stream down her face.

Three months passed. Life at Hendre was difficult. The

atmosphere was bristling with tension and things left unsaid.

John was coldly polite, working as he had to and spending as much time as he could renovating Gelli Galed, making it habitable.

Carrie was monosyllabic except in her conversations with John, usually in the dead of night when all were asleep. She would intrude into his room and they would lie in the dark sharing their dreams and planning the future. John was careful to hide his very real feelings of love for his sister that he knew he would have to control or go mad.

Netta delighted in taunting the children with deliberate comments about their plight, and the tragedy of their father's actions.

But for Jacky, golden boy Jacky, his ambition of being master of Hendre was beginning to pall. The place wasn't so pleasant with this festering rancour around him, growing up like noxious weeds strangling the heart of Hendre, and choking the sunshine out of his life. Netta was beginning to grate on him. She satisfied his basic needs but familiarity had hardened her tone and Carrie's tender young flesh beckoned him. He yearned to caress her youthful sweetness, and longed to taste her innocence.

He missed her infectious laughter and happy chatter. If he was capable of feeling remorse this was the nearest he would come to it. He watched her and talked animatedly to her, hoping to draw her out of this morose state but he was greeted with blank stares and terse answers.

Netta frowned at his continued persistence with the children. She felt it was beneath him to try and maintain the same level of friendship especially when he was forever being snubbed. Netta continued to try and impress Jacky and divert attention to herself. In his eyes, she humiliated herself with her constant preening, touching and kow-towing to him.

Gelli Galed was fitted out bit by bit with furniture from both Hendre and old Tom's. Jacky was sufficiently conscience stricken to be fair in his dealings with the children over the contents and it was to this end he managed to persuade Carrie to journey with him to Neath to buy some extras from 'Uncle's Emporium'.

John had risen early and trekked up to Gelli Galed accompanied by Trix. He'd gone to work on the outside walls.

Netta was sulky on the morning they left and grumbled her way through breakfast bemoaning the fact that she was to be excluded from this trip to Neath.

"It's not that, fy merch 'i," honeyed Jacky, "If we're to bring home the items we need, they'll be cumbersome and heavy. They'll fill the cart and there's only room for a little one next to me. And as we're looking for bits for Gelli Galed, Carrie should have the choice."

Netta huffed and shrugged her stiffened shoulders. Jacky put an embracing arm around her.

"Come on gal, give me a smile. I'll make it up to you, I promise. We'll have a day out ourselves, just you and me on Saturday."

The promise was made and Netta's complaining whine was stilled.

Jacky and Carrie set off in the cart. He sat uncomfortably close to her. His arm was rubbing against hers. His leg was pressing against her knee. She shrank away from him as far as she dare. He whistled cheerily as Senator trotted his way down the mountain track towards the village.

Jacky eyed his surroundings carefully and when they reached Crynant he talked in swift bursts.

"Come on, Carrie fach. Let's make the best of it. I know you feel you've been treated harshly, but I've done no worse than anyone else and many would say better. I didn't turn you out did I?"

Carrie managed a cursory nod and returned the greetings from familiar faces in the village that acknowledged her in the cart as they drove by.

"When we get to Neath, after we've concluded our business and bought what we need, I have to see Mr. Phillips again. While I'm there you can go round the market. I know how much you like to do that. Am I right?" he questioned, determined to break through her icy barrier.

Carrie nodded and sat quietly at his side preferring to look at the countryside around them rather than be drawn into Jacky's chatter.

He tried to muster up some defence of his actions.

"Come on, cariad. You can't blame me for claiming what's mine." There was no answer. "It was your father who insisted we play for such high stakes. I tried to dissuade him." Still there was no response. "Well, when I considered it, starting married life, I thought why not? I promised myself I'd see you and John all right. You can't deny I haven't done that. Besides what if Bryn had won. You don't think of that do you?"

Carrie turned to him, her eyes showing a flicker of interest, "What had you got to lose?"

"My freedom, Carrie. I would have been bound to work for three years for only my keep, not another penny. Imagine what that would have been like with a wife to keep?"

"Dada wouldn't have held you to it."

"No? He held me to a similar bet he won, for three months work on those terms."

"When?"

"Oh, a whole back now. When I first came. That's why I hadn't played cards for a long time, because of that bet."

"I don't believe it."

"All right, don't. But what reason would I have to lie?" And so Jacky continued talking, cajoling, persuading, beguiling but Carrie refused to be drawn. She remained polite but distant.

In divorcing herself from his charms she didn't notice the way his eyes ran all over her budding body. She didn't see his lingering gaze on her immature curves. She was unaware of the way he licked his lips lasciviously as his eyes flicked up and down her body, drinking in her innocence.

If she had not isolated herself in his company she would have seen and she would have been afraid.

Chapter Twenty-Five

Carrie spent a pleasant day in Neath. She enjoyed the hustle and bustle of the market. She even occasionally responded cheerily to Jacky when buying furniture for the house. The cart was packed and Carrie sat outside the office of Phillips, Pugsley and Pugh waiting for Jacky to emerge. She thought about going on without him but decided against it and sang lightly to herself.

A newspaper headline caught her eye:

"Hitler wins majority of seats in the Reichstag. Nazi party sweeps the board. Fourteen million Germans vote for Hitler."

Carrie reflected on this news item. She'd heard of this powerful new leader who promised an end to his nation's problems. Well, he'd talked about it for long enough now he'd have a chance to prove it!

Carrie looked around at the people passing. As the time ticked on she became bored and invented a little game to pass the time away. She gave strangers names, jobs, invented their thoughts and conversations. This started her giggling. The more absurd her imaginings the louder she laughed. She stopped abruptly when Jacky emerged from the office. He stood on the step and warmly shook hands with another man, one she didn't recognise. Jacky patted his pocket and smiled. The stranger disappeared into the pedestrians. Jacky grinned broadly taking in Carrie's expression as she watched him.

He lightly skipped down the steps and jumped into the waiting wagon, clicked an instruction to Senator, jerked the reins and urged the horse into action. They trotted off down the road.

Jacky was silent but smiling in the town. They left Neath on the Cadoxton Road and he began to talk animatedly. Carrie sat there passively, looking neither to the left nor the right.

Jacky chatted on, gradually edging closer. Carrie was disturbed by his proximity. She shrank away from him as far as she dared without falling off the seat.

Jacky was excited by her anxiety. The bulge in his trousers became more prominent as his eyes caressed her young body. But, he was aware that it was not safe to indulge himself yet. There were other travellers on the road and houses with watchers. He'd waited over three years. He could wait a while longer until the road was empty of dwellings and his actions could be sheltered by the woods where he could satisfy his desires uninterrupted and unobserved. He didn't wish to alarm her yet so he eased back in his seat and continued to talk.

Carrie began to relax and resumed her quiet uncommunicative state, staring straight ahead.

They passed through Tonna and Cilfrew and eventually reached the selected woodland. Jacky pulled up Senator and jumped down. Carrie turned in surprise as Jacky secured horse and wagon to a milestone at the edge of the road.

"What's the matter?"

"Senator has a loose shoe. I just need to check it. I don't want him going lame."

"I didn't notice anything."

"Step down. See for yourself." Jacky busied himself lifting Senator's back legs and then squinted back at her when he received no reply.

"No, thanks," murmured Carrie, "It's all right." She shifted uneasily in her seat, uncomfortable in the awkward silence that followed. Jacky straightened up and walked round to Carrie's side of the cart.

"Now, cariad, you and I have something to sort out. You've avoided me a tidy time now, barely been civil," he put his hands on the seat next to her.

"You know I've always been fond of you, Carrie fach." His words lingered in the air, their real meaning raining like darts in her ears.

The shadow of a cloud started to mask the face of the sun and the woods began to look gloomy and forbidding. The bird song was stilled and the green of the leaves darkened.

In a minute the cloud had passed and the sunlight was shafting down through the trees, streaming its ribbons of light onto the grassy path below. The bird song resumed, but the threat of his words lay suspended in the air.

Jacky placed his roughened work hands onto Carrie's skirted thighs. She flinched away from him. He gently stroked the inside of her legs through the coarse cotton. His eyes locked onto her startled face.

A bird shrieked in the woods alongside shocking Carrie into action. She slapped at his hand but his grip tightened. He grabbed her flailing arms holding her wrists together with one hand, as one might hold a chicken's legs waiting to be plucked. His other hand stopped kneading the inside of her thigh and with a feral light burning in his eyes he grasped her around the neck and pulled her forward. Her feet kicked and scraped futilely as she struggled to be free.

Jacky pulled her down from the cart and she tumbled onto the grass verge below. Senator whinnied softly, his animal senses warning of some impending doom.

Jacky yanked her to her feet, half dragging, half carrying her squirming body to the shadowy forest path. She screamed shrilly, disturbing a bird from the bushes, which flapped and circled anxiously.

There was no one to see and no one to hear.

Carrie started to sob as the brambles and thistles scratched at her legs; and like the taloned fingers of malevolent spirits they plucked and grasped at her clothes.

Jacky could hardly contain his excitement as he carried her off into the enveloping trees that cloaked them in secrecy, swallowing their presence so that he could satisfy his years of longing.

She twisted one hand free and brought it up to his face in a sharp stinging slap, then raked her fingers down one side of his cheek drawing tiny droplets of blood.

He stopped momentarily, his complexion white except for the red imprint of Carrie's fingers. His dark eyes filled with lust and he snarled in animal anger bringing his hand crashing against her cheek.

A livid purple welt raised itself on her milky white skin.

Jacky threw her down on a bracken bed and feverishly tore at her clothes.

By now, Carrie's frail thrashings had ceased. She was still, too terrified to move and whispered pleadingly, "Please don't hurt me. Please. I'll do anything, but don't hurt me."

Jacky's lips curled into a leer as he ripped her bodice and exposed her adolescent breasts. His hot mouth fastened onto hers silencing her. Carrie's eyes widened and stared in abstraction at the leafy ceiling dancing with the afternoon sun.

Grunting like a hog on heat he snatched up her petticoats, pulled at her cotton knickers and fumbled crazily with his trouser fastenings releasing his swelling, throbbing manhood. He forced her legs apart and searched hungrily for her virgin maidenhead.

Carrie stifled a cry of pain when she felt the rough intrusion that violated her. She suffered his pinching fingers on her developing breasts. She withstood his pawing hands that opened the most secret parts of her body. She endured the rhythmic pounding that culminated in a spasmodic twitching that spewed hot semen into her.

Her body was still but her mind raced. Carrie survived this evil assault on her innocence with the fire of her thoughts that blazed behind her dry impassive stare.

This wanton act of vandalism would not destroy her. If thoughts were bullets Jacky would already be dead. His heart and entrails would have been cut out of his living body and fed to the dogs before his eyes. Then she would tortuously mutilate his maleness, safe in the knowledge that he would never harm another living soul.

Gratified with her plan of vengeance, she mercifully allowed herself to slip into the dimmest recesses of her mind, divorcing herself from all that was happening to her body by effectively blocking it out and retreating to a small box in her head where she felt safe. She lay still and unresponsive, her mind hiding from what was being done to her.

Jacky's whole body tingled in ecstasy at the forbidden fruits he had harvested and tasted. He rolled off Carrie and stroked her enflamed cheek already turning a bruised blue. He sucked at her forming nipples while rubbing himself to hardness again. His fat finger explored her anus and he brought his mouth down on the inside of her thighs, wriggling his tongue over her maidenhead. Then, as her thigh muscles started to shake and tremble in a near state of collapse, he entered her again; glorying in the exquisite tightness and pleasure her sweet youthfulness was giving him.

Carrie was ravaged brutally until the evening sun had faded and the twilight hours were upon them. Finally satiated from his Bacchanalian orgy he redressed himself, tidied her clothing and put her back in the cart. He would take her home. He wasn't too worried by the consequences. He wasn't staying.

Chapter Twenty-Six

Carrie sat numb and silent. Her wide eyes unblinking, staring blankly ahead, distracted and in shock. Her breath juddered irregularly in her chest. She moved a protective hand to her chest and fumbled with the collar button of her blouse.

Jacky sat quietly, reins in his hand and said not a word for the rest of the journey. The only sounds were Senator's hooves, the rumbling cart and Carrie's snatched gulps of air.

Jacky emanated an almost proud air of cool arrogance, of someone who had satisfied a need regardless of the cost. It was nothing to him that he had so cruelly ruined the lives of the Llewellyns. It was nothing to him that he had deceived in pursuit of his own selfish desires and pleasure. It was nothing to him that the children had lost their birthright or that he was about to destroy the life of another hapless woman.

Jacky believed himself to be in control, all powerful, that nothing could touch his supremacy at Hendre and his dealings, but he was wrong.

The wagon trundled its way up the mountain track. The evening mists had begun to thicken as the twilight hours faded from dusk into night.

The oil lamps, now lit, swung on the sides of the cart beaconing their approach to Hendre. Trixie set up a joyous barking as Senator's hooves clip clopped into the yard.

Netta opened the door to greet them. The light spilled out onto the stones in a muddy orange glow. Jacky called for John to unharness Senator and take him to the stable.

Carrie still sat frozen in the cart. Her eyes were staring and she was mute. The shadows of her horror reached out from the dimmest corners of her mind and leered up at her, growing and stretching like some misshapen demon with grasping hands threatening to suffocate her sanity. All her terrors paraded before her and a wave of nausea flooded through her.

Forced into life, by the rising of stomach acid into her mouth Carrie snapped into action, jumped off the cart and vomited violently into the drain outside the house. She coughed and retched until she had emptied her stomach.

John emerged from the house to stable Senator. Jacky swaggered past Netta indoors to look for his supper. He had worked up an appetite.

Netta looked suspiciously at his hastily misbuttoned waistcoat, and the protruding tail ends of his shirt. She smelt the familiar aroma of wheat germ semen and pheromones that had excited her in the steamy sex sessions with Jacky in the bedroom at night.

"What's the matter with her?" she asked, indicating Carrie.

"Something she ate at the market," came the glib reply. "She's been feeling rough all the way home. She'll be all right now she's brought it up. What's for supper? I'm hungry."

Carrie wiped her mouth on her sleeve and moved painfully to the glasshouse steps. She was finding it difficult to walk and paused to rest against the wall of the house. Raised voices came from within.

"You smell like a tomcat who's been locked in a cattery. You can't fool me, Jacky Ebron."

"Stop your whining and get my supper, woman. I'll not stand for your accusations and suspicions."

"What did you do?" Netta needled. "Leave poor Carrie to wander the market while you pleasured yourself in some whore house, I'll be bound."

"If you don't stop your tongue, I'll stop it for you." Jacky menaced.

"Raise your hand to me would you? It's come to a pretty pass. Well, you just try it and I'll have you out of here so fast your feet won't touch the ground."

Jacky was crafty enough to realise that letting his temper fly would do no good, so he switched tacks.

"Aw come on, Netta. Don't let's be arguing. You know there's no one in the world but you. Look, I'm sorry I'm in such a bad temper. Carrie was complaining all the way home with bellyache. It just got on my nerves, that's all."

Netta sniffed disdainfully. "Well, why do you look as if you've spent all day in bed with Madame Pompadour then?"

"I don't know. Senator had a lose shoe and I spent an age figuring what to do. I had to buy a hammer and nails to fix it in case it didn't last the journey home. I suppose with all the scrabbling about I did I must look a bit dishevelled, especially with all the bramble scratches," he added touching his injured cheek. He smiled beguilingly at her showing his perfect film star teeth.

"Why is your waistcoat buttoned wrong?"

"Because I took it off to see to the horse and I couldn't be bothered to redo it. Now, come here and give Jacky a kiss."

He slid his arm around her waist and pulled her in close. "Now, just for that and when I've eaten my supper, I'll show you what I've been thinking of all day and then, I'll fill you up," he added suggestively placing his hand on her bottom and grinding his hips against her.

Netta released herself from his embrace and the semblance of a smile graced her lips. She arched her back seductively.

"Now then, Jacky Ebron, you behave yourself. Eat your supper first," and she smiled coquettishly at him.

Jacky's lips smiled as a steaming plate was placed before him laden with meat, vegetables and gravy. But his eyes remained cold and distant while he calculated in his mind what to do next.

John came out of the stable and saw Carrie leaning against the wall, clutching her stomach in distress. He rushed to her side. "Cariad, what's wrong?"

He received no answer. Carrie doubled over and sank to the floor a dark stain spreading through the cotton of her skirt. He called helplessly to his aunt, "Aunty Netta!"

Netta presented herself on the doorstep, took one look at Carrie and rushed to help John. Between the two of them they managed to lift her up the steps and into the house. Carrie's face was deathly white and Jacky feigned concern.

"It must have been worse than I thought. If you get her to bed I'll go for the doctor."

"I've just unharnessed Senator, besides the cart's full of furniture," flustered John.

"There's no time to lose, you stay with her I'll run for Dr. Rees," the words came readily to Jacky's lips and inwardly he smiled. This was working out better than he had hoped. True, he wouldn't be able to take everything he wanted, but he had enough and now was the time he needed to move on.

"I'll just get a coat and a lamp, someone's bound to lend us transport in the village. It shouldn't take too long. At least I'll be travelling down the mountainside. Take care of her. Poor Carrie," and he looked down at her pale face and gently stroked her wild hair.

Jacky ran to his cottage and hurriedly collected some items together. He changed into his clothes of the road and patting his pocket with the bill of sale and eight hundred and fifty pounds, he grabbed a lamp and made off down the track. He took one last look at Hendre and all he was leaving and trying to suppress the whistle that rose cheerily to his lips started off into the night for pastures new.

"If the cart wasn't full of furniture, I could have gone with Jacky for the doctor," whispered John as he looked down at Carrie's pale face. "What if Dr. Rees isn't there?"

"It's no good worrying about that. Jacky will get help. That's all there is to it." Netta sounded more confident than she felt. She didn't like the look of the child who appeared to be in a severe state of shock, and whose left cheek was puffy and bruised.

"I'm going after him," said John.

"That won't do any good, besides you're of more comfort to Carrie here. Wait, he can't be much longer."

"That was over two hours ago, something's wrong. I know it. It's no use trying to stop me. I'll ride Senator to the village."

"Suit yourself," said Netta tartly, "I'll sit with Carrie although I'm sure she'd prefer you to be with her."

John leaned over his sister and stroked her forehead, carefully pushing back her wild mane of hair from her eyes. Her eyes momentarily lost that blank distracted stare and she looked up at her brother giving the first signs that she recognised him and that she knew where she was.

"I'm home?" Carrie questioned in a tiny little voice.

"You're home, cariad, and safe," murmured John.

"Thank God!" she uttered, and closed her eyes as if to sleep.

"That settles it!" Netta said acidly, "It's no good you going. Carrie's not that fond of me, she'll be needing you. I know, I know..." she waved him quiet, "It's years since I've ridden, but if you saddle up for me I'll go down to Dr. Rees. Come on, you know it makes sense. Besides, I feel I owe it to her."

John nodded. He realised his aunt was right and he went out to the stable to tack up the horse.

Netta mounted Senator gingerly. He whinnied sensing her inexperience, but being an unusually even-tempered horse he allowed her rough handling of him without complaint. John urged him on to the village with a slap and it was almost as if the horse knew the urgency that was involved and he trotted off across the yard and disappeared down the track.

John retraced his steps to the house and kept his lonely vigil at Carrie's side. Not even Trixie's company and consoling licks could ease the pain and distress he felt at seeing his sister like this.

Netta cursed as brambles and branches plucked at her clothes. She was feeling saddle sore and she was worried. Horse and rider seemed to slither down the few remaining yards of mountain track and Netta was glad to reach the more level surface of the road.

Netta tried to spur Senator into a trot and headed for the crescent where Dr. Rees lived. The streets were silent save for the clattering of hooves and in the gas lit street it was all too clear when she approached number ten that the lights were on and people were at home.

She lifted the heavy brass knocker and rapped loudly, half expecting Jacky to come to the door to say he was waiting for the doctor.

The door opened and there stood a diminutive Mrs. Rees,

looking enquiringly. "Yes? Can I help you?"

"Is the doctor in?"

Expecting a negative answer, she was surprised when the door opened wider and Mrs. Rees ushered her in. She apologised for her dishevelled state as she stepped into their sitting room.

"Don't worry about that," smiled Dr. Rees, "How can I help?"

"Has Jacky not been here?"

"Jacky? Oh, Jacky the farm worker you're to marry?"

"Yes," muttered Netta.

"Not to my knowledge. We haven't been disturbed all evening. Have we, Millicent?"

"No."

Netta pushed her thoughts and fears to the back of her mind and blurted out, "It's Carrie. There's something wrong, we don't know what. She's been vomiting and she's bleeding, there." She pointed roughly to her groin area and blushed with embarrassment.

"I see. Anything else?"

"She appears to be in a state of shock, not talking or anything. She only just recognised John before I came down."

"I'll get my bag." He turned to his wife, "Don't wait up, Millicent. I'll be back when I can. If there are any emergencies, I'm at Hendre." He spoke again to Netta, "Is the cart outside?"

"Only Senator. The cart was full and we didn't have time to unload it."

"Thomas Mitchell should lend me his mare. Millicent will you run down to number five and ask while I get my things together?"

Millicent Rees hurriedly put on her coat and hat and went out into the night. Some fifteen minutes later she returned leading a young chestnut.

The doctor secured his bag to the saddle pack and mounted. His wife called to him, "Thomas said there's no rush for the horse just as soon as you can make it back is time enough." She looked anxiously at Netta, "I hope young Carrie is all right, and that nothing has happened to your young man."

In the fifteen minutes Netta had been waiting, her mind had run riot, she had convinced herself that Jacky was lying somewhere injured, in a ditch, and that was the reason he hadn't turned up at Dr. Rees' house. Anything else was too awful to contemplate.

Mrs. Rees waved her husband goodbye and the unlikely duo started towards the edge of the village and the mountain track.

Senator followed in the wake of the mare, Jessie who valiantly scrambled up the steep slope. Not a word passed between the two riders who needed all their strength to keep the horses moving.

It was Trixie who alerted John to the arrival of the doctor and the return of his aunt. Ashen faced he went out to tie up the steeds and then made haste inside to hear what the doctor had to say.

John met Netta outside Carrie's bedroom door.

"He shooed me out while he examines her," she explained. John nodded in acknowledgement and the pair waited quietly outside her room.

Inside, a grim faced Dr. Rees was looking at the extent of Carrie's injuries. He gently pulled back the covers on the bed and tucked the coverlet around her.

"Who did this to you, Carrie fach?"

Carrie removed her blank gaze from the wall and turned to look at him, a spark of fire returned to her eyes, now that this other violation of her body was over. She recognised the doctor and knew he was there to help.

There was a barely discernible pause before her lips formed the words and she whispered, "Jacky," and the shock and humiliation she had endured came bubbling to the surface and she started to weep.

"There, there!" Dr. Rees soothed, "You're safe now, there's no one to harm you here. And I doubt whether we'll see the likes of him again."

Dr. Rees strode to the door and ushered in Netta and John. "The child has been raped," he said baldly. "She has suffered severe internal bruising and injury."

Netta staggered back, white faced, stifling a small cry of alarm. "Nooo!"

Before John could get out the words, "But who...?"

Netta knew, as she always knew, and she didn't want to admit she knew but she murmured, "I know... Jacky."

John stood stunned, hardly able to believe what he was hearing as Dr. Rees assented.

"I'm afraid so. The child told me herself. I'm sorry Netta."

Netta clutched at her throat and a low rumbling howl rose from her throat. She fled from the room and down the stairs with only one thing on her mind. Murder.

Chapter Twenty-Eight

Netta flew from the room with its hushed tones and accusations. She ran down the stairs into the yard where the sickness flooded through her and she retched violently into the drain. She wiped her mouth with the back of her hand and then, drawing herself up to her full height walked with an exaggerated air of defiance back into the house.

She lightly rinsed her mouth with some cool water, and patted her lips dry with the kitchen towel. Hands on her hips she took several deep breaths in an attempt to calm herself. Her stomach churned uncontrollably as her limbs started to tremble. She strode purposefully to the cutlery drawer and examined its contents carefully. Minutes later Netta had selected a particularly wicked looking blade usually reserved for carving the Sunday roast. She tested it lightly against her thumb and was pleased to see the drops of fresh red blood that seeped so easily through the skin. She sucked at her thumb taking pleasure in the salty, coppery taste. And her eyes burning with a righteous glint seized her coat and hat. Stuffing the knife into a canvas bag she returned to the yard, secured the bag to the saddle, mounted Senator and with Boadicean courage streaked off into the night.

John sat at Carrie's side making comforting noises as he stroked her hair. He was devastated by what he had heard and resolved that one day he would have his revenge on Jacky Ebron for the cruel defiling of his sister. He cursed himself, if only he had listened when Carrie had told him of her fear of Jacky.

Dr. Rees was as much concerned with Carrie's state of mind as with her health and gently broached the subject of the police.

Carrie shook her head, "Please no! No police. I can't go through all that happened with them and have the whole village know. Please!"

Carrie begged pleadingly with her eyes and Dr. Rees sighed, "I know how you feel, Carrie dear, but we can't be letting him get away with it. Or there'll be another young girl in another town or village who will suffer at that devil's hands. Do you want that?"

"I'm sorry... Of course I don't want anyone else hurt but I can't bear to think of everyone knowing. Haven't I suffered enough?"

John turned his sorrowful eyes on the doctor, "Look I understand what you're saying, we all do, but the time's not now. Let Carrie have her wish. Rest assured it won't be forgotten but my first priority is to Carrie and if that's the way she wants it, then so be it."

Dr. Rees nodded slowly, "I see. You've thought about the possible consequences?"

"What do you mean?"

"Carrie's a young woman now, she told me she's started her periods." Dr. Rees' tone was grave, "She could have a baby."

"Is there nothing you can do?" John asked.

"We don't know for certain, so it's best we wait. If she's fallen..." He stopped.

"Come on, Doctor. There must be something you can do," pressed John.

"All right, all right. I'll respect your wishes. I can't blame you for reacting like this. I don't know what I'd do in the same circumstances."

"What about now?" John questioned.

"She must have plenty of bed rest and I'm afraid I'll need to stitch her, so I'll need hot water if you could arrange it."

"Certainly." John rose up from Carrie's side and shouted down the stairs, "Aunty Netta! The doctor needs some boiling water. Can you put the kettle on the range." There was no answering shout, so John called out to his aunt again, "Aunty Netta!"

"Perhaps it would be better if you did it," said the doctor gently. "Your aunt will be in need of some attention herself I expect," and he nodded meaningfully to the door.

John sighed in agreement and reluctantly left the room.

Five minutes later, he was back. "I've put the kettle on, the water shouldn't be long." Then he added, "I can't see Aunty Netta anywhere. I've called and called. Senator's gone too."

"Let her go. She'll need some time alone. It's been a shock for her too, remember. Now, go and fetch the water."

John nodded dully, and went out leaving the doctor to minister to Carrie's wounds. He returned a few minutes later with a jug of steaming hot water and placed it on the wash-stand. "I'll be downstairs if you need me," and with a heart weighed down with sorrow he returned to the kitchen.

Waiting seemed an eternity to John, but in fact only ten minutes passed before Dr. Rees was standing in the kitchen with him again.

He stooped to put his hat on his head, remaining hunched up in the low ceilinged room.

"She's sleeping now, John. Let her rest. I've treated her as best I can and I've stitched her up. There's some lauda-num for her if the pain gets any worse. Use it sparingly and follow the directions." He cleared his throat uncomfortably, "I'll respect your wishes, although I don't agree with them. In my opinion that beast should be hunted down and dealt with by the proper authorities. However, I shall come out again in a day or two and if we feel the need," he gestured upstairs, "To what we spoke of - I'll help all I can." John knew what he meant and smiled limply. Dr. Rees said his good-bye quietly and went back into the yard to Jessie. John heard the faint clip clop of hooves on cobbles that faded into the distance. He put his face in his hands and wept.

Netta was burning with a murderous rage. Her stomach knotted sickly in anguish and jealousy and she chastised her-self for being a fool. Her sister Annie had been right. That fact in itself was enough to fire her anger. But the pain and heartbreak she was feeling now, was like nothing she had ever experienced before. Not even when Penry had died had she suffered such torturing agony. Agony that could only be exorcised by putting a blade through Jacky Ebron's heart.

"The bastard!" she exclaimed, "The lying, cheating bas-tard. I'll swing for him," and she continued down the track and into the village of Crynant.

There she had to stop and think. He was cunning, as sly as a fox. Which way would he go? Netta deduced that if he'd already been to Neath then he would have tied up his business in that area. He was not likely to travel anywhere that would put his life in jeopardy, he would go nowhere that he might be recognised. This meant he could only travel one way, north. She turned the horse decisively. He'd been gone now for nearly four hours and he was travelling on foot. He may have rested up somewhere for the night, but she thought not. Netta determined to press on and find him.

The midnight blue of the sky lightened, as the rosy hues of dawn seeped through the clouds washing the horizon a dusky crimson welcoming the morning. The wakening birds began to ruffle their feathers and chirrup their first song of a new day.

Netta was weary. Her back ached, her bottom was sore but the flame of vengeance blazed fiercely within her driving her onwards. She ignored the complaints of her body and the heaviness of her eyelids and pressed Senator forwards. Unaccustomed to such exercise he had now slowed to a walk.

Netta wiped a dusty hand across her face. Was it her eyes playing tricks or could she really see a figure in the distance? She squinted her eyes and stared hard. A man in black with a bedroll on his back, wearing a preacher's hat. That walk, that arrogant swagger could only belong to one person.

"Jacky!" she whispered, and licked her dry lips in anticipation. Netta kicked the horse's sides hard, forcing Senator to trot and then canter after the man who was just disappearing over the next rise.

A dust cloud whirled under Senator's hooves as he pursued the quarry his rider was hunting down.

If Jacky was disturbed by the approaching rider he didn't show it. He felt no curiosity or concern to make him turn and see who was thundering along behind him.

Netta's unmistakable voice called out to Senator to "Whoa!" and she drew up alongside the man who was her fiancé.

A startled flash of anxiety revealed itself in those darkly

passionate eyes that had so beguiled and seduced her.

"Steady now, Netta fach. Steady!" she told herself as much to stop her from falling for his lies or to forget the mission she had set herself. As he looked at her, she felt that nervous flutter of excitement, that leap of desire, that tingling yearning that spread through her thighs.

"Well, Jacky?" she questioned, she didn't know what else to say, yet. Through all of this night chase she hadn't once planned what she would say if she confronted him.

"Netta, gal. I'm glad to see you."

"Are you?" Her voice was acidly menacing.

"Course I am, fy merch 'i. I was going to get in touch."

"What for? To say goodbye?"

"No, no! You've got it all wrong."

"Have I? Then you'd better put me right."

"Come on. I'll help you down off Senator and we can talk."

"I'm fine where I am, thank you. Talk away."

Jacky cleared his throat, "What's that little minx been saying to you?"

"Little minx? Oh, you mean Carrie. Not much, she's not been in much of a position to, is she?"

"Why what's happened?"

"What's happened? You know full well what's happened. Don't deny it."

"If you know, why are you bothering to ask?" he said quietly.

Netta bit her tongue. She needed to feel some pain, to stop herself from being carried along on his sea of lies.

A sudden flash of clarity hit her and she knew exactly what she would do and how she would do it.

"I can't believe it. That's why I need to hear it from your lips."

"I don't know what the child's told you I only know what she threatened."

"How do you mean?"

"It seems that when she went round the market in Neath she was assaulted by some old man. She ran crying to me and after she calmed down she started hinting things."

"Hinting things?"

"Yes, she said if I didn't give up the idea of taking you as my wife and keeping Hendre that she'd tell everyone it was I who hurt her." He paused to see if his words were having the desired effect.

"Go on," urged Netta.

"Well, she threatened to blackmail me if I didn't. She said the only way I could stop her was to get rid of you and wait until she was older. Then we would be master and mistress of Hendre together."

Netta's eyes glittered with spite and hurt. He was very nearly breaking through her resolve.

"Of course, I told her I couldn't. That I loved you. She went silent then for most of the journey. We had just passed Cilfrew when Senator's shoe came loose... That's when it happened."

"When what happened?"

"I got down to have a look and Carrie said she needed to go to the toilet so she disappeared into the woods. I didn't know, I swear to God I didn't know she had a knife with her. Plucky little madam, so damned determined to have her own way, she cut herself, mutilated herself. Made a good job of it too from the looks of it. Well, when she came back she was in some pain and left me in no doubt that she would keep her word, unless I gave in. When she passed out like that I knew what would happen and I couldn't take the risk. I started out to get the doctor and then my nerve failed me. I vowed I'd get clear of Hendre and the Dulais valley. Then as soon as I was settled I'd write to you and explain. Then if you believed me and still wanted me, I could send for you. Now, do you understand?"

"Oh, Jacky, of course I understand. I knew you couldn't do anything like that why do you think I followed you?"

Netta leaned over and removed her bag. She slid down off the side of the horse and wrapped her arms around Jacky's neck nestling her face in his chest.

She looked up at him and parted her lips for his kiss, arching her back and thrusting her hips into his groin. Jacky flicked his tongue between her lips, probing her mouth, setting up little needles of electricity that fanned her desire.

"Come on," she coaxed, her tongue exploring his ear. "Tie Senator up and let's go in there." She pointed to the sheltering woods where he could sate his desire.

Jacky hesitated fractionally, but when she edged away mouthing and stroking her finger with her tongue Jacky did as he was bid.

Netta ran lightly into the woods, her tiredness forgotten. She took out the knife and hid it underneath the empty bag, placing it at her side. She removed her coat and laid it out on the dew damp grass. She pulled off her hat and put it on top of the bag. Then, she stretched out on her coat, undid the buttons on her bodice and lifted her skirts above her waist. She took off her knickers and parted her thighs in readiness.

Jacky emerged into the clearing and was faced with that fascinating mound of thick dark pubic hair that rose and fell as Netta lifted those hips begging to be entered. She made little animal sounds as her head turned from side to side and Jacky smiled.

He brazenly undid his coppish and struggled to release himself. He walked towards her rubbing himself gently up and down until the tell tale drops of his excitement were visible. He lowered himself onto her and feeling her exquisite heat, he surged into her, exploring her nipples with his tongue as his thrusts became harder and more frantic. All the time Netta whispered, tantalisingly to him, urging him on, fiercely clamping him to her with her strong legs. She stroked his back with one hand whilst she felt under the bag with the other until her hand grasped hold of the handle.

Jacky pushed himself up in a frenzy of delirium as he announced, "I'm coming, I'm coming. Oh Duw!" and he fountained forth within her and as his body reached the heights of ecstasy, Netta plunged the knife into his back. His body juddered with the orgasmic spasms and the sharp pain he felt between his shoulder blades. His eyes registered a look of disbelief as she twisted the blade once more. Jacky Ebron fell forward and died.

Disgusted Netta pushed his dead weight from off her, and she looked on the face of the man she had loved.

She stifled a sob, and willed her trembling limbs to be still. Then, overwhelmed with an inexplicable calm, she kissed his still warm lips and redressed herself. Netta walked back to where the horse was waiting, remounted and began to make her way back to Hendre.

Chapter Twenty-Nine

For the first time Netta looked, really looked at her surroundings. She could hardly believe that she was on the outskirts of Crai, close to the town of Sennybridge, near Brecon. The furthest she'd ever been, apart from Neath, was Seven Sisters where her sister Gwenny lived.

It wasn't long before she approached the signs to the famous Dan-yr-Ogof caves. People came from miles around to see these caves. She suspected that, that was where Jacky had sheltered and slept for part of the night.

Jacky, his name still brought a sigh to her lips and a tear to her eye. Even though she felt she had righted the greater wrong she knew she still loved him.

Senator stopped to browse on the hedgerow before moving off and settling himself to feed on some clover in an unfenced meadow.

Netta sat numbed. She shuddered involuntarily. The memory of Jacky Ebron's thrusting body flashed through her mind. Again she relived the feel of the knife in her hands, the weight of his body on hers and the revulsion with which she had pushed him from her.

She was unaware of the spectacle she presented to the outside world. Jacky's blood had seeped through to the front of her bodice and was still sticky and wet. Her eyes were wide and staring. Her hair had come loose from its restricting bun and straggled down over her shoulders. Her right hand was crimson with his blood. The stain spread darkly up her arm. She sat astride Senator, silent and unseeing except for the violent images that thrashed through her mind.

People were stirring in the outlying houses. Smoke puffed out of chimneys as kitchen ranges were refuelled to boil the pans and kettles set on them.

Senator stirred uneasily and shifted his weight. He brought his head up from where he had been nibbling and whinnied gently as a stranger moved towards them.

The man was young with a spring in his step and he wore the typical garb of a farm labourer. He swung towards them and doffed his cap looking curiously at Netta whose features were frozen in an anguished grimace.

"Are you all right, fy merch 'i?" he asked fearing she was ill. If she heard him she gave no sign. She stifled a wail and brought her blood soaked hand up to her face muttering, "No more! No more! Be still, damn you," and she caught at her throat stilling her cries.

The young man took a step back when he saw her hand. He stared hard at her, noticing her bloodied front and the frenzied look of pain in her eyes. He spoke again, "You're not ill are you?"

Netta, still lost in her thoughts of Jacky, neither heard nor saw him. She whispered to the air around her, "Why didn't I listen? Why didn't I see?" Then, she cursed and swore at her foolishness and a tide of tears coursed down her cheeks for what she had done.

Netta pulled Senator up sharply and dug her heels into his flanks to press him homeward and continued on her way.

The young man shocked by what he had seen, walked on towards the woods on the outskirts of Crai, which he had to cross to reach his place of work. He puzzled over the woman he had seen and her odd behaviour. He would have an even greater shock when he walked further on and discovered Jacky Ebron's body.

Senator plodded on solemnly, through Ystradgynlais and Dowlais. He paused to graze on the common land. Netta too weary to pull him up, let him feed. She sat silently in the saddle remembering her plans and dreams now cruelly destroyed.

She thought nothing of her future now and nothing of her own endangered freedom following the crime she had committed. Her eyes stared dully at the road ahead. It was quite some time before she moved Senator on.

Carrie felt defiled, dirty and degraded. She needed to wash and cleanse herself. John in compliance with her wishes had boiled numerous pans of water, filled the tin bath, and set it in front of the range in the kitchen.

The water was almost too hot to bear but Carrie forced herself into it, her skin turning scarlet on contact. Then she set to, scrubbing, washing, and purging herself of Jacky's filthy touch. She let out an agonised cry of anger as she finished soaping herself for the fourth time. It was as if she would never be clean and she vowed that no man would ever abuse her again.

Trixie whined and scratched at the kitchen door when she heard her mistress thrashing about in the water. John came running when he heard her cry. "Are you all right, cariad?" he asked anxiously.

"Yes, thank you. I just feel so used and dirty."

A lump rose into John's throat and he spoke reassuringly through the door, "Nothing or no one could ever taint your loveliness." He spoke with deep feeling, "You mustn't let this cruelty foul your mind. Together we'll come through this, through everything. You'll see."

Carrie wished she could believe him, but she knew she'd been robbed of her innocence in a particularly horrific manner and although the physical scars would eventually heal she doubted if her mind would. Carrie said tremulously, "Oh John, the only man I could ever trust in the world now, is you."

Carrie's words filled him with delight as well as guilt, and he said softly, "Your fears are but shadows on the moon, they make the night seem black and long but they always pass; and then the moon shines all the brighter to make up for having its light stolen away."

Carrie controlled the sobbing that was rising in her breast and in a trembling voice called out, "John, come in and hold me. I need you to hug me and tell me it will all get better."

John gently lifted the latch. Carrie beckoned to him to fetch the towel warming by the fire. Just as their mother had done when they were little children, he wrapped her up and briskly rubbed her dry. She sat quietly at his feet, whilst he towelled her damp, fiery tresses and when he had finished, she sat on his lap in the rocker, still dressed in her towel and he cradled her in his arms, singing to her gently until she was asleep.

It was late afternoon when Senator clattered into the yard with Netta. She had travelled slowly, burdened by the enormity of her deed.

Netta looked a broken woman as she stepped over the threshold. Gone was her proud bearing and majesty that had been apparent to all. Gone was that spark of fighting spirit that had always glimmered so dangerously in her eyes.

She sat in the fireside chair opposite the rocker, where Carrie, now dressed, sat on her brother's knee and stared into the heart of the fire as the flames curled and danced over the coals.

"I've killed him," was all Netta said. She looked up at them both. And there was silence.

The three of them sat quietly and unmoving until the evening sun was fading in the sky. They were still sitting quietly when the police came.

Trixie fell to a sudden and ferocious barking that belied her nature and scratched on the glasshouse door. John eased himself out from under Carrie who sat rocking gently, her eyes no longer blank but alert. Carrie turned her head and watched John, "Who is it?"

"I'm not sure. I'm going to look."

Carrie stood up and followed her brother out to the yard where the village policeman, Trevor Pritchard, and two constables from Sennybridge stood.

"Sorry, Master John," said Trevor. "Is Netta there?"

"Yes, she's in the kitchen. Why?"

"It's a hard thing we have to do but your aunt is to be arrested for the murder of Jacky Ebron." Trevor shifted uneasily in his boots, "May we come in?"

"Of course," said John and opened the door wide to let them through.

When they entered the kitchen Netta was standing defiant at the dresser. She had pulled herself up to her full height and no longer looked cowed and weak. She was just slipping on her gloves. She turned and looked at them, "I'll just get my hat and then, I'll be ready to go." She picked it up from the floor at the side of her chair, and pinned it securely to her head.

"Right. Ready when you are," she announced in a matter of fact tone, "John, you can take my things to Mam-gu's can't you?"

John nodded and then she continued, "I'm sorry this had to happen. That I was too blind to see." She sighed primly, "You may not believe it, but it's true. Forgive me if you can."

With that she turned smartly on her heels and accompanied the police outside to the waiting wagon, which rolled out of the yard and down the mountain slope.

"Well cariad, it's just you and me now," and he placed a protective arm around his sister's shoulder. She looked up trustingly at him and together they walked back into the house.

Chapter Thirty

Jacky Ebron's body was recovered. Netta admitted her guilt and stated that she was fully prepared to take the consequences.

The whole of the village was awash with the news. There was gossip in every yard, accusations at every turn, whispered mutterings in huddled corners and throughout it all the family retained their distance and maintained their dignity.

A large sum of money had been found on Jacky's body. The police were uncertain as to whom it belonged and it was to be held by them until the courts could decide.

Carrie and John were gradually becoming used to having Hendre to themselves. It seemed as if right was finally on their side and that they would no longer lose their birthright. They rejoiced in that fact but they were taking too much for granted too soon.

It was early on Saturday morning and Carrie was emerging from the milking parlour carrying a bucket full of fresh warm milk. So full was the pail that the creamy smoothness slopped over the side and onto the ground where Trixie was ready with her tongue to lap up the warm goodness.

Trix stopped short, looked up and gently snuffed the air and then set up an excited barking such as they heard when visitors arrived.

Bespectacled Mr. Phillips, the Neath solicitor, was strutting into the yard accompanied by the gentleman Carrie had seen outside the lawyer's office with Jacky, on that fateful day.

"Ah, Carrie, my dear," puffed Mr. Phillips. "This is Mr. Lawrence." He said this as if the words were explanation enough.

Carrie squinted in the brightness of the day, her fiery hair a spangle of lights in the morning sun.

"Yes?" She looked questioningly at the lawyer that she neither liked nor trusted.

"Surely you know the name?" he blustered, turning pink with embarrassment.

"I'm sorry?"

"Oh dear, this is really most awkward. I really don't know what to say."

"Try the truth," said Mr. Lawrence.

Carrie looked at the stranger again. She put down her milk bucket and shaded her eyes from the glare of the sun and studied his face. He was in his early twenties, of medium height and build with rich brown hair and pale grey eyes that had a hint of steel. His chin was firm and strong, his complexion clear and he had an air about him that suggested he was someone used to being obeyed.

"Well?" probed Carrie, "Please be quick, I haven't got all day."

Mr. Lawrence smiled. It changed the whole of his expression hinting at an abundance of personality and humour. Carrie felt herself smiling back.

"I'm the new owner," the gentleman said.

"What?

"Hendre. It's mine," he added looking bemused.

"No. It can't be!" She turned to barn owled Mr. Phillips, "Tell me it's not true. That it's a cruel joke."

"I only wish it were," panted Mr. Phillips.

"Why? What's the problem?" Mr. Lawrence asked, puzzled at the response.

"It's all very involved," grunted Mr. Phillips. He looked despairingly around as if the words he needed would somehow come from the air. There was nothing for it but the truth so he took a deep breath and tried to explain. "Jacky, came to me some time ago,"

"Jacky!" hissed Carrie derisively.

Mr. Phillips continued, "Jacky came to see me and asked if I could find a buyer for Hendre. He didn't want it advertised, to safeguard your feelings from a lot of gossip was how he put it."

"I see," she said coldly.

The young man turned to Carrie somewhat surprised at the embittered expression that had fixed itself on Carrie's sweet face.

"I don't understand, your uncle said you were looking forward to moving."

"Uncle!" she snorted, "Is that how he described himself? Well Mr. Lawrence, Hendre is not up for sale, and never will be. So take your offer and look elsewhere."

The young man's facial muscles began to pulse. He drew his lips back and said firmly but quietly, "Now you just listen young lady. I don't know what I've walked into here, but I paid good money for this house and land. I had an agreement to visit a fortnight before I would be ready to move in, to give me time to conclude my affairs and to give you time to move out. Now my part has been accomplished and I am giving you order to quit a fortnight today."

With that he turned on his heel and strode through the yard to the gate leaving Mr. Phillips fumbling an apology. "So sorry, my dear, but it's all true, every word. The money changed hands the last time you visited Neath with your uncle... er Mr. Ebron."

Carrie's hands had started to shake, not with anxiety but with pure rage. She knew that if she spoke she would fly off into a screaming paddy and end up in tears of frustration and anger. She took a deep breath and tried to control her words, "Take your briefcase and your buyer and leave my land. I think you said we had a fortnight?"

"Yes, yes a fortnight," fussed Mr. Phillips, "That's all right then?"

"No, it's not all right, but if you mean will we be gone, then I believe we have no choice?"

Mr. Phillips nodded and scrambled after the waiting Mr. Lawrence, fawning apologies.

Carrie stood her ground and watched them leave the yard. She picked up the milk pail and returned to the house, a crispness in her stride that contradicted the turmoil boiling within her.

She was stung to the quick by this disastrous turn of events. She thrust the bucket down and hammered on the table, numb to the bruises that would show themselves later. Her crystal clear voice now roughened with passion cried out to the house, "So Jacky Ebron, even from your grave, you manage to work your mischief. But you'll not break me. I'll suffer no more of your tormenting."

Carrie washed and dried her hands and changed from her working clothes into one of her mother's suits. It was a little big, but she wanted to appear somewhat older and more mature to make her look less vulnerable. She tried to tease her wild fiery hair into some order, covering it with a felt cloche hat. Carrie secured it with a pearl hatpin and using her mother's little used powder and puff tried to conceal her youthfulness.

Carrie hastily scrawled a note to John and robbing the jar of its kitty went to harness Senator to the cart and drove into Crynant.

Carrie took great pleasure in rattling past a perspiring Mr. Phillips and his client, forcing them into the undergrowth of brambles and nettles. Ignoring their startled cries she careered on down the mountain slope to the level road and into the village.

She pulled up outside Evans the death, the undertaker, secured the horse and marched in primly. Her fingers drummed lightly on the counter top whilst she waited in the darkened shop front that respected the dead.

An unhurried Talfryn Evans came noiselessly from the back room where he did his embalming. He was tall and gaunt with a mournful appearance that well suited his job. He was somewhat surprised to see Carrie standing there in clothes too big, and her carefully ordered hair now a tangled mass whirling out from under her hat as a result of her ride down the mountainside.

"Yes?" he enquired in a servile manner, his hands clasped in front of him as if in penance.

"Jacky Ebron's funeral is to be Tuesday, yes?"

"Why yes."

"Good, then I'm not too late. The funeral is being paid for, am I right?"

"Well yes, the gentleman had more than enough money on him to cover my costs. The police have dictated that the dead man himself should pay for the burial."

"Excellent. Well, what I want is quite simple. Has anyone ordered a headstone?"

"Why no." His eyes glinted greedily, "The police weren't prepared for anything more than a name plate on a simple stone cross."

"Well, I wish to change that. I want you to place a stone weighing one ton over his grave. Surround it with iron railings and inscribe the words, in capitals, 'God have mercy on your soul'. Can you do that?"

"But Miss Carrie, where am I to get a stone that size? Are you sure you wouldn't like an angel with a book? I've got a lovely one here, 'God forgives all' it says. Surely that's the same sentiment?"

"No! I want to make sure he can never leave his coffin in any form or spirit. He'll never cheat or harm another living being again. Now, how much will that cost?"

"But it's such short notice. I don't know even if I should do it. By what authority do you make such a request?"

"He had no next of kin. He was to be married to my aunt that makes me his niece. Is that authority enough?"

"Well, I suppose so, yes," said the undertaker his greasy servility forgotten, "But I still don't think..."

Carrie cut him off mid sentence and took out a large white five-pound note from her purse. His avaricious eyes brightened when he saw the proffered money.

"Will this do to be going on with? I'm sure it'll spur you on to find the stone. I don't even mind waiting until after the funeral if you're sure you can get it done." She pushed the note tantalisingly close to his long, lean fingertips, then added, "Of course if you think it's impossible then I shall take the business to Neath. I'm sure someone there can help me."

The note brushed his fingertips and he grasped hold of it firmly, "There's no need to dally with Neath. I'm sure I can fulfil your wishes."

"Good, then take this on account and I'll pay the rest on completion."

"But, don't you want to know how much it will cost?"

"Mr. Evans," she said soulfully, "I'm sure you'll do right by me. You wouldn't cheat an orphan would you? And now, if you don't mind I must visit the police and inform them of my transaction and discuss the question of some missing money."

Startled by the mention of the police his previous humility returned, "Of course, of course."

Carrie threw him a charming smile, removed the constraining hat and pin, and shook out her wild mane of hair, "Well then, I'll bid you good day," and she gracefully turned and left the shop, leaving the shop bell clamouring loudly in her wake.

Carrie smiled delightedly, she knew Mam's clothes would help her. And help they had. Her mother had plenty of spirit and was never afraid to stand up for her rights. Carrie knew in her own clothes she wouldn't have been so brave, but in her mother's... She knew she felt, looked and sounded different. On she went through the streets to find the village policeman.

Trevor Pritchard was relaxing in his armchair listening to the wireless, a mug of tea in his hand, jacket undone and his tie loosened. He moved nimbly when he heard the door open but relaxed when he saw it was Carrie Llewellyn. There was something not quite right about her. He couldn't put his finger on it she just didn't look quite the same. "Carrie," he acknowledged.

"Mr. Pritchard, I've come about the money that was found on Jacky Ebron's body. It belongs to us."

"Carrie fach, we've been through all this before. You both said you had no idea where the money came from. I can't just hand it over to you without proof. Besides the court has directed we hold on to it."

"And if you've deposited it in a bank, you'll be making a tidy profit from it I expect," retorted Carrie surprised at her growing confidence. She continued, "Jacky Ebron sold Hendre, which didn't belong to him and I need the money to return to the buyer or we lose our home."

"Well now, even if that's true and I've no reason to doubt your word, you Llewellyns have always been a honest bunch, it will take some time to establish your rights to it."

"Time is something I don't have much of. What do you

advise?"

Trevor Pritchard took a lengthy statement from Carrie, which he promised to present to the courts, then added, "Look, take my advice, get yourself a lawyer. Someone you can trust to handle this affair. Not anyone who had anything to do with Ebron."

"Don't worry, I wouldn't trust Phillips, Pugsley and Pugh anymore than I would a hungry ferret down a rabbit hole," she said using her Aunty Annie's phrase.

"There's plenty of choice in Neath. Find someone who comes recommended."

"Whom do you recommend?" Carrie asked sweetly.

"I've never had no dealings with lawyers. Not even to make a will. I know I should, but they cost so much," he paused. "Ask Gareth Williams or Dr. Rees, they'd know. They'll see you all right."

Carrie smiled, thanked him politely and left. The contest of ownership was in her hands now, and with the strength of her mother's spirit she would use everything at her disposal to regain the family home.

Chapter Thirty-One

Carrie was waiting anxiously for John's return from Neath. She sat in the rocker springing it fiercely back and fore, her fists clenched white on the padded arms. The grandfather clock sliced away the minutes with each swing of its pendulum.

The waiting was unbearable. She stood abruptly, leaving the rocker scraping crazily on the slate, ran to the glasshouse door for the fourth time in twenty minutes, and gazed across the yard. A minute later she was back and resumed her frenetic rocking.

Trixie looked up from the rag mat and whimpered, sensing Carrie's agitation.

Carrie looked down at the dog and smiled, "I know, I know. I can't sit still. I'm worse than a bug on its back. Got fleas nesting in my knickers is what Aunty Annie'd say!"

Carrie rose again and walked into the pantry. She hunted through the jars on the shelves until she found what she was looking for. She took a piece of liquorice root and started to chew on it while she resealed the Kilner jar.

She liked the twiggy feel to the stick and its chewiness. She resumed her seat and concentrated hard on flattening the end, sucking all the taste out of it. Carrie used her nails to pick at the woody bits that stuck in her teeth whilst carelessly humming a tune to herself.

Trixie raised her head from her paws and stood up, shaking her coat and wagging her tail. Carrie knew this meant John was approaching Hendre.

Sure enough some minutes later Carrie heard the wagon's iron rimmed wheels rolling into the cobbled yard. She sprang up from the rocker, tossed her sweetmeat on the fire and ran to the door and out into the yard bursting with questions for John.

"Let me get in first, cariad. I'll see to Senator and then I'll tell you everything." He paused changing the subject,

"What's for supper? I'm starved."

"Come on, John, don't keep me in suspense. Is it good news or bad?"

"Both, I'm afraid," he sighed as he unharnessed the horse. "Let me stable him and I promise you I'll explain. Go on, go in and get supper."

"The table's all laid, the food's keeping warm." She hesitated by the door and watched John.

"Carrie!"

"Oh all right!" she said grudgingly and flounced off.

John allowed a grin to spread across his face. She was an impatient little madam; a proper funny ossity. No one was going to persuade her to shop when she didn't want to that was for sure.

But, John felt a flicker of pride; in spite of all she'd been through she had grown in strength. And she was still as stubborn now as she ever had been. She was becoming more like her mother every day.

Carrie's torment was soon to be over. Once John was settled and tucking into his food he recounted the day's events.

"So, you see cariad, although everything *seems* to be legal like, with Dad signing away the house and only leaving us with Gelli Galed. It seems the *way* Hendre was lost was illegal, making the contract null and void. Also, Jacky Ebron has no close family and he describes us as his nephew and niece in all the legal documents the solicitor holds. Now, Mr. Bridgeland thinks that we can lay claim to the money paid for Hendre and he will write to this Mr. Lawrence and explain the full truth surrounding the sale and ask if we can buy Hendre back paying him the standard rate of interest on top of the house price for the length of time since the purchase. This will save us bringing a civil action, which could take anything up to two years or more to be heard. So, our hope is that this Mr. Lawrence will sell"

"Do you think he'll accept?"

"I don't know. You spoke to him what do you think?"

"I'm not too sure. I wasn't very pleasant to him."

"Well, we'll just have to wait and see. Anyway, it's not so bad, if we do get the money and he won't sell it back at least we won't have to go half crease and owe anyone anything. We'll have enough to buy our own stock and build ourselves up just like Dadcu did until such a time as we can win our court case and reclaim Hendre. We still have to live."

"How long before we know about the money?"

"That could take a while. But Mr. Bridgeland is almost certain that we will get it."

"Almost certain?" Carrie said wistfully.

"All we can do is be patient and wait."

"Easier said than done." grumbled Carrie who always found it difficult to wait for anything.

"So what about moving out?"

"Well, we'd best be prepared. I'll make a start sorting out what we need to take with us tomorrow. It'll give me more pleasure if I think we may be able to put it all back."

Carrie sighed soulfully. She'd always been an optimist but so much had happened to her she felt it would be better to believe the worst and then she wouldn't be disappointed.

That week Carrie and John were kept busy packing and clearing the house. It was a time of laughter and tears. Forgotten treasures were rediscovered. Carrie wept when she sorted through her father's things and bundled his good clothes into a box. These she would keep, thinking they may be of use to John later on.

Old clothes and other oddments that were not to be kept, she offloaded onto the minister at the chapel who promised to deliver them to the mission in Neath and thanked her for her charity.

Each day she waited for news from Mr. Bridgeland, the Neath solicitor who had taken up their cause.

The following Wednesday a letter arrived. Carrie collected the letter from the box by the gate and studied it carefully. She slowly walked back to the house turning the envelope over and over in her hands. She recognised the name on the back of the envelope as the Neath firm in which Mr. Bridgeland was a partner.

Trixie padded along at her side, wagging her tail.

Carrie was filled with a cold dread. The waiting had come to an end. At least no news had left her with some hope, but she feared the worst.

The letter was addressed to John. She wanted to tear it open, or even throw it on the fire. She was filled with such confusion, wanting to read it and yet still remain in the blissful state of ignorance. She knew she could wait no longer. With her heart thumping and a curious fluttering in her stomach akin to fear, she broke into a run and yelled across the yard as she ran, "John! It's come. Quick, open it."

John heard her screams from inside and dashed out fastening his waistcoat as he came. He met her on the glasshouse steps. They both fell silent and not a word was said as Carrie solemnly handed him the letter. He too studied the envelope in silence before ripping at the flap with his thumb and forefinger. With trembling hands he teased out the headed notepaper and unfolded the letter.

Carrie anxiously watched his face as he read. His hands dropped to his side and the letter slipped from his grasp to flutter to the ground.

Carrie searched his eyes for some clue in his expression then snatched up the letter before an errant breeze could steal it away.

She struggled her way through the solicitor's jargon and looked up, "He won't sell. The bastard won't sell. Oh John, what'll we do?"

"Nothing. We'll move as planned. He may own Hendre temporarily, but he will never own its heart. He'll find it harder than he thought to take over our farm. You'll see cariad, in two years he'll be begging us to buy it back."

"Why? How?"

"We've got friends here, Carrie. That's more than Mr. Lawrence has. I don't think he'll find it easy living here."

John took the letter from Carrie and screwed it up into a tight ball and flung it onto the range as soon as he entered the kitchen. It popped lightly as the flames licked round it. Soon all that was left were some charred fragments. "Well, time to set to girl. As soon as we've had breakfast we'll start taking our things to Gelli Galed. I need to get the range lit and warm up the house. All the work we've done on it has paid off. It should be in a reasonable state for us."

They ate breakfast in silence and spent the day moving their boxes and belongings to the house on the side of the hill known as Hard Living, Gelli Galed.

GELLI GALED

HARD LIVING

Gelli Galed

One

Carrie paused, misty eyed, in the cobbled yard. She turned back to look over her shoulder at Hendre, the old home the name taken from her great grandfather who had helped to build it. The time had come to leave. Only her pale porcelain skin and the suggestion of dark rings around her large haunted eyes, reflected the ordeals of stormy times past.

John had gone on ahead with the last wagonload. Carrie had remained to check that nothing of importance had been left.

It had been a lonely walk around the house as she inspected each room with its shadowed corners and memories. The echoed murmuring of voices whispering goodbye and the etchings of family faces seemed indelibly imprinted on the walls as the essence of three generations melded with the emptiness that begged the future not to leave.

It was hard to say adieu. Carrie sighed, with her face looking determined to face any challenge she turned to the track and started the slow ascent to Gelli Galed and a new beginning.

Carrie glanced down and ruffled the fur of the collie looking adoringly up at her. "Well Trix, it's you, me and John now."

Carrie's spangled hair blew gently from her face. She looked more than her sixteen years. Head up, shoulders hunched against the wind, she shook off the despairing cloak of sadness that had displayed her loss to the world, and adopting the mantle of hope, of new beginnings, and with increased enthusiasm she stepped out onto the hillside to the renovated property that was now to be her home.

Half way up the path she stopped to rest, "I don't know, Trix. I'm feeling tired all of a sudden".

Carrie had been feeling off colour the last few days. She

had put it down to the pressures of the move and her distress of leaving the home she loved. But, now she was aware of other changes taking place in her body.

She felt a pleasurable tingling sensation in her breasts that were now extremely sensitive. They felt as if they were filling out. She'd noticed her nipples were darkening and enlarging. She was experiencing a slight ache in her lower back and undue fatigue after completing the least energetic of tasks.

Carrie smoothed the collie's velvet black head and looked sorrowfully into the dog's gentle brown eyes, "I know what I must do, Trix. Check the calendar. That's what Aunty Annie'd make me do," and she resolved to study her diary when she reached the house.

Carrie took a deep breath and resumed her climb. It was some thirty minutes later that she reached what was before a rickety wooden gate, now repaired, shiny with paint and newly hinged. She walked to the front door with its brass fox head knocker and before she had a chance to put her hand on the handle the door opened with a flourish and John stopped her from entering.

"No, cariad, no! For good luck let's cross the threshold properly."

He scooped her up into his arms, planted a kiss on her laughing face and carried her into the house where he placed her down in the newly painted hallway.

"I thought it was only married couples did that," giggled Carrie.

"Well, what's good enough for them's good enough for us. Besides we need all the luck we can get."

Carrie gazed around the hallway and passage. John had worked hard to repair and paint the house inside and out. Familiar treasures looked down on her and the leisurely tick of the grandfather clock welcomed her. This, too, was a house of memories of generations past. The spirits of the Llewellyn's ancestors were here too, as well. Carrie could feel it. She could feel their pride, their hurt and their power willing her on to succeed.

The passage to the kitchen was long and gloomy in spite

of the light, freshly painted walls.

"We must hang a lamp each end by the doors to make it brighter and more cheerful," she prompted. "And we must get help. There's much to do to get the fields in order. Too much for you."

"You are right, but I don't fancy advertising in the paper like Dad did."

"There's no need. Let's ask old Tom. Just to begin with, as a temporary measure. There are plenty of people looking for work. We'll take someone recommended. Someone we can check out and trust."

John sighed, "It makes sense, but that could take a while."

"That's why I think old Tom would help us until we found someone. He did say, remember?"

John had to agree that this seemed a sensible solution and they decided that while Carrie finished the unpacking, John would visit old Tom at Cilfrew to see if he would be prepared to come and help.

Trixie followed Carrie up the narrow spiral staircase and accompanied her beloved mistress on her inspection of the rooms.

John left Carrie exploring the house and went outside to the barn where Senator was stabled. He saddled up and left for Cilfrew.

Carrie heard the sound of horse hooves clattering out of the yard. She sat down on the feather bed in her room and looked wistfully at the naked walls, the dresser bare of trinkets and the wardrobe empty of clothes. She rose up from her seat and rummaged through a packing case, took out her mother's silver vanity set and proudly displayed them on her dresser. She unwrapped a velvet backed little bull that stored the few hatpins she had inherited from her mother and her mother's wooden and ivory jewellery box. They shared the space on the dresser.

Carrie couldn't help feeling saddened as she handled these items that had meant so much to Miri. She caught sight of herself in the mirror and was overwhelmed by her resemblance to her mother, especially with the changes that were taking place in her body. Her hips were becoming more rounded, there was a narrowing of her waist.

Inexplicably Carrie felt drained. She forced herself to resume searching through the packing cases until she found her diary. Turning to the calendar pages she started to count the days. She counted again. Her cycle was always regular. There was no mistake she was eight days late. With everything else she had been feeling, she was convinced she was pregnant.

Carrie rubbed at her small, flat tummy. The thought that she was carrying Jacky Ebron's child filled her with both dread and revulsion. She had to do something. "I've got to get to Dr. Rees as soon as possible," she murmured aloud.

Trix pricked up her ears attentive to Carrie's gentle tones.

"He promised he'd help," she explained to the dog, who cocked her head on one side and listened.

Carrie ruffled Trixie's fur, sighed and sat back down on the unmade bed sinking into its softness.

There was plenty for her to do, the beds to be made up, clothes to unpack. There would be time enough to see Dr. Rees when John was back. Carrie ran her fingers through her fiery curls,

"Right, my girl, this won't knit the baby a bonnet." She laughed wryly at the unintended pun and rolling her sleeves up, set to.

"Come on, Trix, all hands on deck!"

The animal followed her around as she worked, before finally settling on the sheepskin rug by the window of the main bedroom that Carrie had taken as her own. The collie watched Carrie lazily with one eye as Carrie deftly made the beds. The rooms with their musty unlived in smell mingled with the odour of fresh paint, and gradually transformed to a more homely appearance. Carrie opened the window to air the room and let in the warmth of the morning sun.

She did what she could upstairs and then moved down to the dark kitchen with its newly lit range. The dog followed her. She popped the freshly filled kettle on the coals to boil, "Thirsty work this, Trix," smiled Carrie and she sat in the rocker and waited for the water to heat up.

Carrie looked critically around the dark kitchen, the cream paper looked brown in the gloom. She pondered the question of how to make the room look brighter.

The big, black kettle started to steam and the lid jiggled and rattled in the pot as the water began to bubble. Carrie took the knitted kettle holder, she had made at school, from off the hook and made herself some tea. She sat in the rocker and sipped it, gently daydreaming, and planning her future.

By three o'clock in the afternoon she had more or less finished her chores. Her mother's brasses adorned the inglenook fireplace and crossbeam. The pots and pans were put away. An old flat iron propped open the door letting the light stream into the gloomy corners of the dim kitchen.

Carrie had stacked the boxes and paper in the outhouse for John to move. The cases and bags from upstairs were tidied away in the box room and the door was firmly closed.

Carrie washed her dust warm hands and splashed cold water on her face. She made herself another drink and sat on the wooden steps of the back veranda and looked along the overgrown path to the vegetable garden and the orchard beyond. That was an area that needed tending. She made a mental note to work on that in the next week or two, once the alterations she had decided on inside were underway.

Trix sat up and followed the veranda around the side of the house and padded in the direction of the front gate, her tail wagging furiously. Carrie set down her cup, shaded her eyes in the afternoon sun, straining her ears to hear a sound.

She stood up and followed Trix to the front of the house. The flimsy cotton print dress clung to her legs and rippled in the gentle breeze that blew through the hills to the valley.

John appeared leading Senator accompanied by someone she didn't recognise. Carrie slid under the wooden balustrade dropped down onto the path and went to meet them.

The stranger was a small barrel chested man with a rubicund face, bright twinkling eyes that creased up in the corner either from squinting at the sun or from lots of laughter. His upper lip sported a grey, whiskery toothbrush moustache. His cheeks gave the impression of being rosy but were coloured by a network of tiny red, thread veins that weaved crazily across his cheeks.

He followed John, a pace or two behind, and Carrie noticed that he had an irregular step. He clutched a brown paper parcel tied with string that he tucked under his arm. With his other hand he swept off a black beret revealing a balding head. Wiry tufts grew in sparse clumps at his temples. His eyebrows bushed out in front.

He wore a small pair of half spectacles that lent him a scholarly air. His waistcoat was too tight and as he waltz stepped to Carrie one of the buttons flew off and landed at her feet. He apologised profusely, "Iechy dwriaeth, so sorry!" He gave a stiff, formal little bow and turned to look at John.

"Where's old Tom?" questioned Carrie, uncertain as to what was going on.

"I couldn't ask him, cariad. You wouldn't believe how he's aged. Lean living and the depression has taken its toll. He suffered badly in the winter, nearly died with pneumonia. His sister pulled him through. It's left him with a weakness in his chest. He's too frail to work here."

"So?"

"So I paid our respects and asked his advice."

"And?"

"And here we have Ernie Trubshawe."

Ernie Trubshawe beamed at Carrie. He had a lopsided grin that showed an uneven bottom row of teeth. His two front teeth crossed and his incisors either side overlapped his front ones. He had a small gap top left. As Aunty Annie would say, 'Teeth more crooked than a cemetery, a bankrupt dentist's delight.' Ernie's eyes crinkled up in pleasure, "There's glad I am to meet you." He had a catch in his voice as if he needed to clear his throat.

Carrie found herself doing it for him. "Ahem, ahem," she coughed, "I'm Carrie, John's sister."

"And even prettier than old Tom described," said Ernie.

Carrie blushed. She remembered old Tom with great affection, and was sorry that he wasn't to be with them but there was something about this character in front of her that she liked. She warmed to him. She felt herself smiling back.

His grin was infectious.

"Ernie's coming to work for us. He doesn't know for how long. He tends to stay on a farm three to six months, sometimes more and then moves on."

"Working my way to Vaynor Pendarrin, got family there, see. I need to go with a bit of a nest egg, then they'll have me and let me settle. That's why I need the work. I'll ask you to keep my pay. John says I'll have my grub. If I need anything, shoes or whatever, you can buy it out of my wages for me, see. That way I'll be able to save." He winked at Carrie and she giggled, his ears twitched as he talked.

"Comes well recommended, Carrie," interrupted John, "Tom speaks well of him, but says it's no good giving him his pay."

"No. Blow the lot I would. You'll be doing me a favour."

"He does want to get home, he's got a daughter he's never seen."

Carrie's nose wrinkled up into a smile, "Welcome to Gelli Galed, Ernie. We're glad to have you. Come into the house and I'll show you your room."

"Begging your pardon like, I don't mean to be rude but I'm a bit of a man of the road, I'll be happier in the barn on a bed of straw and hay. I'll be only too glad to eat with you, but I'll wash by the pump. My feet get bored if I'm in a house too long. That's another reason why I keep moving, see."

Carrie smiled again, "That's fine by me. You make yourself comfortable in the barn then come into the kitchen and I'll make us a cup of tea. You must be thirsty after your journey."

Ernie Trubshawe nodded, "I've got a thirst like a dredger and my knees are all out of breath after that climb." He laughed, replaced his beret and scrambled after John who was already leading the way to the barn.

Ernie looked an odd little figure but Carrie knew instinctively that if old Tom had recommended him then he must be all right.

Carrie tossed her fiery hair and with her head held high, and an easy swing of her hips, she strolled into the house.

No sooner had she entered the kitchen and set the kettle on the range when Trix set up a whimpering and barking by the door.

Carrie let the dog out who raced down the path to the once rotten gate to greet the visitor.

Carrie paused in the doorway squinting in the afternoon sun. She shaded her eyes and could then make out the features of Trevor Pritchard; Pritchard the police.

His face was red from his climb. Beads of sweat glistened on his forehead and upper lip. He dabbed with a handkerchief as rivulets of sweat dribbled down the sides of his nose.

"Constable Pritchard, what brings you to Gelli Galed?"

The policeman tried to speak in between snatches for breath,

"Well, it's not a social call I'll be making all this way. Duw, Duw, there's a climb. I could see your brother ahead of me but I couldn't attract his attention. My shouts went to nothing in the breeze, blowing the wrong way it is."

Carrie smiled, "Come on through and sit a while. I'll get you a drink you look as if you could do with one."

"Thanks, Carrie. I'll be able to talk a bit better once I've got my breath. I can see why they call this Hard Living. Working the fields on these slopes must be murderous," his cheeks flushed redly and he floundered an apology, "Sorry, nothing intended."

"It's all right really, no offence taken. Come on through take a seat on the back veranda and I'll get that tea."

Constable Pritchard was soon recovering from his exertions, and sitting on the wooden bench on the back porch sipping his tea. Feeling more refreshed he struggled to find the words to explain his visit. "Well, it's tricky, see. I've come on your Aunty Netta's behalf. She's due to stand trial and she refuses to see a lawyer till she's spoken with you. In fact she insists upon it, not John - you."

Carrie didn't respond.

"Well, no one can conduct her defence if she won't talk to them. Stubborn woman your aunty."

"It runs in the family," said Carrie.

"Well, will you see your aunt or no?"

Carrie thought carefully before answering, "I don't know. Oh, I know I should. That we're family, but I don't know whether I'm up to it."

"Well, what message can I take back with me?"

"None," said Carrie simply, "Look finish your tea. I'm going to find John, after I've spoken to him, you'll have your answer."

Carrie left the policeman drinking his tea and wondering at the poise of young Carrie Llewellyn. She certainly seemed to take after her mother. She had the same obstinate tilt of chin and the same resolve reflected in her eyes.

Carrie found John with Ernie in the barn. Ernie had selected a corner of the hayloft out of the way of draughts, banked high on either side by bales of hay. Carrie was amazed to see it already resembled living quarters.

The brown paper parcel was unpacked, blankets laid on a bed of straw, an orange box placed neatly at the side, housing a shaving brush, soap, mug and razor; and a few other trinkets, fob watch, penknife, a Bible; two small photo frames, one containing a middle aged lady in black with a lace collar; the other of a young woman with glorious sausage curls adorning her face who was smiling angelically at the camera.

Ernie pulled off his beret and bowed stiffly at Carrie.

"Sorry to interrupt," she smiled at Ernie, then turned to John, "Constable Pritchard is here. Netta wants to see me. What shall I do?"

John looked at his sister, "The decision is yours, cariad, no one can make it for you."

"She says she won't see a lawyer till she's spoken to me."

"It's up to you."

"She can't have a proper defence unless she co-operates."

"Sounds like you've already made up your mind."

Carrie thought for a minute, nodded in acknowledgement and turned away without another word. She returned to the veranda and Constable Pritchard.

She leaned against the balustrade and looked at the policeman. He rose from his seat.

"Tell Netta I'll see her."

Gelli Galed

Two

"I'm glad you came."

Netta stood straight and tall in her prison clothes. She wore a thick coarse cotton skirt and yoked top of navy gabardine. Her hair was tied back and her face was devoid of any make up.

Her face looked thinner, pinched. She waited by a scrubbed wooden table bereft of varnish, then sat in a hard backed chair. She gestured Carrie to sit in the seat opposite her. A prison wardress stood at ease by the door, hands behind her back. Although the wardress gave the appearance of not listening, Carrie felt self-conscious in her presence.

Carrie and Netta faced each other across the table. Carrie sat demurely, her hands in her lap, not knowing what to expect whilst Netta leaned forward and studied her niece's face hard.

The unflinching gaze unnerved Carrie somewhat and some of her old fears and prejudices about Netta returned. But a voice inside her head seemed to call out to her to be calm. Carrie took a deep breath and in level tones conveying no emotion, and certainly sounding more confident than she felt, she coolly returned her aunt's unblinking stare.

"You wanted to see me?"

"I did."

There was a pause while they both eyed each other.

"Let's get one thing straight, there was never any love lost between us. I know how you felt about me and I know you only tolerated me because I was family. Carrie, I made a mistake in my judgement, gave my loyalty to the wrong person and I'll pay for that mistake but now I need to set things right with you."

Carrie bit back the recriminations that were ready to flow from her lips. She would wait. She would listen to what her aunt had to say.

"I can't change what's happened but I can try and salve my conscience. I've had plenty of time to think in here and some of the truths I've faced about myself are not pleasant."

Netta paused and cleared her throat. The words were not coming easily to her lips and she was finding it difficult and humiliating to speak.

"Go on, they say confession's good for the soul." prompted Carrie.

"If it's a confession you're after I'll not give you that, but I will apologise. And, in return for your help, I have a tidy little nest egg saved. It's yours and John's, to help you through at Gelli Galed."

"We don't need your money. We can manage on our own."

"Maybe. But if you have any hope of regaining Hendre, you'll have to pay a price. Let me help with that."

Carrie looked at the pleading eyes of her aunt. Never had she seen Netta look more sincere or more in need of kindness. Carrie made up her mind. "Nothing you can do or say will make me accept anything." She was gratified at the sudden stab of pain that rippled through those dark eyes. She tried to soften her words, "You never know when you may need the money yourself. You've a court case coming up."

Netta stiffened her back and sat straight in her seat, "I knew you would be hard to convince, so I'm not going to try. I accept what you have said. But I still have something to ask," she glanced up quickly at the wardress, staring blankly ahead and lowered her voice, "I'm bored in here cariad, I need something to do to occupy the time. Will you bring me some knitting needles and wool?"

Carrie looked surprised, "I never thought you were one for knitting. I thought it was Aunty Annie that had the talent."

"It's never too late to learn," Netta said acidly, then softened her tone, "It's just something to try, perhaps you could find a simple pattern, maybe one of Annie's leavings. I know she showed you how to knit and left a few bits and bobs with you."

Carrie nodded, slightly bemused by what her aunt was asking.

"Oh, and one more thing."

"Yes?"

"My blood's in a terrible state here. It's the food I think. I've always been anaemic. Could you bring me some 'Steel and Pennyroyal' pills. I've run out and as I can't pop out and fetch some more..." She left the sentence unfinished.

"Is that all?"

"That's all." Netta watched Carrie carefully.

And Carrie swallowing her misgivings, nodded, "All right."

"I'll need them as soon as possible." Netta added hastily. "Maybe, I won't be so tired or so bored then."

"I'll fetch them for you. If they let me come back this afternoon you can have them then."

Carrie rose from her seat, the interview was over but she had to speak. There could never be true peace between them but she felt Netta was in her own way trying to make some sort of recompense.

"Netta? Why did you kill him?"

"Why? Because I loved him," she thought for a fraction of a minute and added, "and because he wasn't going to beguile or despoil anyone else. He had it coming to him. No matter what had happened between us no man should have done what he did to you. For that I hated him and he deserved to die."

"Are you sure there's nothing else to ask me?" probed Carrie.

"Like what?"

"If the courts knew the truth, they wouldn't prosecute you for murder. The charge would drop to manslaughter."

"I couldn't ask you to do that for me, you've been through enough."

Carrie lowered her eyes before turning silently to the door then, she said clearly, "Aunty Netta, defend yourself. Tell the truth about what happened, I'll survive."

"Carrie?"

This time Carrie, turned back and looked directly into her aunt's eyes that were shining with unshed tears. Netta's voice was full of emotion, "Thank you."

Carrie impulsively moved to her aunt and took her hand; she squeezed it, then signalled to the wardress that she wished to leave, gracefully departing from that barren room with her head proudly aloft she proceeded down the corridor and heard the door clang solidly behind her. Taking a deep breath she went out into the welcoming sunshine in search of a pharmacy.

Back in her cell Netta had the semblance of a smile playing around her lips. Once Carrie returned she could do something to get rid of the brat developing inside her body. She would do away with it before she could feel any motherly tendencies awaken within her.

It didn't take Carrie long to find a wool shop where she could purchase a selection of needles and yarn. She even asked advice on a simple pattern and came away with something that she felt Netta would enjoy making whilst helping her to pass the time.

Carrie did, however, encounter a little difficulty at the pharmacy. After scrutinising the shelves and not seeing the product she wanted she went up to the counter. "Excuse me," she said awkwardly, "I'm after some Steel and Pennyroyal pills."

The assistant gave her an odd look and disappeared out to the back of the shop and returned with the white-coated pharmacist who peered at her over the top of his glasses. The assistant pointed at Carrie.

"Yes, Miss? Can I help?" He had a sibilant 's' that sounded like an escape of steam when he spoke.

"I'm after some Steel and Pennyroyal pills, please."

"And might I ask what for?"

Carrie was puzzled by his interest but answered truthfully, "My aunt's anaemic. She's unable to get out and asked me to buy them for her. She's feeling exceptionally tired all the time."

"There are other products on the market," he hissed.

Carrie noticed he was also incapable of saying his 'r's. She always thought that was such a pity in a man. Carrie coolly returned his gaze. "There probably are, but that's what she asked me to buy. I don't think I ought to get anything else."

"I'm sorry I can't help you then." and he returned to his dispensing room at the back. The assistant who had been standing behind him gave a shrug and when the old man was out of earshot she whispered to Carrie, "It's urgent is it?" Not fully understanding Carrie nodded.

"Try Potters in Bath Road. You should have better luck there. Old man Davies makes his own rules here. Good luck."

Carrie left the shop its bell clanging away and moved in the direction of Bath Road. She wondered at the old man's behaviour and what it was she had said that had caused such a stir.

Ten minutes later she reached Potters, walked in and purchased a bottle of the pills without any questions or bother. She found a tearoom and ordered herself something to eat and drink. While she waited for it to arrive she removed the bottle from its bag and read the label. There was nothing sinister there. She replaced it and settled back to enjoy her tea and toast. Thoroughly refreshed she returned to the police cells and passed over the items Netta had requested, promising to visit her again the following week.

Carrie stepped back out in the sunshine to resume her shopping trip. It would be a pity to waste the rest of the day by going home. She headed for the High Street.

She wandered into a haberdashery and purchased some thread and sewing items. She browsed the many rolls of fabric and selected some clean looking material from a bolt of cotton and linen mix but was overcome by a wave of nausea.

She left the shop hurriedly suppressing a bout of sickness. This decided her. She would curtail her shopping expedition and call on Dr. Rees on the way home.

Gelli Galed

Three

Dr. Rees peered at Carrie over his half spectacles as she stood up from the examination table and straightened her clothing. "Well, it seems you are right, are you sure it's what you want to do?"

"Dr. Rees, I'm not happy about waiting for the result of some test when we both know the reason for the changes that are taking place in my body. I trust your opinion more than any test. I'm pregnant, aren't I?"

"Yes, Carrie. I believe you are."

"I'm pregnant, through no fault of my own. Will you help me?"

Dr. Rees cleared his throat uncomfortably, "Well, Carrie fach, it's highly unethical but I agreed. I'll not break my word. I'll not let you suffer a lifetime for someone else's sins. Wait here."

A few minutes later the doctor was back with a bottle of white liquid. On the side of the bottle was a glass measure.

"When you get home, go to bed with a hot water bottle. Take a measure of this in some warm water. Repeat the dose if necessary in the morning. If nothing's happened by the evening take another. If there is still no sign of your period, come back and see me."

"What is this?"

"Ergot."

"What's that?"

"It contracts the uterus. I use it sometimes when a patient has had a difficult or exhausting birth and the placenta hasn't come away or it's adherent. The ergot works on the uterus and expels it."

"Does it hurt?"

"You'll have stomach cramps, that's why a warm bed will help. And be ready with towels in case you flood. There could be a lot of blood. Come and see me afterwards, just for a check-up."

"Thank you, Doctor." Carrie hardly dared to ask the next question. "What if it doesn't work?"

"We'll cross that bridge when we come to it."

"Dr. Rees?"

"Yes?"

"What are Steel and Pennyroyal pills?"

Dr. Rees paused for a moment, flummoxed by the change of subject. "Let me see, Steel and Pennyroyals... purify the blood; improve the iron, the red cell count. Usually taken by those with some form of anaemia, why?"

"Nothing else?"

"Well, I have heard of maids who have taken them in large quantities to induce a period. But that would be a silly thing to do, Carrie."

"No, not me."

"Who then?"

"Netta, Netta asked me to get some. She said they were for tired blood."

"Well, they are." Dr. Rees looked quizzically at her, "As long as you are not being stupid, Carrie."

"No, no. I'll do as you say, with your supervision. It just made me wonder that's all."

"Some pharmacists are reluctant to sell it, especially to young girls because of the implications."

Carrie smiled tentatively and put the potion in her bag, knowing that Dr. Rees was helping her already more than he should.

She pulled her cloche hat down firmly on her head and stretched out her hand to the doctor. The doctor grasped it, and shook it firmly. Carrie released his hand and left the surgery with a quiet dignity reminiscent of her mother Dr. Rees thought.

Carrie returned to find John and Ernie enjoying a mug of tea on the front porch. They were discussing the merits of rotational farming. Ernie was stressing the need for deep ploughing to rid the ground of the troublesome coltsfoot and suggested that by planting winter corn they could overcome another bugbear of farmers, thistles.

Ernie stopped and doffed his cap, "Miss Carrie."

"Ernie. Is there any tea left in the pot, John? I'm parched."

"Oh, I think we can squeeze one out. How was your day? What did Netta want?"

"I'll tell you all later, now I need to put my feet up and have a cuppa. Do you mind?"

"No, no, you carry on."

"What's for supper?"

John looked across at her sheepishly, "Sorry, cariad, I haven't thought."

Carrie pulled a face, "I thought you might have prepared something."

Ernie Trubshawe looked from one to the other. He saw the tiredness and strain in Carrie's eyes and the helplessness in John's who was not used to tending the kitchen. Ernie's eyes twinkled merrily and his whiskery toothbrush moustache bristled his top lip into a smile.

"Now then you two. Let Ernie handle it! I know exactly what to do. Carrie you go in and rest awhile you're looking drained. I'll call you when supper's ready. John you go and wash up, treat that hand that's blistered, it's been a hard day for you too."

Carrie moved to protest but Ernie silenced her with a shake of his head. "No arguments please! Do as Ernie says."

Carrie smiled weakly, nodded and went inside.

John tried to apologise.

"No need to, bach, no need. I won't offer every day, make the most of it," and he winked.

John smiled gratefully and rubbed his hand through his rebellious hair and he too went inside.

Ernie set to in the kitchen. Carrie lay flat on the bed upstairs listening to the sounds of pots and pans clattering in the kitchen and Ernie's less than tuneful voice singing out robustly the words of Sospan Fach.

Carrie stared hard at the bottle of white medicine standing like an obelisk on her window shelf. Her eyelids became heavy and still wearing her felt cloche hat, she drifted off into the realms of sleep.

Carrie dreamed she was running through a poppy filled meadow in a white broderie anglaise cotton dress with Trix chasing at her feet. She was heading towards the old ash tree, laughing and giggling when a cloud obscured the sun. The meadow was robbed of its warmth and the air appeared a thundery black. Out from the shadows from behind the tree stepped Jacky Ebron, his arms stretched out to her, his face twisted in an evil leer. Carrie stopped in dismay. She felt a flooding and looked down in horror to see her blood seep through the white cotton of her dress.

Jacky Ebron whispered huskily, "The stone didn't hold me, cariad. I've come for you."

Carrie stifled a scream and sat upright on the bed with a gasp. She was fully awake and sweating. Her hair stuck inside her hat was damp. Carrie pulled it off and took several deep breaths to calm herself. She glanced at the clock, it was five past seven. She had been asleep an hour. The aroma of onions wafted through the door to her. She scrambled off the bed and lightly ran to the window, throwing it open, and took in three lungfuls of fresh air. She steadied herself. The dream had been so vivid. She felt a tremor of fear judder through her and a sick twisting in her stomach.

A knock on the door interrupted her thoughts. She managed to keep her voice level. "Yes?"

The latch lifted and the door swung open to reveal Ernie. He did a funny little jig culminating in one of his stiffly formal bows.

"Dinner is served, Carrie," he announced shaking a tea-cloth over his arm in an attempt to imitate a photograph of a silver service waiter he'd once seen in a newspaper.

Carrie laughed in spite of herself, "All right, Ernie. I'll be down in a minute."

He nodded and left, calling out, "Hurry up or it will get cold, you must eat it while it's hot."

Carrie removed her coat, which had deep lapels that broadened to a point above a one button fastening. Her heart was still racing. She sat at her dressing table and tugged at her fiery tresses with the silver brush trying to bring some order to her wild, unmanageable curls. Her pulse was still throbbing frenetically inside her head.

As she struggled to regain control of her breathing and composure she studied her image in the mirror. A smattering of freckles adorned her neat nose contrasting sharply with her fine porcelain skin. Only a fleeting shadow of the horrors from her dream remained reflected in her eyes and they were gradually fading like spectres in the fog as Carrie regained control of her emotions, turning fear to anger.

She slammed down the brush and turned knocking over her padded dressing table stool. Her hands stayed fixed on the dresser, behind her. She leaned back against it and stared at the white medicine bottle that seemed to loom larger the longer she stared at it.

Carrie knew that after dinner would be the time, when she would mentally be more prepared. She propelled herself forward and with her head erect she moved through the door, down the stairs to the tantalising smell of savoury onions and mince slices.

That supper was one of the heartiest and cheeriest she had had since Annie had left. Carrie felt a small lump rise in her throat as memories of Annie intruded into her thoughts.

Ernie Trubshawe had cooked a tasty and nourishing meal. His chatter at the table had the Llewellyns laughing and giggling like school children.

He regaled them with stories of his youth and nomadic wanderings and his accounts of working on various farms until Carrie had to plead, "Enough! Enough, my stomach's hurting. I can't laugh anymore," but of course she did and Ernie was rewarded with a healthy blush of colour to her pale cheeks.

The chime of the grandfather clock striking eight roused Carrie from the table, and like Cinderella fearing the stroke of midnight, she rose unsteadily to her feet.

"It's been a wonderful meal. But I really must rest now. John, will you see to the dishes?"

"Course, fy merch 'i. Anything wrong?"

"No," she hesitated, "Nothing that can't be put right."

John raised an eyebrow and was about to question her further when Carrie raised her hand, "Not now. I'll talk tomorrow. Promise. Now is there any hot water on the range? I'm going to take a bottle to bed."

"This weather?" John gasped.

"Yes, more of a comfort really. I get cold easily when I'm tired," she lied, anxious to avoid the truth for the moment.

John seemed to accept her answer and foraged around in the under stair cupboard for the stone water bottle, which he filled for her. Carrie kissed him goodnight and clutching her bottle and a glass of water went up the stairs to her room.

Gelli Galed

Four

Netta took a careful look around her to make sure that she was unobserved. Lights were out and she felt reasonably safe that her actions would go undetected under the blanket of night.

Slowly she removed the knitting needle she had hidden in her bed. The other needles, wool and pattern had been taken from her as possible offensive weapons, but not before she had managed to secrete one needle down her stocking under her skirts and lose its partner through a crack in the floorboards. Netta had also safely stashed away her pills, which had so far managed to escape detection.

She gently eased up her legs and spread them apart. She probed with her fingers inside her until she managed to retrieve the glass bottle of pills from their hiding place. She slipped the bottle under her mattress.

Netta was ready. She eased the pillow under her buttocks and spread her legs again. She took the knitting needle and inserted it into her vagina, slowly pushing the instrument up inside her.

She tensed with the effort but the thought that one slip could seriously damage her was enough to unsteady her hand. Netta soon hit the round button of her cervix and although her aim was to push the needle through this into her womb, she started to shake. "Esgyrn Dafydd! I can't do it. I can't." She cried softly to herself whilst removing the needle with care. She lay tense on the bed until her fears subsided and then reasoned with herself,

"Come on gal, all you've got to do is push it up far enough, pierce the foetus and no more brat!"

But Netta had strong doubts. What if she damaged some internal organs? She did not intend to take her own life or reduce the quality of her life by maiming herself in some way. No, no this was not for her. Her iron resolve on this occasion failed her. The only other alternative was the pills and they weren't guaranteed to work.

Netta silently dropped down from her bunk and feeling with her fingers found the site of a button on her mattress. She pushed in the needle at an angle, inserting it well into her mattress and then adjusted the button over its entry point.

Netta clambered back into bed, an exhilarating mix of fear and anticipation heightening her senses. She reached for the pills and sitting upright emptied them into her hand. She shovelled a handful into her mouth almost gagging on the amount and struggled to swallow them.

Somehow, she managed to continue until she had swallowed every one. Exhausted she flopped back on her bed and slipped away into a fitful sleep.

Carrie carefully measured a dose of the ergot mixture and added it to some of the warm water taken from her bottle. She pulled a face at the bitter tasting liquid but continued to drink it down until the draught was gone. She made herself ready for bed and lay on the thick wadding of towels she had placed underneath her and waited, willing sleep to come.

Morning dawned. The glittering blades of sunlight stabbed through the gap in the curtains pooling in golden patches on the polished floor.

Carrie threw her arms out from under the cover and raised a sleepy head. Then she remembered and hastily raised herself off her uncomfortable towelling base and looked to see the familiar telltale signs of blood. There were none.

Disappointed, she sat on the edge of the bed rubbing her face awake with her hands. She padded across the floor and drew open the curtains flooding the room with the glory of the morning.

Gazing out across the wooded valley, she caught her breath, not with the beauty of the sight in front of her but with a sudden sharp pain. She felt her stomach tighten and harden and a griping ache filled her lower belly. Gently easing herself back into bed, she lay flat on her back and waited for nature to take its course.

Several contractions later she felt a slow but steady trickle of blood dribble down her thighs. Smiling in spite of the pain, she waited for the potion to finish its work.

Netta twisted and turned feverishly in her cot. The pains of Hell were upon her. Her head felt like it didn't belong to her. A pulse thumped mercilessly on through her clouded cotton-wool mind. A terrible pressure was building up at the back of her eyes and her guts were aching. She groaned aloud.

"You all right in there?" came a questioning voice that belonged to one of the wardresses.

Another low moan followed. Netta drew her knees up to her chin to try and find some comfort, some escape from the twisting wrenching going on inside her. Oblivious to the wardress outside she gave a soft howl of torment. This was enough to set the wardress' keys jangling to gain entry to the cell. One look at Netta's unnaturally sallow complexion that was drenched with a feverish sweat and she was running to the phone for help.

Netta leaned over the side of her cot and vomited. She brought her knees up and tucked them up in front of her once more before keeling over and lying in a foetal position. She was barely conscious when a trolley took her from her cell and wheeled her to the prison hospital.

Carrie watched the spider on its web by the open bedroom window, carefully shortening its supporting strands.

"Rain must be on the way," she murmured aloud. Carrie found that spiders were most reliable at foretelling the weather, even better than the wooden and brass barometer hanging in the hall that relied on air pressure. She watched as the spinner worked away, shortening and strengthening its supporting strands. It was a sure sign that rain and gales were on the way.

Carrie felt drained of energy. Pale and weak from loss of blood she carefully cleaned herself up. She hid the blood drenched towels in a sturdy brown carrier bag with string handles at the side of the wardrobe until she knew she could sneak them downstairs and wash them.

Carrie also knew she had to get to Dr. Rees for him to check her over and make sure all was well. She had carefully inspected the mess that had come away from her and had wrapped the gelatinous blob, which she presumed to be the embryo in a wad of paper to show him.

The thought of what might have been sickened her and she was thankful that the Doctor had acted as her friend.

In spite of her initial relief, Carrie felt an inexplicable wave of emotion surge through her over her loss. She was having difficulty reconciling this feeling with what her head dictated she should be feeling. It was yet another contradiction in her young life. But Carrie knew she must put these worries out of her mind and concentrate on living.

Netta was suffering the torment of the devil. Her stomach had been pumped by forcing a rubber tube down her throat. She was lying on her back with her feet in stirrups.

The doctor wagged a finger at her. "What were you thinking of? Didn't you know you were pregnant? You could have damaged the child. You could have damaged yourself."

Netta flopped feebly to one side. A nurse came to her aid and helped her up supporting her head over a bowl while Netta was sick yet again.

She wiped her mouth and took the proffered glass of water rinsing away the sour taste. Her dark eyes flared with intensity as she raged at the doctor. "So I'm pregnant," she snorted, "Don't you think I know that?"

"You mean you don't want the child?" gasped the nurse who was Catholic, "That's a mortal sin."

"Come, come," said the doctor, "You must rest. You can talk later," and he ordered she be put on a saline drip.

Whilst Netta lay on her back with intravenous tubes spiralling out of her arm and twisting like spaghetti into clamped bottles on stands she had time to reflect on her future. A future it seemed she would be sharing with a child; Jacky's child. The thought did not fill her with pleasure and she schemed and plotted on how to rid herself of her tiresome burden.

Gelli Galed

Five

"Cariad, why didn't you tell me?" John's face was white with shock.

"It didn't seem right to bother you. There wasn't anything you could do. I just had to let nature and Dr. Rees' medicine do its work."

"Are you all right?" John's voice was filled with concern.

"I'm fine," Carrie smiled, "Honest John, there's no need to worry. It's all over. Now, I can look forward to living again."

John took his sister by the shoulders and sat her gently in the rocker. "I could have shared this with you. Your problems are mine, Carrie. We only have each other." His eyes searched hers.

Carrie met his gaze, her obvious independence and confidence unsettled him. He feared she was growing away from him. He was afraid of losing the closeness that had been theirs.

Carrie saw the worry in her brother's face and took his hand.

"John, every thing's okay. Really. We've just got to put this behind us. As Annie would say, we must be prepared as there's dark days ahead!"

"I dread to think what else can happen!"

Carrie put her arms around her brother's neck and they stood up together. She nestled into the safety of his arms. He gently kissed her hair. Carrie sighed, unaware of the racing of her brother's pulse. Tenderly, he disentangled himself from her embrace.

"Annie's right. Things aren't going to be easy."

"We'll come through it," whispered Carrie, willing herself to believe it, but in her heart she feared the prejudice from folk in the village with narrow minds, once Netta's story was told in court. That would be a testing time.

John was more concerned with the everyday running of the farm. He needed more help but knew they couldn't afford it. The stock would take time to become acclimatised to living on the side of that particular mountainside. Ernie had said it could take generations. Even worse, new sheep introduced would face their worst enemy, that of other sheep, poisoning fresh grazing.

Brother and sister clung to each other, each with their own fears and worries.

Carrie's sixteenth birthday came and went. She had now left school and busied herself on the farm. The season marched on toward their first Christmas at Gelli Galed.

The family had never been used to holidays as such. They had always shared the work between them to allow for a day or two off. But now they were lucky if they could have half a day for Christmas. Carrie decided that somehow they would all sit down together for Christmas lunch and she would make it special.

With this thought in mind, she took the cart down into the village to do some shopping. She bought some fine lawn cotton to make a shirt for John and went to Segadelli's to buy a cherry wood pipe for Ernie with some tobacco.

She stood waiting in Segadelli's, conscious that Mrs. Chappell was eyeing her curiously. Carrie turned to her. "Is there something wrong, Mrs. Chappell? Do I have smuts on my face or something?"

"No! No! Forgive me staring but there've been so many rumours going round the village. I was just wondering in the truth of them that's all."

"Well, that would depend on what they were," Carrie said with feigned sweetness. "Perhaps you'd care to repeat them to me."

"Oh no! I couldn't possibly. And then again..." She tailed off as the shop bell jangled announcing the entry of another customer.

"Mrs. Chappell. Miss Llewellyn," Mr. Lawrence doffed his cap.

Mrs. Chappell nodded and smiled but Carrie turned her back on the man and refused to acknowledge him.

"You were saying?" Carrie prodded.

"Oh no, Carrie, not in front of a stranger," gestured Mrs. Chappell.

"In that case, you can have the potted version!" exclaimed Carrie aware of the acute discomfort she was causing bird eyed Mrs. Chappell.

She took a deep breath and believing it better to get the truth out now she launched into a tirade. "My aunty's fiancé cheated my father out of his home, swindled him and sold Hendre out from under our feet. Not content with that he raped me and as punishment my Aunty Netta killed him. To cap it all the person who bought Hendre illegally, refused to sell it back to us claiming to fight us in the court to the bitter end. Not a pretty story."

Mrs. Chappell blushed as pink as her bonnet and stuttered something about being sorry.

Carrie purchased the pipe and left the shop buzzing with chatter.

"Miss Llewellyn! Miss Llewellyn!" Mr. Lawrence ran up the road after her.

Carrie stopped and turned to face this man, usurper of Hendre, "I have nothing to say to you. Now, if you would kindly let me be on my way."

"Listen please."

Carrie resumed walking, closing her eyes and ears to the man. He grabbed her roughly by the shoulders and spun her round to face him.

"How dare you touch me? Let me go at once!" she bridled.

He let her go as if he had been burnt, "I'm sorry, I just want you to listen."

Carrie sighed, "Very well. If it will prevent a scene in the strect."

"It doesn't appear that scenes alarm you, judging from that little episode in there."

"Mr. Lawrence," said Carrie in an overly patient tone as if dealing with a difficult child, "I'm not standing here to be insulted. Say your piece and let me be about my business."

"I bought Hendre in good faith. If you were cheated then

so was I."

"Cheated! How could you possibly know the meaning of the word?"

"I invested all my money in Hendre. My savings from business deals in order to start a new life."

"Money we offered to repay with interest, for our home, built by our family." Carrie could not keep the heat out of her voice or to stop it rising in anger. "You could have started your life elsewhere, on some other farm. Heaven only knows there's enough farms in trouble looking for a buyer. You could have picked one of them and let us have what's rightfully ours."

"A pretty speech, but you don't know all of it. I wanted a profitable farm not one struggling to make its way."

"So people's feelings don't come into it; you just selfishly march in here, even when it's explained that our home was taken illegally you pay no regard. Don't even try to put it right."

"Now, hold on a moment," he blazed. "I was trying to explain to you that I'm not as black as you paint me. But if you're not prepared to listen then to Hell with you! My life hasn't exactly been made easy since I moved here."

"I wonder why," Carrie bit back sarcastically.

"I won't give you the satisfaction of burdening you with the details but I've not been made welcome."

"Nor will you be, Mr. Lawrence. Folk round here know what's right. They know the rightful owners of Hendre." Carrie turned to go.

"I'll be damned if I'm going to belittle myself to you. I'll speak with your brother maybe he's more tolerant than a small minded village girl."

"Do what you like! Nothing you do or say will make you right," and with that she left Mr. Lawrence. Her words stung him. Boiling with silent fury, he watched her go.

Ernie and John had made a steady profit from the sale of useful store pigs averaging £2.0s.0d. a piece. They bought only when good stores could be obtained for twenty shillings or less, and feeding regular quantities, according to age, of carefully balanced rations so that they always knew their costs. They sold as soon as they could see £1.0s.0d a head, over and above the cost of feeding stuffs and weaners. Pigs gave them a quick turn over in capital and with this profit they managed to buy a second hand tractor. This was going to make life a little easier for them in the fields.

Ernie suggested they plant winter corn and thus help rid the fields of troublesome weeds. Cattle and wool could be sold to pay for living expenses and wages. Return from corn sales could be used for debt repayment and improvements. John was growing more confident each week. He was certain that with Ernie's help, they would make Gelli Galed pay!

The bitter chill of the winter air prised its fingers under the door of the kitchen where Carrie was boiling pans of water to take a bath.

"One of these days when we've got money I'll have a quality bathroom installed. No more heating water for a tin bath in front of the fire, but a proper enamel one with fancy taps."

"One day, Carrie. We'll have it all," said John.

John stepped out of the kitchen to leave Carrie in privacy and stood on the veranda looking across at the bleak barren fields. The now iron ground freshly ploughed had frozen in ruts with the frost. The farmland looked hostile and unyielding. It was a struggle to farm here but farm they would. Their first Christmas was fast approaching. Together they could begin to catalogue their successes.

Trix started to bark and wag her tail. John, thinking it was Ernie back from feeding hay to the sheep, stepped off the veranda to meet him at the gate and was surprised to see the figure of Mr. Lawrence approaching.

He was carrying a holly wreath. His breath puffed in smoky clouds before him. John stopped and narrowed his eyes. Carrie had told him about the incident in the village and he didn't know quite what to expect.

"Phew! That's quite a climb. I'm glad I don't have to do that very often."

"Mr. Lawrence," greeted John cautiously.

"Merry Christmas, Mr. Llewellyn. I brought you a wreath."

John had a smart answer ready on his lips but he stopped himself from speaking and just managed a nod.

"May I come in? It's pretty damned cold out here once you stop moving."

"My sister's taking a bath."

"Oh..." There was a pause and finally John grudgingly offered, "I suppose we could sit in the parlour. Come inside."

Mr. Lawrence hung the wreath on the doorknocker as he entered and he followed John down the passage to the parlour.

"What can I do for you? I take it this isn't just a social call?"

"Partly. I feel we should get to know each other being neighbours and because I need to talk or more correctly, I need you to listen."

"Well?" John gestured him to sit and he perched uncomfortably on the settle.

Mr. Lawrence cleared his throat feeling awkward. "I don't know how to begin except that you haven't heard the full story."

"My sister feels we know enough."

"With all due respect, I understand how both you and your sister feel but it's not as cut and dried as you think."

"I'm listening."

"You see, the money Jacky Ebron had on him was the second instalment. I paid double that amount for Hendre."

"Can you prove that?"

"The solicitor has all the details. I explained this at the time of your offer, obviously, the information was not passed on. We need to discover what happened to the rest of the money and then I feel sure we could come to some arrangement without all the expense of a court case."

"I've no idea where that money could be and we certainly don't have that sort of cash."

"As I imagined, that's why I thought to put another proposition to you."

John narrowed his eyes, wondering what was to come. Mr. Lawrence cleared his throat.

"I dislike what has happened and the way business has been conducted, I can't excuse what happened, but I can in some way try to put it right."

"How?"

"If the missing money is recovered then I accept your original offer and no harm is done. If not..." and here he paused, choosing his words carefully, "You pay me the half that's due when you get it, allow me to continue to work Hendre for a further four years to build up my capital and we do a straight swap, Gelli Galed for Hendre."

John thought for a moment. By his reckoning Lawrence could make his profit and at the same time run Hendre into the ground whilst at the same time Gelli Galed would be beginning to make itself pay. The sums seemed too heavily weighted in Mr. Lawrence's favour, all the same John knew that his heart, as well as Carrie's belonged in Hendre.

"If the case comes to court sooner than expected you will be evicted anyway. You have a solicitor's contract that's null and void as it was founded on deceit. It's only a matter of time and we can retrieve our property without paying you a penny. Why don't we exchange properties now, and pay you the money when it comes?"

"Because I haven't your expertise and talent. Hendre is relatively easy to run, apart from the problems I'm experiencing in the village and at market."

John's eyes gleamed when he heard this. His loose talk in the village had paid off. He knew folk wouldn't want to know the outsider once they knew how he had come by Hendre.

"So what are you saying? That you haven't the knowledge to run Gelli Galed?"

The brass door handle turned and Carrie entered, "I thought I heard voices..." She stopped and stood there wrapped in a bath towel her skin moist and pink. Her face, already reddened from her bath, flushed angrily when she recognised the visitor in the parlour. Her voice was quiet and full of icy menace. "You are not welcome here, Mr. Lawrence. I suggest you leave. Now!"

"Carrie," John interrupted, but Carrie ignored her brother. She felt no embarrassment at being caught in a state of undress, only wild fury at seeing her enemy.

Mr. Lawrence was taken off guard by the unexpected vision before him. Carrie Llewellyn was indeed a beautiful woman, even if a trifle young. He stampeded these thoughts out of his brain and missed the next thing that was said.

The door was opened and he found himself being ushered out. John was politely apologetic, "I'm sorry, Mr. Lawrence. It's best that you leave now. I'll talk to my sister and see what she says."

"Don't count on it," blazed Carrie from the hallway. You're in for a big shock if you think we're giving up without a fight."

Mr. Lawrence tried to explain again but Carrie gave him no chance and ripped into him with words like knives that only served to fuel his own anger.

"You're not welcome in this village, Mr. Lawrence and I will see that life is made extremely difficult for you. You may feel a little awkward now, but I assure you I haven't even started yet."

"I came here to try and make peace, to come to some sort of arrangement that would help us both. It's obvious now that I was wasting my time. Even your brother has no influence on you. You are the most intolerant, pig headed, stubborn woman it has ever been my misfortune to meet. If it's a fight you want, you can have one. I wouldn't be so sure of your ground either. I'll have the best lawyers working for me, possession is nine tenths of the law!"

"Get off this property," screamed Carrie, "Or I'll put the shotgun on you."

Michael Lawrence walked away down the path. The wreath thudded on the ground behind him. He didn't look back but strode on toward the gate and out of sight.

Carrie fell into John's arms sobbing with frustration and anger. He led her inside tenderly and she sat on his knee in the rocker still clad in her towel.

John didn't quite know what to say, he gently kissed her wild spangled curls and lovingly removed the hair from her eyes. His hand lovingly caressed her tear stained cheek and he placed his soft lips on her eyes licking away her salt tears, kissing her eyelids and forehead. A fierce passion raged inside him and losing all control he showered her face and neck with his kisses until finally his lips burned down onto hers in a frenzy of excitement.

Carrie's arms twined around her brother's neck drowning in this show of affection, but when the affection turned to urgent passion Carrie flustered in confusion. She ached to respond to her brother's searching desire but horror and revulsion swept through her. She pushed away her brother's searching hands losing her flimsy covering. They stood up and he caught her by the wrists and pulled her in so close that she could feel his breath on her cheek and his pressing desire. She shook her head, this wasn't right! A thousand alarm bells seemed to clamour inside her head.

"John! No! No! Paid, stop it!" she screamed. Finally, her words broke through and John dropped her hands, letting her recover her fallen towel, which she clutched to her.

The full shame and realisation of what he'd done and what he'd nearly done hit him. His face drained of colour and he started to tremble, "Oh cariad," he sighed, "I'm so sorry, please forgive me. I don't know what happened."

Carrie edged towards the door, "I'm going to get dressed. We'll talk later." And she left the room. John collapsed in the rocker numb with shock and shame.

Gelli Galed

Six

Ernie looked across from sister to brother. Something wasn't quite right between them. The meal that Carrie had taken so much time and trouble to prepare should have been relaxed and enjoyable. There was tension in the air. The atmosphere was like that of a violin string tightened to breaking point. Ernie could almost hear the discordant notes of a fiddler's bow, scraping along untuned strings.

Ernie tried to lighten the proceedings, to bring the couple so distantly polite back to normality. "Come on then, how about a game?"

"I'd love to but I've got all the dishes to do."

"Blow the dishes! You did all the cooking, John and I will see to the washing up."

"No, it's all right. Really. I know you've got the cattle to see to and the sheep to feed."

"Yes and so we shall, but for now it's Christmas. And Christmas isn't Christmas without fun and games. There's plenty of time."

Carrie relented and laughed gently, "All right. You win, what had you got in mind?"

"Oh, I've a wealth of ideas under my hat," and he pulled off his black beret revealing a tiny black duckling."

Carrie giggled delightedly, "Oh, Ernie where did it come from?"

"The mother kicked it out for some reason. I always feel sorry for the runts. So I popped it down my vest and then when it was warm enough, under my hat it went. They need warmth see, at this age. Time enough for it to eat and drink tomorrow."

Carrie scooped up the little chap with its orange and black webbed feet. It had tiny yellow markings round the eyes like a mask.

"I know! We'll call you Bandit!" she exclaimed.

"Where are we going to keep him?" John said, as practical as ever, joining in the conversation.

"Surely we can find a stout box, fill it with straw and wood chippings. If we cover it with chicken wire we can keep it by the range until it's old enough to go out."

"I tell you what, you two see to the duckling, I'll get the dishes done then, if you and Carrie see to the sheep I'll deal with the cattle. That means we can still have an excellent Christmas night and do all the things I've got planned. We've yet to exchange gifts," winked Ernie as he undid yet another button on his already tight waistcoat. "There that's better. I can breathe again. Got a belly on me like a porker pig. Much more of that tasty fare and I can say goodbye to my feet."

Carrie smiled, "Come on, John, let's find that box."

John allowed a shy smile to lift the corners of his saddened mouth. A lock of his hair fell down into his eyes, Carrie moved towards him and brushed it away, her hand lingering on his cheek.

"Come on, what do you say?" She put the duckling down her front, carefully supporting it with one hand. "Race you to the barn. Bet I'll beat you!"

Carrie raced out of the door, down the passage and into the yard. John followed closely, all traces of sadness gone.

Carrie ran to the barn and up the ladder into the hayloft giggling deliciously. Puffing and panting she threw herself down on the hay. John crashed down beside her.

"Remember at Hendre," said Carrie her breathing becoming more even and her eyes misting over.

"The hayloft?"

"Right. We used to take it in turns to jump off the ladder into the hay, a rung at a time."

"I never could beat your record."

"That was just foolishness, I twisted my ankle one day."

"Stubborn little tyke you were, just like Mam."

"Oh, John," Carrie sighed.

"Don't say it. I know."

"I'm sorry."

"No, I'm the one who's sorry. I don't know what happened. I was trying to comfort you, all upset you were and then somehow..." he tailed off.

"There's no need to explain. For a second, a part of me wanted you too. But we mustn't, it's not right."

"I know. I do love you though, cariad."

"I know and I love you too," and the way she said it he knew she meant as a sister. "We'll just have to be careful it doesn't happen again."

"It won't," he said softly.

Brother and sister paused and looked at each other. John wanted to tell her she'd misunderstood. That he loved her not as a brother but as a man. He wanted to hold her, to kiss her, to make her, his. Instead he stood and pulled her up onto her feet. "Come on let's find a box for that orphan."

Carrie leaned across and softly brushed her lips like butterfly wings on his cheek. "All better," she said, in a voice from their childhood.

John's heart leaped and he tightened his grip on her hand. Together they went to search for a box.

Netta had finally decided to co-operate. And after the preliminary hearing a date for trial had been set at Cardiff Crown Court.

Further attempts to lose her baby hadn't succeeded. She had punched herself in the stomach, thrown herself down the iron staircase when leaving her cell for exercise in the yard and all she had managed to do was break her arm while the baby stubbornly developed inside her.

Netta stood in her cell and ran her hands over her stomach barely beginning to pop and she felt a fluttering like a moth's wings around a candle flame inside her. With each movement inside her Netta's iron backed will slowly crumbled.

She sat on her bed and wept. Feelings that she'd never before experienced bubbled up inside her, feelings belonging to a fiercely, protective mother.

Netta knew now that she wanted this baby and that nothing would change her mind.

"It will prove excellent for the case," said Netta's lawyer.

"A pregnant woman will invoke the pity of the court. This coupled with the story you have to tell could get you off with probation."

"Will we need Carrie's evidence?" asked Netta.

"Of course. You did say she'd agreed?"

"Yes, yes. It's just I didn't want to put her through the trial unless it was absolutely necessary."

"I'm afraid so. We need her to corroborate your story. I will have to see her soon to discuss her evidence. Are you sure she won't change her mind?"

Netta's dark eyes smouldered, "No, Carrie won't let me down." Netta knew the determination and strength of character of her niece and was convinced.

Carrie stood in front of the wardrobe mirror and stared hard at her reflection. She was growing up. Her mother's clothes would soon fit her perfectly.

Carrie chose a sombre coat with deep wide lapels that fastened with one button and her felt cloche hat. She hoped she would retain her poise in the courtroom. Mam's coat would help.

Carrie sighed and turned away from the mirror.

There was a knock on her door. John opened it and looked in. "Are you ready, cariad?"

"As ready as I'll ever be."

"Right!" He paused, "The wagon's all set. Are you sure you want to go through with this?"

"I'm sure. What time's my train?"

"Ten-past-eight. There'll be people from the village there."

"I know."

"The case has attracted a lot of local publicity. It's even hit the nationals. You can still change your mind."

"No. I've given my word. I'll go through with it."

John knew his sister well enough that when she made up her mind to do something nothing would break her resolve. He put his arms around her and held her close. "I just don't want to see you hurt, cariad."

"I know, I'll be all right, really." She stepped back and

looked John calmly in the eyes, reached deep into her pockets, took out her kid leather gloves and eased them onto her fine hands.

"How do I look?" she said and tilted her chin upward.

"Like Mam, stubborn and proud," smiled John.

"In that case, I'll do," said Carrie and gracefully walked to the door.

The courtroom was filled with the chatter of excitement from the spectators' gallery. The clerk of the court in his official black attire called for all to rise as the judge entered.

The visiting judge settled himself at the bench. The hushed assembled company shuffled into their seats when told to sit. A few nervous coughs broke the otherwise tense silence of waiting.

The coldly efficient announcement came, "His majesty the King versus Netta Sarah Llewellyn."

The clerk faced the prisoner in the dock standing boldly defiant. "Netta Sarah Llewellyn, you are charged that on the 26th October 1934 you did willfully murder one, Jack Abraham Ebron. How do you plead?"

Netta's barrister rose to his feet. "If you please m'lud, my client pleads not guilty whilst the balance of her mind was disturbed."

The case proceeded. The prosecution painted a dramatic picture of a woman full of spite and vengeance who had set out to take the life of her fiancé with no proof of his guilt in his alleged crime.

Dr. Rees was called to the stand as his evidence was vital to Carrie's story.

"So it was obvious from your examination that the child had been raped?"

"She had suffered severe internal injury and bruising, and required stitching. The injuries received were conducive to that of rape. She had received a blow to the face and had been subjected to what must have been an horrific attack."

The prosecution interrupted, "May I remind my learned friend and the jury that the dead man is not on trial for rape but Netta Llewellyn for murder."

The courtroom burst into a frenzy of excited chatter. The judge called the court to order and Dr. Rees was allowed to continue with his evidence.

The morning progressed. The young worker who had discovered Jacky's body told his story and when asked to identify the strange woman in blood soaked clothes, on horseback, he pointed his finger straight at Netta.

"That's her. I'll never forget those dark eyes. She's the one all right."

He lowered his eyes from Netta's cool gaze and mumbling an apology made a move to step down from the witness stand.

"Don't step down yet, Mr. Crighton." said Norman Parrish rising. When you first saw Miss Llewellyn did you speak to her?"

"Indeed I did, a number of times."

"Why?"

"She looked unwell. I thought there must be something wrong."

"Did she answer you?"

"No Sir, she didn't seem to hear me. It was as if she was in some sort of trance, bewitched like, distracted."

"As if she wasn't normal?"

"Objection. Leading the witness."

"Sustained. Move to strike the last remark. The jury will disregard the last question."

"Very well. When you spoke to her why then did she not answer?"

"She was distant, in shock it seemed."

"And yet you did not stop to try and help?"

"I was afraid to. I didn't want to get involved. There was something strange about the way she was acting."

"How do you mean?"

"She was mumbling to herself and cursing."

"Could you hear what she said?"

"Only bits of it. She seemed deranged, like a woman possessed."

"Objection, conjecture. Mr. Crighton is not an expert on the human mind."

"Agreed. Mr. Parrish, please refrain from this line of questioning."

"Sorry, M'lud, but I needed to establish that my client was not in her usual frame of mind as described by other witnesses. I've no more questions."

"Thank you, Mr. Crighton, you may step down." ordered the judge.

More witnesses were called to testify to Netta's character delivering a portrait of a tragic figure, who after the death of her fiancé devoted her life to her widowed mother until a chance for happiness had come along with Jacky Ebron.

However, not all witnesses could testify to the good of Netta's character.

"Is it true that Netta Llewellyn had a reputation for cruelty?" barked the prosecuting counsel, Mr. Tynan.

"As a child she got into mischief sometimes."

"Just confine yourself to the question, yes or no?"

"I can't possibly answer as baldly as that. We all did things that could be deemed to be cruel."

"Mrs. Morgan, if you please, just answer yes or no."

"Objection, badgering the witness when she has no simple answer."

"M'lud, I intend to show that Netta Llewellyn had a vicious streak as a child, out of which she did not grow. She tortured animals and enjoyed giving pain."

Evidence faded in and out and Carrie waited outside the huge double doors waiting to be called.

By the end of the first day, Carrie was still waiting.

"You realise they'll try to discredit you." warned Norman Parrish, Netta's lawyer. "It will be hard up there on the stand with all eyes on you. I'll be as gentle as I can. Just answer my questions and tell the truth."

Carrie nodded. Inside her heart was hammering, but outwardly she exuded a calm that belied her feelings. "I understand."

At 11.26 precisely Carrie was called as a witness. She straightened her mother's coat, stubbornly tilted her chin and with her head held proudly she pushed the heavy, oak, double doors of the courtroom.

All eyes watched her proceed down the central aisle on the worn, wooden parquet floor. The walk seemed endless. She flicked her eyes up to the balcony. Carrie saw a blur of faces. She quickly levelled her eyes and tried to look neither to the left nor right but fixed her gaze on the witness stand ahead of her that seemed to rise out of the ground like a tower, grim and forbidding.

Carrie felt a slight sweat break out on her upper lip. She clenched her teeth, swallowed hard and strode purposefully forward.

She mounted the steps to the witness box slowly and deliberately, and took a deep breath as she turned to face the court.

A Bible was thrust in front of her, she placed her right hand on the book, raised her left hand and read from the card. Her voice was quiet but not hesitant. "I promise that the evidence I shall give shall be the truth the whole truth and nothing but the truth."

"You are, Caroline Jane Llewellyn?"

Carrie's mouth was dry. She took a sip from the glass of water on the desk. Her inner strength surged to the surface and in a voice that was clear and even she replied, "I am."

"Where do you reside?"

"Gelli Galed, Near Crynant, Neath."

Norman Parrish spoke gently, "Carrie, may I call you Carrie?" Carrie nodded. "I want you to tell me in your own words what happened on that fateful day, October 25th when you went to Neath with Jacky Ebron."

Carrie could feel everyone in the spectators' balcony straining forward to listen. Carrie knew she had to blot them out and concentrate on Mr. Parrish.

She cleared her throat nervously, and started quietly, struggling to keep the emotion out of her voice.

It was a painful and distressing interview. Carrie had to stop several times. Norman Parrish could feel the effect Carrie's story was having on the assembled courtroom. The whole company were shocked by Carrie's ordeal and sympathised with the fresh open-faced teenager who retained her modest poise throughout. Carrie's evidence would certainly make a difference to Netta's defence.

Norman Parrish played most of his defence directly to the five female members of the jury sensing how they empathised with Carrie.

"Miss Llewellyn." The prosecuting counsel stood up. Carrie lifted her eyes and looked at her interrogator.

Each of his questions came exploding out, one after the other, barely giving her time to draw breath. A still small voice grew inside her urging her to be calm, persuading her to answer as best she could. Carrie knew it would do no good to allow her temper to bubble and boil. It would help no one's case if she allowed herself to become rattled by his persistent questioning, inferences and slur on her character.

The faces of Mrs. Chappell and Mr. Segadelli loomed out of the crowd of faces in the balcony. Carrie wondered what they were thinking.

"Well, Miss Llewellyn?"

"I'm sorry, what did you say?" Carrie asked suddenly aware that everyone was waiting for her answer.

"Let me put it another way, I think Miss Llewellyn that you are not the sweet, naive innocent you purport to be."

"Objection, supposition."

"Sustained. Counsellor, hearsay is inadmissible as evidence, you will please confine yourself to the facts."

Carrie swallowed hard, in an attempt to keep calm she had allowed her thoughts to wander and had obviously missed something very important, something very damaging to her character.

"Thank you, Miss Llewellyn. You may step down for the time being. M'lud I intend to call a witness to testify that Miss Llewellyn did deliberately excite and enflame Jacky Ebron's passions."

"Objection, as my learned colleague has so aptly said, we are not here to try a case of rape, but one of murder and I fail to see what this has to do with proving Miss Llewellyn's guilt."

"Mr. Tynan, I have to agree with Mr. Parrish. Where is this line of questioning leading?"

"M'lud, I believe that if you allow me to continue I can

certainly discredit Mr. Parrish's theory that Netta Llewellyn was not in full control of her sensibilities."

There was a low rumbling of voices in the courtroom.

The judge looked down the bridge of his sharp aquiline nose and made a decision. "Order in the courtroom or I will have it cleared. Mr. Tynan, you seem unable to convince me of the suitability of this proposed evidence, therefore it is disallowed."

There was a sudden rush of whispers and the judge glared at the gallery. One by one the spectators fell silent.

Carrie left the courtroom as she had arrived. Inside she was trembling but outwardly she was her mother's daughter. Proudly and gracefully she glided down the wooden floored aisle, back through the double doors where she collapsed into shuddering sobs on the wooden bench reserved for witnesses.

John came running down the wooden staircase from the gallery and hastened to her side. "There, there, cariad, the worst is over. Hush now."

"Oh, John I feel so dirty, so used and humiliated. That man was so unpleasant I shall find it hard to look anyone in the eye again."

"Nonsense. You told the truth. The jury are on your side. Everyone felt your pain. No one blames you."

Carrie turned to her brother and sobbed in his arms. "Please, John," she managed to say, in between sobs and snatches for breath, "Get me out of here."

They left the courtroom with the trial still in progress and made their way to their humble lodgings in Station Road. There they sat and waited for news.

Gelli Galed

Seven

The trial dragged on painfully for four days. Finally, Netta was called to the stand. She rose to face the assembled courtroom her pregnancy made more obvious by the plain cotton smock that she wore.

The courtroom was silent, the tense atmosphere of waiting amplified by the people gathered, almost afraid to breathe. Netta took the oath and because of her condition the judge allowed her to sit.

"You are, Netta Sarah Llewellyn?"

The pinched tones that had been hers, softened. It was as if she had been coached and rehearsed in her speech. Her voice came out clearly and well modulated, "I am."

John and Carrie had returned to the court to hear Netta's evidence. John hardly recognised his aunt. Pregnancy had gentled her proud bearing, had softened the nettle sharp mouth, her thick, glossy hair was tied in such a way that it flatteringly framed her face rather than when scraped back in a harsh bun. She looked like a woman wronged.

"I want you to tell me, in your own words what happened the night you went in pursuit of Jacky Ebron."

Netta took a deep breath as if to calm herself, then sipped from the glass of water at her side. Using her newly discovered tones she started apprehensively, stopping and starting as she found difficulty in speaking. Gesturing with her fine hands and tapering fingers, she lightly stroked her throat suggesting that a choking lump had manifested itself there, restricting her speech.

Norman Parrish took this advantage and spoke soothingly, "Take your time. There is no need to rush. Just tell your story to the jury."

Netta managed a half smile in understanding and with a trembling voice began. "After my Penry was killed in a mining accident I never believed I'd find happiness again. It had fallen to me to look after Mam. You see, my sisters were both married and my brother had Hendre. I saw it as my duty and I locked away all my womanly feelings, hid them from all, for what I thought was forever."

"Was it hard to see your sisters so happy and you left with the work of looking after your mother?"

"Sometimes. I felt bitter when I saw what they had, knowing I would never know the joy of a husband and family."

"Objection. I fail to see what this has to do with the case in question."

"M'lud, I intend to show in addition to the evidence we have already heard that Netta was duped by the man Ebron and carried out the act of murder whilst the balance of her mind was disturbed. Furthermore, I shall show that the charge should be lessened to manslaughter. Her own story is vital to my case. A woman's life is at stake and she should be afforded every opportunity to save it."

"I don't need a lecture, Mr. Parrish. Pray continue. I will allow the evidence."

Netta took out a small lace handkerchief and twisted it in her hands.

"After my brother had his accident, my sister, Annie had to return to her own farm. She asked me to stay at Hendre for a while until the family could cope. Also, she was suspicious of a farm worker who had come to work for Bryn." Netta faltered, and Norman Parrish gently urged her on.

"Go on."

"He was the most wonderful man I had ever met. Perfect film star teeth, full of charm and good humour. I could scarcely believe it when he turned his eyes on me."

Netta continued with her story. The jury appeared sympathetic nodding in understanding as she unfolded her tale.

Netta talked for over an hour. By this time she was physically and emotionally drained, the sweat was running off her brow, which she dabbed at frequently with her lace hanky.

"Netta, when Dr. Rees informed you that Carrie had been raped, what was your initial reaction?"

"I was shocked, flabbergasted. A pain shot through my

heart like hot coals. It was all my fault. Carrie's plight. I should have seen it coming, but I was blinded by my love for the man.

I knew before the doctor said, who it was. In my heart I'd always known, I just didn't want to admit it." Netta stifled a sob. "I'm sorry..." The court waited while she regained her composure and then she continued.

"Passion, rage and shame flooded through me. My hurt was anxious for revenge, my heart wanted to forgive, my pride wanted to kill. A multitude of conflicting feelings swept through me. I knew I had to get out. Get out of the room with its unspoken accusations. Get out of the room with its suffocating pain. I ran. I don't know where. I don't know why. Maybe I wanted to believe there had been some terrible mistake, maybe I needed to face my true self, maybe I wanted to die."

There was a quiet murmur of whispers in the gallery while Netta struggled to carry on. She took another drink from her replenished glass.

"I had to be punished, I had to die. I don't remember what happened then. The urgency of my emotions drove me on. I had no control over my movement, as if I was outside looking on, observing, playing no part in this drama. I watched with the detached interest of an audience, everything was in slow motion, voices echoed inside my head but I knew I had to keep going. I remember finding myself out on the road to Crai. I wanted to remove myself as far away from Hendre as I could. I didn't realise I'd travelled so far."

Netta took a shuddering breath and twisted her well-wrung hanky.

"I saw in the distance a man with a bed roll walking over the rise. I spurred the horse on until I caught up with him. My eyes clouded over and suddenly I saw very clearly what I had to do. I had to stop him from ever hurting another woman again." Netta swallowed hard.

Norman Parrish prompted, "Go on."

"A terrible rage bubbled up inside me. The red of blood flooded my eyes, I remember sliding down off the horse. I remember the feel of his kiss on my lips. I know I yearned to become intoxicated with his embrace. His hips melted into mine and I remember no more."

There was a quick burst of chatter from the gallery, which quickly lulled with the next question.

"You don't remember killing him?"

"I remember feeling his dead weight on my body, and the disgust I felt pushing him off. I had a knife in my hand. I was sticky with blood, his blood. Shame and fear overcame me as I realised I must have so savagely taken his life. I was shaking with regret and sorrow that I had eclipsed the life of the man I loved."

"Then what did you do?"

"I don't remember... I must have got back somehow because I remember sitting in the chair waiting for the police to come as I knew they would."

"Thank you. No further questions for the time being."

It was then the turn of the prosecution. Netta was questioned and harassed. With every answer the barrister sought to confuse, to anger, and to humiliate her.

She stood her ground alarmingly well.

"Do you still deny that without malice or forethought you set out to wreak vengeance on Jacky Ebron, to murder him in cold blood?"

"I have already testified to a thousand different emotions spurring me to flee from Hendre, one of which was to take my own life, but to murder him ... No. In spite of all I loved him.

"But you couldn't bear the fact that he had left you. In fact you would rather kill him than let him go to another woman. Is that not right?"

"No! I loved him. I also hated him for what he did to Carrie. I hated myself for my own stupidity. But, I don't think I planned to kill him."

"Think? You mean you don't know? Then why did you take the knife?"

"I don't know. I was numb. I needed to feel some pain, some hurt."

"Are you suggesting that you planned to self mutilate?"

"I don't know, I don't remember."

"That's all very convenient for you isn't it?"

"Objection. We've already heard testimony that she was in a state of deep shock when she left the house. He is merely trying to antagonise the accused."

"And are you afraid of what she'll do or say if I do?" burst in the prosecutor.

"Mr. Tynan, you are over stepping the mark." reprimanded the judge.

"I apologise your honour. No further questions.

There were no more witnesses to be summoned and the prosecuting counsel was called to deliver his final speech. He castigated Netta, painting her as a sadistic, scheming woman who was cleverly playing the system to excuse herself from murder.

"There is only one punishment, fit to be meted out to a woman of her kind. Jacky Ebron lost his life, and no man or woman has the right to take a life. We cannot play God. If you find as I do that this was a premeditated act then there is only one verdict you can bring in and that is one of guilty."

Mr. Parrish rose for his closing speech, "The burden of proof throughout the trial rests with the prosecution. So far he has produced little to substantiate his case against my client except hearsay. Through her own admission she has pronounced herself guilty of Jacky Ebron's death although her mind was in such a state of turmoil that she does not remember the act. Trusted and learned medical practitioners have testified on the state of her mind. You have heard the evidence from five different experts in their field who agree that Netta should plead guilty to manslaughter on the grounds of diminished responsibility.

You the jury have heard the most terrifying tale of rape and murder and cannot fail to have been affected by it. Uncontrollable impulse has never been recognised as a defence in English law, but how many of us would have wanted to do to him what Netta did after his crime against Carrie? Let's not forget her suffering.

The defence has established proof on behalf of the accused on a balance of probabilities that she was in such a state of deep emotional shock that it substantially impaired her mental responsibility for her act in killing the fiend, Jacky Ebron.

It is the duty of the jury to consider the issue broadly and if there is the smallest doubt in your mind, and we have seen plenty of medical evidence to support the fact that she did *not* set out to kill him; you must return acceptance of a plea of guilty to manslaughter.

There is also the evidence of extreme provocation and if you feel that any reasonable man or woman would have acted this way in these self same circumstances you must acquit or pardon the accused for her crime. Look at her. Has she not been punished enough? Also, she is carrying Jacky Ebron's child. A child she promises to cherish. Can we deny that child its mother? I think not."

Excited whisperings broke out in the gallery once more that were shushed into silence as the judge shuffled his notes. He began his summing up, highlighting facts presented to the jury that he insisted they consider.

Finally he concluded, "In this trial for murder it is for the jury to consider whether there is such evidence of provocation on the part of the victim, as put forward by Mr. Parrish. Evidence, which the jury could reasonably so find, exists and I have drawn your attention to it. As to the degree of provocation involved, I beg to differ from the prosecuting counsel. Where on a charge of murder there is evidence on which the jury can find that Netta was provoked by things done and said, to the extent that she lost her self control, the question whether the provocation was enough to induce any reasonable man or woman to do what Netta Llewellyn did, shall be left to the jury. In determining that question the jury shall take into account everything both done and said according to the effect, which in their opinion, would have been committed by a reasonable person. The defendant is to be treated as a reasonable person placed in the relevant circumstances. The reasonable person will not, of course, be quick to wrath, over irritable, or unduly pugnacious. Testimony has been given to her good character.

But it must be stressed that what is 'reasonable' is here solely a question of fact to be decided by the jury in relation to the actual circumstances of the case. Should provocation reduce the charge to manslaughter and I direct the jury to consider this most carefully, then should there follow a finding of diminished responsibility or acquittal or even pardon? I will leave you to deliberate." He shuffled his papers together again and rose.

"What does that mean?" Carrie whispered to John.

"It means if the jury feel that the circumstances were such as to justify her actions, then they should let her go."

The jury left the courtroom to make their decision. They were out for five hours.

Gelli Galed

Eight

A feverish ripple of mutterings spread through the gallery as the jurors filed in to the courtroom and resumed their seats. The jury had discussed, argued and debated every aspect of the case before finally agreeing.

The whole courtroom waited in nervous anticipation, not least of all, Carrie and John.

The shuffling and whispers ceased as the foreman of the jury rose to his feet.

The judge asked, "You have reached a verdict and are in agreement?"

"We have M'lud."

A piece of paper was handed to the clerk of the court who in turn passed it to the judge who unfolded and read it. Netta was ordered to stand and face the court.

The question was asked, "On the charge of murder how do you find the accused Netta Sarah Llewellyn?"

"Not guilty."

A babble of voices erupted from the gallery. The foreman cleared his throat and continued.

"We find the accused guilty of manslaughter due to extreme provocation and request the court's leniency." He sat down looking embarrassed.

The judge peered at Netta down the bridge of his nose. "Netta Sarah Llewellyn you are found guilty of manslaughter. The jury has decided in its wisdom, that extreme provocation was involved that would compel any reasonable man or woman to have acted accordingly. It is my duty, therefore to respect their plea for leniency. You will leave this court and be detained at His Majesty's pleasure for a period of six months after which you will be placed on probation for not less than three years, the terms of which are to be determined between your probation officer and the court."

"All rise."

The judge left his bench and spectators left the courtroom in an effusion of sound. Reporters raced to catch the final edition of their papers. Netta shook hands with Norman Parrish and thanked him.

"You need to thank your niece. We wouldn't have done it without her."

A policeman came forward to take Netta down to the cells beneath the court.

"Tell Carrie thank you. I'll not forget." And bearing her pregnancy proudly, she left the court.

Norman Parrish conveyed Netta's message. Carrie queried, "How long will she be in prison?"

"With the time she has spent in remand, she has just two months left to serve."

"Not long then?" Carrie nodded in satisfaction. She felt justice had been done.

Back at Gelli Galed there was no sign of Ernie. The animals had been fed and watered but neither John nor Carrie could find him anywhere on the farm.

"I trust he hasn't upped and gone," worried John. "Old Tom did warn me he's likely to just disappear."

"I hope not!" exclaimed Carrie. "I've grown really fond of the old man. Check in the hayloft. We called out to him but we didn't look to see if his things have gone."

John dutifully obeyed while Carrie built up the fire on the range and began preparing their meal.

A few minutes later John was back, "He can't have gone far. His things are still there."

"Well, that's a relief. I was wondering how we'd manage without him."

She turned on the wireless.

"As the fingers of the depression reach further across Europe, so, too, is the situation in our own country worsening. One thousand more jobs have been lost in the shipyards at Humberside and further cuts are expected.

Germany is in the news again, Herr Hitler has announced in defiance of the Versailles treaty that he is to bring back conscription. This announcement comes the very day after the French have voted against stepping up their military service to two years. A strange contrast, and it seems the League of Nations will do nothing to restrain Chancellor Hitler. This is certainly a testing time for the League..."

Carrie switched the broadcast off. There was too much doom and gloom. She could well do without it.

She pulled off her hat with a sigh and set the kettle on the range and flopped in the rocker.

John returned from scouring the farm. "I can't think where Ernie's got to!" he muttered in exasperation.

"Well, I shouldn't worry too much, he can't have gone far. The animals seem to be well tended so he's not been gone long."

"But, I do worry. We desperately need Ernie to keep this place going. Apart from all the valuable advice he's given me. It takes both of us every hour in the day just to keep ticking over. I don't know how he's coped these last few days alone. He couldn't have had much rest."

John looked out of the window at the pinky grey sky. "Besides, it looks like snow. It's cold enough."

"I hope not. I thought we were over the worst of the weather," said Carrie.

"Not necessarily. If it does snow we'll have to be extra vigilant. Snow on this hillside is a killer to man and animal alike. It only needs the gentlest of breezes to set drifts. We've a lot of sheep in lamb. We could lose the lot."

"Don't be such a pessimist, John. You always fear the worst. Try counting our blessings instead of glowering on the black side."

They were brave words but as Carrie looked out of the window at the snow sky, she knew they could be in serious trouble.

Thick woolly flakes started to wisp down from the sky gradually becoming thicker and heavier. The ground was like rock and this snow would have no trouble settling.

Trix whined softly in her throat and stood up wagging her tail. The kitchen door opened and Ernie came in bringing with him the chill of the evening air. He was covered in snow and resembled a Christmas dwarf from a fairy grotto. His whiskers and eyebrows were frozen. The snow had become encrusted on his black beret, which he removed for Carrie. She took it and hung it over the range where the snow melted and dripped, sizzling on the hot coals.

"Duw, Duw!" Ernie exclaimed, "I'm potch!" He shivered as the melted snow dribbled down his neck and soaked his vest.

"Ernie! What have you got on?" said Carrie, looking for the first time at Ernie's smart blue black attire with red flashes.

"Posh, isn't it?"

"Yes, very. But where did you get it?"

"Well, badly in need of a suit I was and with you saving my cash I hadn't the money to buy one. So I joined up."

"Joined up!" John and Carrie chorused in horror.

"Yes. The Salvation Army. They give you a free uniform, when you enlist. That'll do me nicely."

"The Salvation Army! But Ernie don't you realise you'll have to work for them?"

"Yes, you'll have to live in Neath near their hostel and leave us."

"Esgyrn Dafydd, no one told me that. Seemed a good way of putting clothes on my back. I only had to promise a few things."

"Ernie. It'll have to go back. You'll have to explain that you didn't understand what was required. John'll go with you."

"Not tonight we won't. As soon as the snow's cleared. Then, we'll go." John decided.

"But what about my clothes? I gave my others in exchange for these. I've nothing to wear."

"Don't worry about that. We've still got some of Dad's clothes. I'm sure I can alter something to fit you," smiled Carrie.

"I hope so. I've nothing else to wear."

"We'll fix you up, right after tea."

"Then we must see to the sheep. I don't like the look of

this snow," murmured John.

Before John took the tractor out with bales of hay for the sheep, they made sure that the cattle were warm and safe in the sheds and ready for milking.

"You see to the milking, I'll get out on the hillside. I'll be back in time to help move the churns to the end of the lane, ready for loading."

"Right you are," said Ernie. "You go careful now, don't go crawling in any holes for shelter. The snow's coming down thick and fast. You stop to rest in this and ..." Ernie made a strange rattling sound in his throat, "It'll be curtains!"

"I'll be fine. Don't worry so," grinned John. "See you later." John went off whistling into the wild evening.

He drove the tractor right to the edge of a terraced field. He wouldn't go right in, it was too risky on the terraces and he didn't fancy overturning the tractor and getting caught under its weight. He jumped down and hauled a bale off the back and thrust it in the feeding trough. The sheep bleated around it vying for a place to feed. He fetched another two bales and placed them in the feeders and then stopped to count his flock.

He was five short. He noticed that one of his ewes that was very near her time could not be seen. Another mother with sturdy twin lambs that had returned to the flock after the initial beginnings in the barn was nowhere to be seen. And an older sheep was missing; he called down the field as he manoeuvred his way across the terraces.

"Hoah! Hoah! Hoah!"

The snow thickly drifted down, no longer aimlessly but it seemed intent on covering every spare inch of ground. It was crunchy and powdery underfoot and by the time John reached the bottom of the field his walk dragged with the weight of the snow on his clothes.

He was getting tired, of that there was no doubt. The snow no longer seemed a cold black threat but a warm, comforting covering. John felt his eyelids getting heavy. He squinted up at the evening sky, a dusky pink grey that swirled and whirled with fleecy flakes that relentlessly spiralled down.

As he reached the gate at the corner of the field he saw where the snow had drifted up the side of the hedgerow. He thought he caught a glimpse of wool amongst the snow and dug at the drift with his hands.

The snow burned like fire, too late he blew on his hands trying to generate some warmth, some feeling into his numb fingers before reaching into his pockets for his gloves, which he struggled to put on before resuming his digging.

After about ten minutes he had dug out the old ewe that travelled with the flock. She had given birth and the tiny lamb was shivering under the weight of its mother's body. Sadly, the old ewe had suffocated in the drift. John knew he had to get the little scrap of life back home to the dry barn and a good bottle, but it was comforting in this drift. There was shelter from the fierce biting wind that chilled him through his clothes. It was warm next to the old sheep's body and he yearned to rest just for a moment before making his long trek back up the hillside.

"I must keep going. I mustn't stop," he told himself.

The cloudy pink haze of snow that tumbled down from the sky seemed strangely soothing and welcoming.

The night was getting darker now and colder, he would need to rest. Perhaps if he kept the little lamb close to his body they would retain their body heat? Maybe, that would be easier if he pulled the old sheep around them under the hedge?

John tugged and pulled at the stiffening body until there was a barrier between the hedgerow and the sheep in the middle of which John and the lamb sheltered.

The snow continued to fall heavily and John started to slip away into a gentle sleep. Weariness overcame his limbs, which melted into warmth. As he hugged the little lamb to him his conscious mind floated into a drowsy peace. His aching body craving rest, slumbered.

"Surely he should be back by now?" worried Carrie.

Ernie looked out at the hillside, pretty under its snow blanket that deceptively hid its dangers.

"That hillside is like alien territory with the snow and ice. I'll get off up there. Have you got a bottle and a sledge?"

Carrie nodded, "I'll fill the two stone bottles and pack a tot of brandy in some hot water in Dad's old hip flask. Anything else you need?"

"Some blankets, an old sheep fleece, anything to keep him warm. Did you say you had got a sledge?"

"We've got an old wooden board on runners. Dad used it in bad weather to carry the bales to take to the field."

"That'll do. Can you find it?"

"It's in the workshop at the back of the orchard. I'll get it."

"No. I'll do that while you sort the rest out."

Ernie put a scarf round his head and ears before donning his beret. He put on a thick pair of gloves and old socks over those. Then he muffled himself up in his coat and went to search the workshop. He soon found what he was looking for and returned to the house, by which time Carrie was filling the two stone water bottles with hot water. He packed them inside the blankets, covered the bundle with a piece of tarpaulin and bound it to the sledge with baling twine.

Carrie watched him as, by lamplight, he trudged his way down the path to the gate and the treacherous mountainside. Mother nature's violence was rendering the fields a deadly place to be.

Time ticked on. The pendulum hacked away the minutes. The minutes turned into hours and Carrie waited anxiously.

Two hours and forty minutes later Trix clambered off her rag mat and whined softly. Carrie was instantly alert and rushed to the door to see Ernie dragging a bundle on the sledge down the path. She rushed to his aid and between them they managed to lift John into the house and the warmth of the kitchen. The little scrap of a lamb was set in front of the fire and Trix nuzzled up to the baby warming it with her own body and licking it with her hot, moist tongue willing it to survive.

Not a word passed between them while they took off John's outer clothes and tended to his needs.

The tips of John's fingers were frostbitten, as were the

end of his nose and the tips of his ears.

"Can you feel that?" Ernie asked as he squeezed John's thumb.

John, barely awake, shook his head and murmured, "No".

"I can see by the pallor of his extremities that he's been affected."

"What do we do?"

"Firstly, we must get his body warm, then slowly warm the affected parts with water heated to blood temperature. We must send for Dr. Rees as soon as possible."

"Blood temperature? What's that?"

"About 98.6 from what I remember."

"Will he be all right?"

"As long as we keep him warm and keep the affected areas covered with clean dressings. I think the frostbite is superficial. If it is, the dead skin will blacken and fall off. If it is more severe, and I hope not, it could take many months for the dead tissue to separate. He may even need an operation to remove the dead skin or a finger. But let's hope we got to him in time."

Ernie and Carrie set to work with urgency. Carrie boiled some water whilst Ernie covered and wrapped John in blankets.

"Do you know that this little lamb may have saved his life? Cuddled together they were, all cwtched up behind an old ewe."

"Where's the ewe?"

"She was dead. They were using her as a shelter. I was lucky I found him when I did; they were completely hidden by snow. John left the tractor outside the gate to the field so I knew roughly where to look. I tied the sledge to the back of the tractor and drove back otherwise we might still be out there."

"How come you know so much about it?"

"My Dadcu lost all his toes on his right foot through frostbite. I've never forgotten it, or how to prevent it."

"How will I know when the water's the right temperature?"

"Use that old thermometer from the parlour. That'll do.

Take it off the window and put it in the bowl. Not too hot mind, or the glass will crack. Stick a spoon in to take away some of the heat."

Carrie did as she was bid.

John started to come round as his chilled body became warmer. "Thanks Ernie, Carrie."

"Ssh. Don't try to talk. Just rest," whispered Carrie tenderly stroking his brow.

"Ernie, there's some sheep missing!" he exclaimed trying to sit up.

"Don't you worry about that. They're all accounted for. The pregnant ewes are safe in the warm. I put them in the barn. We've only lost the old ewe, mother to that little tot by the fire."

"That's one lamb that won't go to market. Saved your life she did. What are we going to call her?"

"Lucky! Because you're lucky to be alive," exclaimed Carrie.

"Lucky it is," beamed Ernie. "Now Carrie, as soon as the snow stops falling I'll see about getting down to Dr. Rees."

"No you won't. You'll stay put. I remember stories Dad told me about this place. There were times when the family were cut off for weeks and when someone went for help the fresh snow that had fallen on the old iced stuff was so dangerous it caused a slide."

"You mean an avalanche?"

"That's right. So no one moves until we are sure it's safe."

"But John will be needing painkillers. As he starts to recover, the pain in those affected parts will be severe."

"I can manage," grunted John. "Yes, it's uncomfortable but we've got some laudanum in the medicine chest if I need it."

The snow continued for six more days. It was a bleak existence on the mountainside.

Carrie said many a prayer of thanks for Ernie Trubshawe.

Gelli Galed

Nine

"You've done a good job, Ernie," said Dr. Rees adjusting his glasses.

Ernie beamed with pleasure, his rosy countenance becoming more pronounced.

"Many would have rubbed snow into the affected parts and that would have only stirred up more trouble."

"I thought I'd heard something about that," murmured Carrie.

"Old wives tale, Carrie. It would have done more harm than good. As you can see John wasn't seriously affected so it won't be long until he's fully healed. But it could have been a different story. You were lucky Ernie knew what to do."

"I bless him every day for that," smiled Carrie.

"Iechy dwriaeth, anyone would have done the same," Ernie blustered.

"Praise be where it's deserved. Take it in the spirit it's meant," chided Carrie.

"Er.. well," said Dr. Rees packing his bag, "Just keep changing the dressings and there shouldn't be any problems. If there are you know where I am."

Carrie ran for the stone jar and offered the doctor his fee.

"Don't worry about that. You're still covered by the miners' health scheme aren't you?"

"Yes. It's been a struggle but we've kept up the payments," returned Carrie.

"In that case I can wait a little while. I know things are difficult at the moment."

"Thank you, Dr. Rees."

"Tell me Carrie, have you seen or heard anything of your neighbour, Mr. Lawrence?"

"No, I don't want to and I don't care."

"Yes, I heard that you were at odds with each other. He's

not been having an easy time of it you know. Several shop-keepers refuse to serve him. He has to go into Neath to buy his groceries. The animal feed merchants are charging him over the odds, I know that for a fact."

"So, what's it to me?" replied Carrie tartly, stubbornly clenching and unclenching her fists.

"I just thought I'd let you know. Also, I haven't seen him in the village since before the snow. I was wondering if eve-rything was all right. He's not an experienced farmer. I im-agined the Llewellyn's generosity of spirit might have ex-tended to him in spite of everything that's happened." Dr. Rees looked enquiringly over his spectacles at Carrie who squirmed uncomfortably under the doctor's scrutiny. "I think I'll call in on the way down just to put my mind at rest."

"There's no need, Doctor," said Carrie feeling guilty. "I'll look in. Just to please you mind," she added ungraciously.

"Very well. Look after your brother, I'll see you soon."

Carrie saw the doctor out and stamped her foot hard as she closed the door. "Now why did I let myself get talked into that?" she rasped furiously. "Lawrence is the last man I want to see."

Ernie grinned, "Took advantage of your special nature, made you feel uncharitable. Don't worry I'll come with you. You won't be forced to speak to the man."

"Thanks, Ernie. Dr. Rees has been so good to us I don't want to let him down. If you come with me you can see to him but at least I'll feel as if I've done my duty," smiled Carrie thankfully.

"I've heard he's not been having an easy time of it. Can't get farm help, either. He has someone a while, they hear what happened to you two, leave and look elsewhere for work. He's advertising for someone out of the area who doesn't know the farm's history."

"How do you know all this?"

"I keep my eyes to the ground and my ears open, folk don't know I'm listening. You pick up a lot that way."

"You've never said."

"Not my place. Besides I didn't think you'd be inter-ested."

"I'm not! I don't want to waste my time talking about him."

"That's what I thought," nodded Ernie sagely.

"Oh Ernie," laughed Carrie and stretched her arms round the plump little man, "You're manna sent from heaven!"

"Ersgyrn Dafydd," chortled Ernie with embarrassment and flushed with pleasure.

Carrie hugged him and nuzzled his barrel chest with her fiery hair, "What's the time?"

Ernie disentangled himself and took out his pocket watch, "Just coming up to five past eleven," he answered.

"Right, we'll have some elevenses and then get down to Hendre. Shall we walk or ride?"

"We'll take the sledge. It's still pretty thick out there. Trix can come too, just in case."

"In case of what?"

"In case," Ernie affirmed.

Carrie laughed and tossed her wilderness of curls as she set the mugs on the table for their morning tea.

"You know," said Carrie as she picked at a biscuit, "I'd have thought Lawrence wouldn't have had any trouble getting workers in this day and age with the current employment problems."

"There you are, folk round here have got long memories and loyalty to their own, in spite of the depression."

"Yes," mused Carrie as she watched Ernie dunk his biscuit and dribble bits down his front, "It's quite comforting to know that."

She looked at the mess on his shirt and remonstrated with him, "Look at you, you slop! Come here, let's wipe you off. Can't have Mr. Lawrence thinking we're pigs."

Ernie grunted at her and winked as he allowed a damp dishcloth to be scrubbed vigorously down his front. Carrie gave a cheeky swipe at his mouth and Ernie laughed.

"Ach y fe! Leave me be!"

Carrie giggled and drained the last of her drink. "Come on then, we'd better shape it if we're to get to Hendre and back before lunch."

"Right, you see to John and then get yourself wrapped up

warm I don't want you getting frozen to the bone. I'll meet you by the gate in ten minutes. Oh and Carrie?" She turned and looked at him. "Be prepared for a late lunch."

She looked puzzled. "Why do you say that?"

"Just a feeling."

"Well, I hope you're wrong," she muttered as she left the kitchen and went up the stairs to see John. She didn't notice the worried frown that had manifested itself on Ernie's normally jolly face.

Gelli Galed

Six

Carrie and Ernie trudged out onto the bleak and frozen hillside with Trix diving through the snow like an antelope on the run. Carrie giggled and chatted about her childhood memories of outings on the sledge and when they came to a steep banked field she couldn't resist boarding the sledge. She squealed loudly as it skied down the slope catapulting her into the hedge. Trix came running down after her anxiously, worried because her mistress was half buried in snow.

Carrie came up covered with a dusting of snow. She rejoiced in the fun of it and laughed loudly at the dog's obvious concern that turned to tail wagging delight when the collie saw it was just a game.

As they approached the final bend in the track that led to Hendre, the way was deceivingly dangerous. Fresh snow was covering layers of ice and that too was now freezing. It was then Carrie really looked at Ernie and noticed the rucksack he was carrying on his back.

"What have you got there?" she asked.

Ernie gave a solemn smile and muttered, "Just in case!"

It took them only five more minutes to reach the cobbled yard. Carrie stopped and looked across at Hendre, the old home. A fierce passion burned inside her. The whole place held many poignant memories and she choked back a lump that had risen in her throat.

"Well, let's get it over with," she said bravely.

"Wait!" gestured Ernie, "Listen!"

They paused and listened to the silence that only comes with the snow clouds of death. All was quiet. Not a sound, not a movement, not a track from the front door. Nothing to show that anyone lived there.

"What's wrong?" asked Carrie.

"No life," whispered Ernie as if afraid of breaking some

enchantment, "No smoke from the chimney, nothing."

"So, maybe he's out."

"And not leave a fire? And no footprints from the door. Look at the door, Carrie."

Carrie looked. The snow had drifted up three quarters of the height of the door where the wind had blown it. She recognised the seriousness of the situation and struggled as quickly as she could across the yard to the house. Tremulously she glanced across at Ernie who took out a small hand shovel from his pack and he started to dig. She scraped away some of the snow with her gloved hands and Trix joined in thinking it was some sort of game. Now Carrie knew why Ernie had said, "Just in case."

Gelli Galed

Ten

Ernie hammered on the door, "Hello! Anyone home?" There was no response. He called out again.

"I'll feel a right goody-oo if he answers the door and everything's all right," muttered Carrie.

"Somehow, I don't think he will. Is there any other way in?"

"The door that we used at the back is solid oak. There is a door at the side that leads into the passage by the cloakroom, but it was always kept bolted. We never used it."

"That doesn't sound very promising. There's nothing for it, I'll have to break the glass."

"Be careful, Ernie. Don't go cutting yourself. It's a wonder the pane isn't already cracked with the weight of the snow and ice."

Ernie took a small towel from his bag and wrapped it around his gloved hand, "Stand back Carrie, fach. Keep Trix out of the way."

Using the small shovel, Ernie took a swipe at the window above the wooden half of the door of the glasshouse, which gave way with a crack, and splinters of glass flew off to be concealed in the snow. He struck again and this time it broke completely leaving jagged edges surrounding the frame, which Ernie proceeded to knock out. Once it was safe to put his hand through the gap he felt on the other side for the lock and bolt. He turned the key and drew back the sliding bar enabling the door to be opened from the outside.

"Mind where Trix walks, we don't want her ripping her pads on the glass. Wait a minute."

Carrie restrained Trix who was excited to be back at Hendre whilst Ernie threw the small towel over the glass shards on the floor.

The trio entered. Carrie felt a strange awkwardness on coming back to Hendre. Her heart belonged here but it was almost as if she had become a stranger.

She looked at the glasshouse with its pump and basin, inside drain and washing line. The plants she had left on the shelves had been forgotten; they had rotted and turned black in the frost. The whitewashed walls, always kept so scrupulously clean, were pitted with some sort of creeping black fungus. It smelt musty and damp. In winter she had always taken care to scrub the walls once a week with a bleach solution that had kept these parasitic invaders at bay. She clicked her tongue disapprovingly.

"What's the matter?" whispered Ernie.

"Hendre," she answered. "He's letting the place go to rack and ruin. It'll need all hands on deck to get the glasshouse back in order."

"That's not your problem now. Where do these doors lead?"

"The French windows lead into the parlour, the pine door into the kitchen. It doesn't lock so we should be able to get in."

"Well, there's something stopping me from opening the door. Something wedged against it. We'll have to try the French windows."

"They were always kept locked. Look, the key's the other side," said Carrie blowing on the frosted pane and scraping away the crystallised ice. "We'll have to break it."

"No, we won't. Hold this a minute." Ernie passed her the shovel and rummaged in his rucksack once more. He took out a thin piece of wire and a sheet of sandpaper, which he slid under the metal-framed door just in line with the door handle. Then he pushed the wire through the iced lock and wiggled it about. The key freed from the lock dropped to the floor and onto the sandpaper, which Ernie gingerly pulled back under the gap of the door.

"It's a good job these doors were not well fitting, we don't want to do any more damage than we have to," puffed Ernie.

"That's why we kept them locked. The frames were once made of wood but they warped so Dada retrimmed them in metal but he couldn't get them to fit snugly. It was something we were always going to see to and never did."

"Well, it's just as well. Come on let's go through, you know the way."

Quietly they made their way through the parlour and into the passage. Carrie pointed to the kitchen door, "You go first."

Ernie turned the handle and walked into the cold room. A small sob escaped from Carrie who had always remembered the hum of warmth and life in the heart of this house, the kitchen.

Lying on the floor by the door to the glasshouse was Michael Lawrence. Next to him was a small terrier, collie cross, which looked up weakly at the intruders and bared her teeth. The dog struggled feebly to his feet and stood unsteadily, trying to hold his ground in protection of his master.

"Can you see to the dog?"

Carrie nodded. She talked soothingly to the frightened animal, slowly moving forward and offering her hand for him to smell. It was as if the effort to stand had been too much and he sat down again and whimpered softly.

Carrie gently ruffled his fur and scratched him behind his ears. He whined in his throat and licked at her hand.

"Here boy, come on, come and have a drink."

While she went to get the dog a drink Ernie tugged Michael Lawrence away from the door. He turned him over and placed a cushion from the chair under his head. He loosened his clothing around his neck and checked for a pulse.

"He's still alive!" shouted Ernie, "And he's breathing but only just."

Carrie came back from the scullery, "The water's frozen. This little dog needs to drink."

"Fill his bowl with snow let him lick that. Quickly though. We need to get this man warm." Carrie did as she was asked and placed the snow bowl in front of the terrier cross who nervously licked at the contents.

"Carrie, you lie with him, try and warm him while I find some blankets."

"No, thank you! You can lie with him and I'll find the blankets."

"Come on, Carrie there's no time to waste. Please."

Very reluctantly Carrie lay down on the floor and half-heartedly snuggled up to her enemy.

"Put your arms round him. Hug him to you," ordered Ernie.

Carrie sighed impatiently but did as she was told. She breathed her hot, sweet breath onto his face. His lips were blue. His face looked ill and haggard. A rush of compassion swept through her and she hugged him more tightly to her. She could hear Ernie crashing about upstairs. He soon returned with an armful of blankets.

"Now, fy merch 'i, we must do for him as we did for John. Loosen his clothing and get as close to him as you can. Try and generate some of your body heat into him and I'll wrap you both up in these. Then, I'll try and get a fire going."

The next thirty minutes passed quickly and without words. Carrie, furiously uncomfortable, found herself intimately close to the man she loathed, while Ernie grubbed around for dry kindling and coal to make up the fire.

A makeshift bed was made up on the floor in front of the range and a pillow shoved by the door to keep out the draught.

"We need to get something warm inside him when he comes round."

"I don't want to be here when he comes round," grumbled Carrie.

"Never mind that now, we need water. What did you do for water if the pipes froze?"

"We never got frozen up, only once. There are two wells on the property and Dadcu showed us where to dig in the field by the grain store if all else failed."

"Where are the wells?"

"One in Maes-yr-onnen, but that's too far and one by the pigsties in the yard."

"Right, I'll try there."

Ernie went out with a saucepan, leaving Carrie with Mr. Lawrence.

Trix curled up by Carrie's feet and the little dog wobbled shakily to his master's side and snuggled up to them both.

"Come on Ernie!" Carrie ranted to herself, "I shall die if he wakes up and sees me like this with him."

Carrie studied Michael Lawrence's face. He wasn't a bad looking man. Some would call him handsome. He had fine chiselled cheekbones; dark, long curling lashes, and soft gently curving lips. She shook her head. What was wrong with her, gazing at the man like this?

"Oh, Ernie hurry up do!" she exclaimed as Michael Lawrence let out a groaning sigh. His eyelids flickered and were still.

"Ernie!" Carrie called out huskily, trying not to disturb Michael Lawrence. She was agitated by this enforced proximity, his very nearness and maleness causing a confusion of emotions inside her. She was becoming increasingly distressed as the smell of Michael Lawrence triggered her memory. She remembered with loathing, Jacky Ebron's attack. Damn the man! She could still see him leering at her and feel his body pushed against hers. She felt the tears rise up to her eyes and blinked them back furiously.

There was a clatter of boots on slate as Ernie returned clutching a pan of water. "There was water in the well, but the top had frozen. If it stays this cold you'll have to show me where in the field to dig. How's Mr. Lawrence?"

"Too close for my liking. He stirred once and sighed but he's not woken up."

"I'll get some buckets of snow and melt them on the range it won't be any good for drinking, too full of muck and stuff, but it will be all right to fill a bottle. If we can find one. Then I can relieve you of your post." He grinned mischievously, aware of her acute discomfort and taking a somewhat wicked delight in it. "Where am I likely to find a bottle?"

"I don't know," snapped Carrie. "Try the bedroom. Or we used to keep them in the pantry."

"Where's that?"

"Just next to the kitchen door in the passage. It's a walk in one."

Ernie went to look and came back with two stone water bottles and a large can of soup.

"Success!" He grinned toothily at her, "Now, we'll get these filled, put something hot inside us and see if we can bring the young man round. Then you can get back up to Gelli Galed and John, and I'll stay with him until he's well."

"Oh, Ernie that's no good," groaned Carrie.

"Why?"

"I can't manage the farm. It would be better if you went back to John and I stayed here with him." She sniffed with obvious distaste at the thought of spending any time with the man next to her.

"But I didn't think you'd like to do that," observed Ernie.

"I don't. But it seems the simplest solution. Gelli Galed is such hard work for one who doesn't fully understand the land. If I stay here with..." she sniffed imperiously again, "him ... then, maybe I can see Dr. Rees and we can arrange a nurse or something for him. In the meantime I'm sure my idea is best."

"If you say so," agreed Ernie. "Right, the water's boiling let's get the bottles filled. Come on girl up you get, you can get the soup going."

Gratefully, Carrie scrambled away from Michael Lawrence and with Ernie helped to rearrange the bed, ensuring the man was warm and comfortable.

Time marched on. Carrie and Ernie sat close to the fire. No longer did their breath make smoke clouds in the air. The room was warming. They sat at the table and tucked into a bowl of thick vegetable soup.

"I'll finish this and then I'll make up a fire in the sitting room and the bedrooms upstairs, get the house warmed up. We'll have to look out for cracks in the pipes in the wash-house."

"Glasshouse," Carrie corrected him.

"All right, glasshouse," he said resignedly, "But we'll still have to watch for bursts. Tell you what," Ernie said suddenly, "As soon as we know he's okay I'll get up to John. He must be wondering what's happened to us. Then I'll come back down with some provisions for you. There doesn't seem to be much in the larder."

"What about the animals?" queried Carrie.

"What animals?"

"Well, he had stock with the farm. How have they been faring if he's been like this? It looks like he could have been lying here for days."

A long moan of pain came from Michael Lawrence. He turned his head fitfully and his eyes rolled.

"Quick, help me to sit him up," called Ernie.

They propped him up on a pillow but his head flopped forward onto his chest. Ernie rummaged in his rucksack once more and took out the small hip flask. He poured some brandy into a cup with a little hot water. Carrie held Lawrence's head while Ernie tried to get him to drink. Some of the warm liquid dribbled down his chin and onto the blanket.

"Did he take it?" she asked earnestly.

"Some of it. Let his head go back now. That's it. Carefully does it. Right," he said decisively, "You stay put. I'll be back."

Carrie watched as he wrapped himself up and retreated out into the cold afternoon air.

Carrie looked out at the scene from her beloved Hendre and breathed hard in an attempt to still the rising emotion within her. She looked at the bright sky outside. There was only an hour and a half of daylight left at the most. She hoped there was enough oil in the lamps and gas in the canisters.

Trix raised her head and placed it soulfully on Carrie's knee. Carrie ruffled her fur and studied Lawrence's dog. He was looking better. Carrie had found some dog meat and cereal and the little fellow had at last eaten something. Trix had wolfed down the rest and was now looking for more.

Ernie returned, "The animals are in a sorry state. There's some sheep penned up in the barn that've been without water and a cow that was desperate for milking, which I've done. A sow and five piglets dead in the sties and a collie bitch dead in the cattle shed. I've fed and watered the live ones. They're all right for now. I'll bury the collie and pigs when I get back. I've put them out of the way and covered them over with some oilskin for now."

"Couldn't we eat the pork?"

"No. I'm sure they should have been bled first. I'm not so knowledgeable about slaughtering as I am about keeping live animals, never liked that part. But even if they've died of thirst then if the blood's in them they'll be no good to eat. But if they've died from something other than thirst I wouldn't trust burying them. I think they'll have to be burned. But the rest of the pigs are okay."

"All right." Carrie accepted what Ernie had to say and watched him go for the second time not knowing how long she would have to remain as an unwilling companion to Michael Lawrence. However quick Ernie was, he couldn't be quick enough for Carrie.

She watched the clock as the minutes dragged by and darkness fell.

Gelli Galed

Eleven

Carrie lit the gas mantle in the kitchen and the oil lamps in the glasshouse. She stoked up the fire and sat in Lawrence's fireside chair and watched over him.

He turned fitfully and muttered something. Carrie moved softly to his side. He called again and his eyelids lifted wearily. He gasped when he saw her, "Julie-Ann is that you?"

Carrie shook her head but although he was looking at her he did not appear to see her.

"Julie-Ann, my love, my wife. I've missed you so." He twisted and turned in the bed and was overcome with a terrible shaking and his face contorted into a grimace.

Carrie spoke but he did not seem to hear her words. "It's your neighbour, Carrie Llewellyn, Mr. Lawrence. I'm waiting with you until we can get the doctor," she said with embarrassment.

"Julie-Ann, don't go. Don't leave me, please."

"I'm not Julie-Ann," exclaimed Carrie pronouncing her name clearly to him again.

"Take my hand, let me feel your gentle touch."

Michael Lawrence grasped Carrie's hand, which she gave him reluctantly and she listened to his words of love while her face burned with humiliation and anger.

His hands were clammy. He was clearly in the grip of some fever. Carrie tolerated his tortured words and movement, whilst she longed for Ernie's return.

Michael Lawrence rested uneasily. He needed reassurance that Julie-Ann was with him as he fell in and out of consciousness.

Nine-thirty that evening, Trix warned her mistress of approaching visitors. Carrie had fallen asleep next to Mr. Lawrence and for a moment was disorientated. She stretched trying to ease her cramped arms and legs where she had lain awkwardly on the hard floor. The kitchen door opened, letting in a blast of icy air, and Ernie came in with Dr. Rees.

The doctor moved swiftly to his patient's side to examine him. "I don't know what happened to him, but it's a good job you both came along when you did or he could be dead."

Carrie felt a flutter of confusion within her; she almost wished Michael Lawrence was dead and Hendre would be theirs once more, but a twinge of conscience alerted her that at least she had done as Dr. Rees had asked.

"He's delirious with some sort of fever, not from his fall and the cold. Something else...."

"It looks like Q fever," said Ernie.

"It does, but I don't think so. Carrie, I'll need you to keep a check on these shivering fits, how often and when they occur. I need to return to my surgery for the correct medication. If my assumption is correct I think we have here a case of malaria. I need to be sure before giving him quinine that it's not Malignant Tertian Malaria as that could lead to complications."

"What sort of complications?" asked Carrie.

"Destruction of the red blood cells leading to Black Water Fever. I came across a couple of cases in the war, both men died."

Dr. Rees sighed, "Carrie are you able to stay with him? He'll need careful nursing and you have a talent for that," he said remembering the care she had lavished on her father. "Ernie will be able to cope at Gelli Galed and look after John. I can't think of anyone else in the village who could come."

"What about Morfa Davies?"

"She's busy with her midwifery. Suzy Evans is having another baby. She's suffering from pre-eclampsia toxaemia and needs constant attention if the baby is to live. No, Carrie," the doctor surged on expecting her to protest. "There's no one else. Will you do it until I can find someone?"

Carrie took a deep breath. Her lips set in a rigid line while she thought.

"Come on, Carrie," coaxed Ernie, "Do what's right."

"Oh, very well. But I'm not happy about it."

"It's only temporary, not a life sentence. I'll get down to

the village, and I'll be back in an hour. You'll be all right?"

Ernie answered for her, "She'll be fine. I've brought her provisions and some of her clothes. I'll repair the broken window with some wood to keep the chill out."

"I can speak for myself thank you, Ernie," said Carrie half chidingly. "I'll be all right, Doctor. I've got Trix and as Ernie says he's brought me a survival kit. Oh, did you remember food for the dogs?"

"Yes, I've brought them their grub as well. Now, I'd better see to that broken pane before I go and bury those animals."

"So, that's why you thought it was Q fever?" exclaimed Dr. Rees.

"No. It's pigs that is dead not cattle or sheep, but I've seen tanners and dairymen go down like this before pneumonia sets in."

"Where did you find him, Carrie? He's quite a jewel," mused Dr. Rees.

"I know," replied Carrie, "He's one of the family now."

Ernie rubbed a hand over his bristly chin, "An honorary member until I reach my own kin."

Carrie nodded, "I'd almost forgotten that. I dread the day you go," she said sadly.

"Well, it's not yet, so let's get on with the job in hand, you'll talk your tonsils off if I let you."

Dr. Rees replaced his hat and gloves and went to the door; "I'll see you later. Ernie, Carrie." He touched his hat and left.

Carrie wasn't long in unpacking the bag Ernie had brought. She cut herself a huge slice of bread and sat with it on the toasting fork until it was browned on both sides. She buttered it extravagantly and relished every mouthful.

Ernie had since left for Gelli Galed and Carrie settled herself to wait for Dr. Rees' return.

Michael Lawrence seemed to be sleeping better, but every now and then he would call out in his sleep when he would be overcome by an uncontrollable fit of shaking.

Carrie learned something about herself that night. She learned that she enjoyed being in a care situation and could even bury her personal feelings when working in a sickroom.

Carrie listened carefully to Dr. Rees' instructions and administered Michael Lawrence's medicine as directed. She mopped his brow, she talked soothingly to him and answered when he called her Julie-Ann and suffered his ravings and declarations of love with resigned amusement.

His fever fits fell into a regular pattern of every other day and Dr. Rees diagnosed Benign Tertian Malaria, which although not so serious would still take him a while to recover from, and there was the knowledge of the possibility that the disease would recur in future years.

Carrie had been unable to resist looking over her old home. She was curious to see what changes had taken place. Gone was her mother's rosebud wallpaper. Her own tiny bedroom was filled with boxes and trunks. Only John's room remained unaltered and the parlour. Lawrence obviously hadn't got round to redecorating those into his own very masculine style. Carrie resolved that as soon as Hendre was back in her possession she would search the whole of Neath to find paper the same as Mam had in her room and she would redo it in her memory.

Carrie stood at the window of her mother's room looking out over the yard and the hillside. The snow had cleared. All that was left were a few sludgy mounds of slush by the hedgerows. The clear bright sunshine gently warmed the ground persuading the new fresh green shoots of spring plants to push through the soil and stretch their young leaves heavenward.

Carrie was transfixed, lost in a world of reverie and memories. She didn't hear the soft footfall behind her or the door ease open.

Michael Lawrence's tall frame filled the doorway and he caught his breath when he saw the back of young Carrie with her fiery tangle of curls that flowed wildly down her back.

"Julie-Ann," he whispered, his voice husky with passion.

Carrie startled by this silent entry into the room turned and met the gaze of Michael Lawrence.

"And just what do you think you're doing here?" he

roared when he saw the unexpectedly sweet face of Carrie Llewellyn.

Carrie was for a moment stuck for words. Her patient had apparently made a full recovery and part of her was pleased that her nursing had, had some effect. But the rest of her bridled at the ungracious way he had spoken to her. "If you'll excuse me, Mr. Lawrence, I'll just get my things."

"What do you mean you'll get your things? There's nothing here that belongs to you. What the hell do you think you're doing in my house?"

"You're forgetting, Sir, that this is the Llewellyn's house and it is only a matter of time before it will be again. And now, if you don't mind as you have no need of me now, I'll be on my way."

"What the devil do you mean, 'I have no need of you'? Would you kindly explain?"

He walked further into the room, which gave Carrie her chance to move, she pushed past him and went down stairs gathering her coat and hat on the way.

"Trix!" she called to her dog, and without collecting her few belongings she walked briskly across the yard to the gate and up the mountain track to Gelli Galed. Her face burned with two bright pinpoints of red on her cheeks. Trix and the terrier followed on her heels.

She turned to the little dog whose name she had discovered was Boots. "Shoo! Be off with you. Go on home now. Home, there's a good boy."

Boots stopped and looked at her, his head on one side. He didn't follow anymore but watched her retreating figure disappear up the mountainside then turned and wandered back to his master at Hendre.

Gelli Galed

Twelve

In the two weeks Carrie had spent nursing Michael Lawrence, John had made an excellent recovery. Gelli Galed continued to do reasonably well in spite of the depression. It seemed strange to Carrie that someone with Ernie's know how could be so naive at times. She couldn't understand why he'd never made a success of his own life.

"Tell me, Ernie," asked Carrie as she buttered the bread at the breakfast table. "How did you know there was something wrong at Hendre? You went all prepared and kept saying, 'Just in case.' Had you already been down to see?"

"Wish that I had," muttered Ernie his moustache full of toast crumbs.

"Well then, how?"

"It's not something I like to talk about. It's got me in enough trouble in the past. I don't want you thinking any the less of me," Ernie said quietly.

"Aw come on, wuss, I'd never think the less of you. You know that."

Ernie's eyes sparkled brightly with unshed tears and he sat for a moment munching his toast like an old ruminant goat chewing the cud.

"Some people call it a gift," started Ernie uncertainly, "I reckon it's more of a curse."

"What?"

Ernie gave no reply so Carrie implored, "Please, Ernie tell me."

He returned her questioning gaze and thought for a moment before responding. "Don't you go making light of it. Or tell anyone else. I've kept this hidden a long while. It gives people time to forget. I don't want the past raked up again."

"I promise I won't tell, honest," avowed Carrie.

"Every since I was a boy I've known things. Just a feeling when something very good or bad was going to happen. My Mam-gu said I was fey. I had the Celtic gift of precognition. It ran through all the women in my family but skipped a generation in the men. My Dadcu was psychic, my father wasn't. The chain should have been broken when my mother remarried after Dad died. But I don't know whether it has. I took my stepfather's name to lose all associated with the gift."

"I thought Trubshawe wasn't a Welsh name," murmured Carrie.

"No, my real father's name was Beynon. Is that Welsh enough for you?"

"So what happens? How can you tell when something is going to happen."

"I get a curious uneasy feeling and sometimes I hear a clock ticking like the calling of a death watch beetle. That's usually only in cases of a death to come. My mother used to smell a coffin. She was never wrong. Even my father used to tell a story." Ernie paused. Carrie sat down at the table enthralled. She loved tales like this. It reminded her of her childhood and the stories Bryn would tell.

"Oh go on," she pleaded, "Don't stop now."

Ernie chuckled; he was feeling a little better about his confession and began to unfold a tale that had Carrie wide-eyed in wonderment.

"Dadcu was sitting in his rocker by the fire in the scullery smoking his pipe. He'd been suffering from a vicious attack of foreign flu that had left him quite weak. My Dad was sitting with him keeping him company. No one else was in.

Suddenly, my grandfather stopped rocking and leaned forward as if listening and said, 'Oh, there's beautiful singing. There's wondrous singing.'

My father looked up from his book and listened hard but he couldn't hear a thing. But Dadcu's face was filled with rapture.

He continued, 'Oh! There's lovely music. Run out in the street and see who it is. Quickly now or you'll miss it.'

Dad got up and went to the front door. His eyes searched the night street. There was nothing, just the sound of the wind in the trees and the breeze gently rippling the hem of the sun curtain that kept out the draught. There was not a soul to be seen. He went back and told my grandfather who said, 'Aye it's gone now. Funny that.'

They settled again and my Da returned to his place on the floor reading his book and my Dadcu continued rocking.

He stopped once more, 'There it is again. Oh such harmonies! Sounds like it's coming from, outside old Merlin's house. Hurry now! Go and see or you'll miss it.'

Again, my father ran down the passage, opened the door and gazed down the street. There was nothing. All was still.

My father ran back and told him that all was as quiet as the grave and that there was no music. But Dadcu was insistent, "There is! There is! They're singing my favourite hymn. Run and see.'

My father got quite worried and said firmly, 'Dad there's nothing there!' and as he leaned across and gripped his father's arm he too heard the song. He let go as if he'd been burnt, and never said another word.

Three days later old Merlin two doors along was struck down with pneumonia and died. The funeral procession stood outside his house and sang the very hymn Dad and Dadcu had heard."

Carrie sat spellbound. Her spine was tingling and her knees felt strange. She finally broke the mood by saying, "So, that's how you knew John would get into trouble, and that something had happened to Mr. Lawrence."

Ernie Trubshawe nodded, "Then, it was a blessing. It helped to save lives, but if people know, it can become a pressure and a problem. It's why my wife left me."

Ernie fell silent. Carrie didn't press him anymore she knew he needed this moment to be alone with his thoughts and when he was ready he would tell her anything he wanted to share.

The following Wednesday, Carrie received a letter from Australia. It was full of news of Annie's life over there. Dai had managed to buy a farm and although David was working well and had settled into their new life in Australia, Thomas was becoming increasingly unhappy and longed for the hills of Wales. Annie had ended her letter...

"So, if it's at all possible, when Thomas has gathered the fare home and it's a tidy sum, could he stay a while with you until he can find some property worth farming in the valley? He'll work for his keep. I know from your last letter that you could do with the help and I won't worry so much if I know he's with family. But bear in mind that it could take him a year or two to raise the money. I'll wait for your answer,

Lovingly yours,

Annie."

John and Carrie discussed the letter and agreed that of course they would extend a welcome to their cousin. It also gave Carrie an idea that her hopes and dreams were not as unrealistic as she once thought. And with Thomas' arrival, Carrie could put her own ambitions into action. She wrote to her aunt giving their consent.

She was just signing her name with her characteristic flourish when Trix began barking excitedly in the yard. Carrie walked out onto the veranda. It was a fine May morning. The blossom was budding on the trees, the whistle of bird song could be heard and Carrie felt good to be alive that is, until she saw her visitor.

Michael Lawrence with his easily recognised stride was approaching the house. He was carrying a bag that Carrie recognised as hers. She had been meaning to ask Ernie or John to retrieve the few items she had left at Hendre but there was always another chore to do or another errand to run and it had somehow dropped back from her list of priorities.

She stared coolly at him. He felt ashamed in her presence when he remembered how he'd ordered her out of the house.

"Miss Llewellyn," he cleared his throat awkwardly, "I believe I owe you an apology."

"Do you now?" Carrie was determined to savour every word of this encounter. "And what might that be?"

"Dr. Rees informed me of what happened. He told me I owe my life to you," he swallowed uncomfortably, "And so does Boots."

Carrie said nothing. She regarded him insolently, forcing him to stutter on.

"When I saw you in the house, I didn't understand. These are your things," he offered her the bag, "I think everything is there. If you could let me have your account of what I owe you for food and your time I shall be happy to settle it."

He placed the bag on the veranda and looked deep into her startlingly green eyes and for a moment almost lost himself in their beauty. Then he checked himself and turned to leave.

Carrie almost spat at him, "You don't owe me a thing. You'll need everything you've got when we take Hendre back."

She was gratified to see a sudden rush of hurt flood into his eyes, but strangely enough the satisfaction she received did not last long and she found herself adding, "Mr. Lawrence at least let us try to be civil to one another when we meet. I ask no more." She bit her lip. She knew not why she had said that and in frustration with herself she picked up her bag and re-entered the house.

Michael Lawrence slowly walked away.

Inside the safety of the house with no prying eyes and no one to hear she burst into a fit of sobbing. All cried out she felt better, but still couldn't understand her impulsive comment to him. She set the kettle on the range for tea and resolved to forget the man and all he stood for.

"I need to go into the village tomorrow. Does anyone want anything?" asked Carrie at the tea table that afternoon.

"We don't need provisions, surely?" John replied.

"No. But I need a few things," she said evasively, "And I have to get a stamp to post Annie's letter."

"Oh. Right you are."

"You can get me a pen'orth of mintoes," said Ernie who had a remarkably sweet tooth.

"You'll have no teeth left," laughed Carrie.

"Did I see Michael Lawrence coming up the track this afternoon?" said John changing the subject dramatically. "Only you haven't said."

"Bad things are best forgotten," snapped Carrie her face starting to burn.

"Keep your hat on the right side of your head," said John, "I only asked."

"Sorry," said Carrie meekly. "It's just anything to do with him makes me want to scream. He came to return my things that's all. Do you know he even asked how much he owed me for my time. The nerve of the man."

"I hope you gave him a hefty bill with interest," smiled John.

"I did! Well, more or less, I told him I wanted Hendre."

"Good for you. Is there anymore pie?"

"You can have the last piece, now. I was saving it for your supper but you'll have to shift with bread and cheese."

"That's all right," said John helping himself to the final portion.

"Do you want anymore, Ernie?"

"No thanks, I'm stuffed to my ears. Good job too," he added indicating the disappearing pie. "Iechy dwriaeth, what's that smell?" Ernie coughed wrinkling his nose.

"Duw, there's a niff! What is it?" mumbled John hastily finishing his last mouthful.

"It's enough to choke a giraffe," grunted Ernie, reaching for his handkerchief to mask his nose from the smell.

Carrie looked round to see Trix slink in close to her feet, tail well between her legs, head down and looking guilty. "Out! Come on outside," she ordered.

Trix reluctantly shambled out of the kitchen onto the veranda and the trio could breathe easily again.

"Smells like she's rolled in something," muttered Carrie.

"Fox dung!" Ernie exclaimed, "That's what it is. It'll be a devil of a job to get rid of it." And he rose from the tea table and went out through the other door hastily followed by John.

"And just where do you think you're going?" questioned Carrie.

"We've got the milking to do."

"And the lambs to see to," affirmed Ernie.

"Oh no you don't. Who's going to help me clean Trix?"

But her words fell on an empty room. With half a smile playing on her lips she put the kettle on the range, Trix would have to have a bath.

"So you see, Carrie you're too young to begin training as a nurse. You have to be eighteen. You need your school certificate or to pass an entrance exam in English and Maths in order to start at a teaching hospital. How old are you?" asked Dr. Rees.

"Nearly seventeen. My English is good and I never had any problems at school. Before Dad died I was hoping to go on to further education. I'm sure I could pass an exam."

"But there's still the question of your age."

"Is there nothing I could do? Looking after Michael Lawrence made me realise that I want to do something with my life."

"And a very good job you made of it too..." Dr. Rees paused. "There is one thing you could do and it would give you a head start into a nursing career."

"What? I'll do anything," begged Carrie.

"You could start as an auxiliary. You have to be sixteen for that. You would learn an immense amount and could then apply to a teaching hospital when you're eighteen." Dr. Rees stopped once more and considered the child in front of him. No longer a child in body, only in years. She looked earnest and mature enough to cope with what he had in mind.

"I'll tell you what... My sister is Matron of a maternity home in Aberystwyth. I will write a letter of recommendation for you and we'll see what she says."

"Oh thank you, Doctor," sparkled Carrie. Her face shone with gratification and pleasure.

"Tell me, does John know of your plans?"

"Not yet," Carrie bit her lip uncertainly, "I haven't discussed it with him yet. But he'll have Ernie with him."

"Ernie won't be there forever. He has a reputation. I know he's stayed longer with you than most, but he could up and go at any time."

"I know, I know," Carrie brushed Dr. Rees' protests

aside. "But cousin Thomas will be returning from Australia when he's raised some money, so John won't be alone. Believe me, Doctor. I've thought very carefully about it. It's what I really want."

"Well, you're entitled to some happiness. Heaven only knows life has dealt you some cruel blows so far. I'll write to Moira today. We'll see what she says."

"Thank you so much, Doctor," said Carrie and she almost skipped out of the surgery.

Dr. Rees shook his head amiably, and resumed his study. Carrie was one little lady that would do something with her life.

Carrie lightly ran out of the surgery. There was only one thing left to do. She had to tell John.

Gelli Galed

Thirteen

"No, Carrie you can't!" John exclaimed thumping his hand on the table. Carrie was alarmed. Never had she seen John so angry. She couldn't understand his wrath. She had been sure he would have been pleased for her.

"Your place is here with me," he shouted and he pushed his chair away from the table, which fell back with a clatter to the floor and brusquely he left the room.

Ernie sat silently. Carrie stared after her brother dazedly. "Why, Ernie? Why is he so angry?"

Ernie took his time before answering, "Because he loves you, cariad. You're all he's got. If you leave it's like the whole family has broken up. He needs you more than you need him."

"I thought he'd be happy for me."

"It's a shock. Give him time. He'll come round. He'll eventually see that it's best for you... and him," he added carefully.

"We don't even know if I'll get a placement. I may have to wait until I'm eighteen."

"Leave it for now, cariad. Let him cool off. Once he starts to think about it he'll realise he can't make you stay. I'm sure your happiness will come first. Give him time to get used to the idea."

Carrie smiled wistfully. She knew Ernie was right. John wouldn't stand in the way of her dreams. It was just a matter of time.

She cleared the dishes from the table, keeping the scraps for the chickens. Nothing went to waste in this house. Even the potato peelings would be boiled up to make a mash for the animals.

Carrie sat at the scrubbed table and waited for the water to boil. She loved life on the farm and she hadn't completely forgotten her aspiration to run her own one day. She thought

about everything she did at Gelli Galed, and all her respon-
sibilities; the chickens, ducks, lambs and pigs, not forgetting
the cooking and cleaning, which she admitted she disliked.
She sighed. There was more to life than that. She really felt
needed and useful when she looked after Michael Lawrence.
It was a feeling of pride that made her feel worthwhile and
important. She didn't want to spend her life in the valley
seeing nothing of big city life. But it was her own feeling of
self worth that was important. Carrie proudly tilted her chin.
Once she made up her mind nothing would sway her. John
was going to have to get used to the idea she was not going
to live and die in the valley with nothing to show for her life.
She would live a life that people would remember. Then and
only then would she be content to return to Hendre.

Hendre her family home, they would get it back. That too
was just a matter of time. The jiggling of the lid on the kettle
woke her out of her reverie and she poured the scalding water into the bowl to rinse away the debris of their meal.

Carrie's thoughts wandered back to Michael Lawrence.
The man disturbed her and she didn't like it. She wondered
how old he was. From her guess she took him to be in his
early to mid twenties. Where was his wife Julie-Ann? What
had happened to her? She found herself speculating on a ro-
mantic scenario featuring Michael Lawrence and his wife
and then crossly dismissed her imaginings as absurd.

That evening when John returned he went straight to his
room. He didn't sit up for supper with Carrie and Ernie. Ernie looked at Carrie's sorrowful expression and comforted
her, "I'll talk to him. Just be patient."

Three weeks passed. The tension had eased between
brother and sister. Ernie had spoken to John who reluctantly
accepted that Carrie had her own life to lead, a life that
might not necessarily include him.

Carrie sat at John's feet on the rag mat in front of the
rocker and scratched Trix behind her ears. John was lovingly
stroking Carrie's back. He placed one hand on her shoulder,
"You know, cariad. I only want what's best for you?"

"I know," she answered simply.

"I am just so afraid that there'll be no place for me in your new life. That's all."

"Don't be silly. You're all I've got. You, Trix and Hendre. You can be certain that I'll come back to you and the farm, and fulfil all our dreams. This is something I just have to do. Oh, I know it sounds corny, but it's true. I need to do this, John. That's if I get a chance. Dr. Rees hasn't heard from his sister yet, it may never happen."

"No, it may not happen that you'll go to Aber, but whatever happens you'll go to some big teaching hospital when you're eighteen, won't you?"

"If they'll have me."

"And in the meanwhile, I'll miss you."

"And in the meanwhile," said Carrie playfully, "You'll have Thomas working here with you."

"If he's raised the fare."

"He will," she said simply.

"Come on cariad, on your feet and get the kettle on. I'm parched tickling your back. It's harder work than mucking out the slurry from the cattle. Carrie gave him a cheeky dap, which he dodged. "You get the tea on and I'll see if there's any post. You never know what news awaits us."

He said it half jokingly, but he knew that some mail had arrived by the racket Trix had kicked up at the end of the path. Carrie moved out of the way and dutifully did as she was asked. John went to the door just as a sleepy eyed Ernie entered looking for his breakfast.

"Sorry we're late this morning, Ernie. We've been talking."

"Good, I'm glad to hear it. I hope it's all sorted out now?"

"Well, more or less."

Ernie yawned loudly.

"You look tired. Did you not sleep well?" asked Carrie.

"I was up most of the night with Dora. She was struggling all night to give birth."

"How is she?"

"Mother and calf are doing well, although it was touch and go at one moment. No point in us all being up. Besides,

I knew I could manage."

"I'll pop and see her after breakfast."

"She'll like that. I've also put Bandit in with the rest of the flock. She seems to be doing all right."

"Poor little Bandit."

"Poor little Bandit be damned. We'll have to watch her. At the first opportunity she'll be in her warming her wings in front of the fire."

Carrie laughed and passed Ernie a mug of tea, "There that'll get your taste buds working."

"Carrie! Carrie!" John called excitedly. "There's a letter from Mr. Bridgeland. We've got a date for a preliminary hearing for our civil action against Mr. Lawrence!"

"When?" Carrie asked brightly.

"Thursday September the twelfth."

"That's months away!" Carrie exclaimed in dismay.

"Well, we knew it would take a long time. Anyway, Mr. Bridgeland said there had been a cancellation, someone had settled out of court and we've got their slot. It is only a preliminary hearing, it could take another year or more before it's all sorted."

"Never mind. It's a start. Anything else? It looks like you've got more than a solicitor's letter there."

"Yes and they're both for you. One is postmarked Aberystwyth."

Carrie tore at the envelope feverishly and scanned the contents.

"Well?"

"She wants to meet me. She says I come well recommended. I've got to go for an interview Monday September the second and take a test. If I pass they'll give me a job. I'll be expected to start the following week on the ninth. Oh John, I'm so excited." She squealed and caught him round the waist, jumping up and down with delight.

"I'm pleased for you too, cariad," said John softly. But Ernie saw the fleetingly sad expression that had been in his eyes. "What's the other one?"

"I don't know," said Carrie curiously, turning the envelope over and studying the writing, "It looks like Netta's hand."

"Well open it and see."

Carrie opened the envelope cautiously and took out the plain white paper that sported Netta's fine copperplate handwriting, and read:

"Dear Carrie,

I've served my sentence and have only to endure the terms of my probation. I know I would not be a free woman today if it was not for your testimony and for that I thank you.

I am very near my time now, and have less than a month to go before my given date of 26th July, which is a Friday this year. If the rhyme is to be believed then he or she will be loving and giving, not much like his father then. But dates never work out I suppose it could be anytime around there.

I wanted to let you know that I won't be returning to Crynant. At least, not for a while. Let the dust settle and maybe in a few years I'll come home. I've written to Mam and Gwenny. I would appreciate it if you'd keep an eye on Mam-gu for me. She's not old and doddery yet but her turn will come as it does to us all.

I'm living in Monmouth. My probation officer has got me a job with a milliner. I can work from home and therefore look after the baby at the same time. When I do have to go into the shop I'm assured we'll both be welcome. It's a far cry from Dowds in Neath who would have sacked me on the spot. So maybe your Aunt's life is taking a turn for the better.

I enclose my address, just in case of emergencies. I'll try not to bother you unless it's absolutely necessary. Please excuse the haste of this letter.

Yours gratefully,

Netta."

Carrie passed the letter across to her brother to read who muttered, "I wondered what had happened to her. Are you going to reply?"

"I'll just send a general letter in response to her wishes. Nothing more," she said cursorily.

"Now, I'll have to find out where this place is in Aber and see if I've something decent to wear."

"It may be worth a trip to Neath if you haven't," said John trying to be helpful. "We want you to make a good impression."

Carrie hugged him and stuffed the two letters in the brass holder on the wall and resumed cooking breakfast. The happiness in her eyes was unmistakable. It radiated through every movement. For the moment the sun was shining on Carrie Llewellyn.

Saturday morning, John gave Carrie a lift into Crynant in time to catch the eight o' clock train to Neath. Not being on farm business she could afford the luxury of public transport.

"What time will you be back so I can meet you?" John asked.

"I hope to catch the four-thirty train back like I used to on school days. I intend to have a good day out. If I miss it, I'll get the bus back. They run every twenty minutes, so whatever happens I'll see you between ten-past-five and five-thirty here."

Carrie reached across and gave her brother a peck on the cheek before boarding the train. She looked smart in Miri's plum lightweight summer coat, cut to fit her and her felt cloche hat. She waved at the window as the train gave off steam and whistled its departure to the passengers. John watched forlornly as the engine chugged out of the station until he could see it no more and then returned home.

Carrie was busily looking out of the window, enjoying the countryside. She didn't notice who else had boarded the train. She carefully removed her kid gloves. It was too hot to wear them anyway. The magazine she had bought slipped off her lap onto the floor. She leaned over to pick it up when a masculine hand retrieved it and offered it to her.

"Why thank you," she said automatically, before her eyes came to rest on the person sitting opposite.

"Miss Llewellyn," acknowledged the man and he touched his hat in deference to her.

She recoiled in her seat, her face flushed with colour. "Mr. Lawrence," she replied struggling to keep her voice level in this very public place.

"Going to Neath?" he asked.

"Yes, shopping," and then to prevent any further communication she opened her magazine and proceeded to read it as if engrossed.

The journey seemed painfully long. Carrie constantly referred to her watch. A number of people left the train at Cilfrew, and several boarded. Carrie pressed herself into the corner by the window and appeared oblivious to everything except her magazine, which was not as interesting as she would have wished in such circumstances. Resignedly, she folded it and replaced it on her lap.

Michael's resonant tones broke into her disordered thoughts. "I know you find it difficult to speak to me, but you did say, did you not, that you wished us to be civil when we next met?"

Carrie nodded, aware of the attention such a remark attracted from other people in the carriage.

"Please accept my thanks again for what you did for me."

Carrie was conscious of his grey eyes boring into her, those grey eyes framed by those long, dark, curling lashes. She now was the one who was embarrassed and afraid of a scene and so to avert the curiosity of others she decided to respond. It couldn't do any harm, now. "Anyone else would have done the same if they'd known. I was just being neighbourly."

Her eyes remained firmly fixed on her lap and her twisting fingers pulled at the soft leather gloves. She stuttered, "T..too hot to wear these I don't know why I brought them." She hoped a change of topic might shut him up.

She noticed an elderly lady unashamedly eavesdropping, looking from one to the other.

"Is that what you're shopping for? Something cooler?"

"Partly," she affirmed, "I'm after an outfit for an interview." Carrie immediately regretted the admission, knowing it would only invite more questions. Why was she so flustered? She was angry with herself for not thinking quickly enough and so made up her mind to be politely pleasant until she could leave the confines of the carriage.

"A job interview? Surely, you're not leaving the valley?"

"I don't know. It depends if I get the job," replied Carrie, a little of her old spirit returning.

"May I enquire as to what you are to do?"

"It's no secret. I'm hoping to become a nurse, start as an auxiliary until I'm old enough to train in one of the big teaching hospitals."

"I see," Michael Lawrence stopped his questioning and looked out of the window.

Carrie didn't understand why but she felt obliged to explain herself. "I suppose it's thanks to you that I have discovered my true vocation."

Michael Lawrence smiled and when he did his whole face changed. "Some good came out of my misfortune then?"

"Some," Carrie agreed shyly.

The train started to slow down as it approached Neath station. Carrie rose from her seat and straightened her clothes.

"Miss Llewellyn, I'm in Neath for the day and I would be pleased if you would allow me to buy you lunch. Just by way of thanks."

"Thank you, but no thanks. I don't think we really have anything to say to each other," said Carrie primly.

"Well, if you change your mind I shall be at the Castle Hotel at one o' clock, if you care to join me," and with that he touched his hat to her again and moved off down the train to the nearest exit door.

The engine puffed into the station, its heavy wheels grinding to a halt with a squeal. The doors opened spewing the people onto the platform and Mr. Lawrence vanished into the crowds whilst Carrie picked her way through the throng, deep in thought.

Elizabeth Revill

Gelli Galed

Fourteen

Carrie spent an enjoyable morning in and out of clothes shops trying to find an outfit suitable for her interview for that time of year. She wanted something smart, yet practical, something that would be a useful addition to her wardrobe.

In TT Lloyds near the square she found just what she was looking for; even the assistant said it looked as if it had been tailor made for her. Carrie studied her reflection in the mirror. With the right accessories and blouse this two-piece suit would be ideal.

It was made of a good quality fabric that had some stretch, a mixture of wool and some manmade fibre. At first glance it appeared to be a delicate black and white check but the pattern was more complicated than that with fine threads of red and blue running through the design giving it a pinky hue.

The skirt seemed straight but had two kick pleats in the front and back. The jacket fitted neatly with its nipped in waist. It had a three-button fastening and a hook at the bottom to preserve the neat line, with a revere collar and lapels that turned up to a sharp point and it had flattering, narrow, decorative, side flaps below the shoulder above bust height in line with the angle of the lapels. Matching flaps disguised two small pockets two inches in from the side seams.

It was fully lined in a pinky beige nylon silk and the label read 'original Florian model London WI.' The assistant explained that this particular creation had indeed come from Bond Street in London where one of their chief tailoresses had taken a job but who was still commissioned by them for some work. This suit was one of them.

Carrie knew it perfectly complimented her porcelain complexion and Titian hair. The fine red lines did not clash as one would have supposed but served to highlight her unusual hair colour.

"There's no price tag on this. How much is it please?"

"Well, you have to realise that this was a made to measure garment that was never collected, which is why it is so expensive. I do have other suits at a lesser price."

"No. I want this one. How much please?"

Carrie tried not to alter a muscle when she was told eight guineas. That was as much as many folk earned in a year. But she paid proudly in cash and left the shop feeling very extravagant but never the less highly elated.

She now had to find a blouse, shoes, hat, bag and gloves to match or tone, but first lunch.

Her proud bearing carried her away from Water Street in the direction of the Castle Hotel. She glanced at her watch it was just coming up to five to one. Too late she realised where her feet had taken her. But instead of scurrying away she took a deep breath and walked in to the hotel lobby as if she belonged there.

Michael Lawrence was standing at the desk booking a table. He turned at her approach and his face lit up with delight and he hastily changed the booking to a table for two.

"I'm so glad you decided to come. What would you like to drink?"

"I'll just have a lemonade," she answered politely. He ushered her to a seat where they could wait for a table whilst he ordered their drinks.

He sat opposite her and studied her sweet face while she examined the menu offered by the waiter.

"I shouldn't have come," she whispered, "I don't know why I did. I just found myself here."

"I'm glad that you did. I know that this lunch does little to thank you for your kindness."

"We still have our differences, Mr. Lawrence."

"Please call me, Michael."

"And those differences," went on Carrie boldly, "Can never be resolved over lunch."

"Indeed, I understand. Let's just take a little time out to enjoy the moment."

"Before we return to our warring ways?"

"If you say so. Are we agreed?" he asked.

"Agreed," she affirmed.

A waiter moved across to take their order. "I can recommend the lamb," he smiled, "It's Welsh."

"And local," Carrie observed, looking at the menu.

They placed their order and were shown to a table for two by the window.

"Would you like some wine with your meal?"

"I don't drink," replied Carrie. "Except one at Christmas. I'm not old enough."

"How old are you?" he ventured.

"Mr. Lawrence, one should never ask a lady her age. At least that's what Mam always said. But if you must know I'm nearly seventeen."

"You look older."

"I've had a hard life," she rejoined.

"Not a lot older," he added hastily, "I thought you must have been about nineteen. When's your birthday?"

"August. How old are you?" She asked curiously.

"How old do you think?"

"I'm not very good at guessing, but I'd put you at about twenty-four, or five."

"Not a bad guess. I'm twenty-six."

The waiter intervened then with a bottle of chilled German hock. He poured a sample for Michael to taste who nodded in approval and gestured that Carrie's glass be filled.

"I said, I don't drink, Mr. Lawrence," she reprimanded.

"And I said, call me Michael. Just one glass, Miss Llewellyn. It won't hurt. I'll not press you to take another."

"Very well."

"Besides, we can't go to war over a glass of wine."

The lunch continued politely. Carrie was desperate to ask many questions and the effect of the wine gave her the courage to ask her most burning question. "What happened to Julie-Ann?"

Lawrence's face clouded over, "How do you know about that?"

"I'm sorry, I don't mean to pry but when you were ill, you kept calling for her and often imagined I was her. I just wondered that's all."

"Julie-Ann was my wife. We'd only been married a year when she died."

"I'm sorry."

"She was a lot like you, in a way. I suppose that's where the confusion arose."

"In what way?"

"Not in looks or personality, but that glorious head of hair you have. Julie-Ann's hair was much the same colour and just as wildly unmanageable as yours. I used to love it," he sighed and took another gulp of wine.

"How did she die?"

"It's a long story."

"I've got time," said Carrie, making the pretence of looking at her watch.

"I met Julie-Ann at university. She was the daughter of a wealthy professor and was studying Geology two years above me. We fell in love but she went abroad to Rhodesia to work for a mining company out there. When I completed my degree, there was an opening in her company, I took up the vacancy and joined her. We were married six months later. While we were out there she became gravely ill with TB. She could have survived that if she hadn't contracted Malaria, complications set in and it was Black Water Fever that killed her. I left the company. I'd inherited a fair amount of money so I didn't need to work. I invested some of it and made plans to move into farming. I returned to England and worked on a farm near Hereford to get a grounding in skills I needed to learn. That's where I saw the advert for Hendre. The rest you know."

The mention of Hendre immediately rankled and Carrie struggled to stop herself snapping at Lawrence, but she couldn't let it go. "You know we've a date set for the preliminary hearing?"

"So I believe," he replied, noticing the change in her demeanour. "Look do you mind if we stay off the subject of Hendre at least until lunch is over?"

"It's very difficult Mr. Lawrence, Michael," she added, trying to temper her words. "Hendre has been my whole life. To lose it in the manner we did was devastating and my brother and I will fight you in the courts until we regain what is rightfully ours."

"And yet, if what you say is correct, you are leaving your brother to that fight while you work elsewhere."

"That," she paused, "is something I must do. Something I need to do for myself before I return to Hendre, which will always hold my heart."

Michael Lawrence tried to steer Carrie away from the conversation about the house and managed to persuade her to talk about her proposed trip to Aberystwyth and her aspirations to nurse.

Carrie relaxed a little and even began to enjoy Michael Lawrence's company. She spoke with enthusiasm about her forthcoming interview and even allowed herself to become wistful at the thought of leaving Gelli Galed and John.

"Dr. Rees tells me you're having difficulty buying feed?"

Michael frowned afraid that the conversation would lead back to Hendre and anger. His reply was somewhat guarded, "It's not been easy, Carrie. May I call you Carrie?"

Carrie nodded, "Maybe I can help."

"You," he said incredulously, "How?"

"Well, I can't make the local people trust you. That damage has already been done. On the other hand I don't want Hendre run into the ground when we come to take it over as we eventually will."

Lawrence bit back the remark that rose so easily to his lips and listened. "What did you have in mind?"

Carrie looked him straight in the eye, "We can supply you."

"How do you mean?"

"Ernie has been growing winter corn and we have a surplus of grain. Currently two fields are filled with beets and turnips that's more than enough for our own use, so instead of selling on at market prices we'll sell direct to you."

Lawrence nodded appreciatively. What she offered made sense. He offered her his hand. "It's a deal," as their hands touched he felt a tingling excitement that pulsated up his arm that quite unnerved him.

Carrie appeared not to notice and smiled back. "Then it's

agreed. You can see John and sort out the details," she confirmed hoping that the shake in her hands that had manifested itself when their hands touched was not too obvious. She took a gulp of her wine, her heart was thumping loudly and an inexplicably warm feeling was rushing through her thighs and stomach. She giggled involuntarily and immediately apologised.

"Don't be sorry. Might I share in the joke?" he asked.

"It's nothing really," Carrie replied. "It just seems a little ridiculous that enemies like us help each other."

"I'd rather we weren't enemies," Michael said quietly.

"Mr. Lawrence! Mr. Lawrence!" puffed a small portly man hurrying across to their table.

Michael Lawrence groaned loudly this was one person he didn't want to see, especially now.

"I thought I might find you here. I know you like to lunch at the Castle on Saturdays."

"Excuse me, Carrie," said Michael as he rose from the table and spoke quietly to the man, "Listen can't this wait? I can come to your office on Monday, I don't really wish to talk business now."

"But Mr. Lawrence," blustered the man," I only wanted to let you know that we've managed to engage Christopher Baron for the pending court case. He's one of the finest barristers in the land and feels certain that he can win your suit against the Llewellyns."

At the mention of her name Carrie looked up with renewed interest and a hint of ice entered her voice, "Please Mr. Lawrence, don't let me stop you from talking about your business."

Michael felt his face turn hot, and tried to explain, "Look I don't want to upset anyone. Mr. Pugsley, please let's talk about this on Monday, things may have changed by then," he added with a sidelong glance at Carrie who immediately rose to her feet.

"No need, you can discuss the matter over the rest of the wine. Is that why you invited me here? To improve your argument for your case? Well, it won't wash," she said acidly. "To use an old phrase, a leopard doesn't change its spots."

With that remark she picked up her shopping and left the table. She was furious with herself for imagining that they might work out their differences. And she was even angrier at the way he disturbed her. Carrie felt tears prick at the back of her eyes. She blinked hard and holding her head high in her signatory style she left the hotel. She almost ran down the street away from the curious stares of passers-by until she reached the safety of the park. Sitting on a wooden bench she tried to regain her composure.

Once her breathing had returned to normal and she didn't feel her emotions running so close to the surface she took refuge in the ladies' toilets where she splashed cold water on her face.

Her day of shopping was quite ruined. She still had to buy her accessories but somehow all the joy had been taken out of her trip to Neath.

Gelli Galed

Fifteen

Carrie had brooded on her encounter with Michael Lawrence and was still bristling with anger when she got off the train in Crynant. John was there to greet her. He took one look at the thunderous expression on her face gave a questioning look and received a furious, "Don't ask!" for his trouble.

John knew better than to press Carrie when she was in this frame of mind so he helped her with her packages, loaded them onto the cart and spent the first five minutes of their homeward trek quietly, each one lost in their own thoughts. The rumble of the wagon and Senator's hooves were the only accompaniment to their private wonderings. As they turned onto the old Neath Road John sensed a calming in Carrie and ventured to ask, "Did you get everything you need?"

"Yes, thank you. I think you'll like my choice."

"We'll have a full fashion show when we get in. A proper parade."

Carrie laughed in spite of herself, "Just like old times eh?"

"Just like old times," he agreed.

The rest of the journey passed more pleasantly and soon all trace of Carrie's bad mood had dissolved. She talked with enthusiasm about her model suit and toning accessories. John knew she would tell him in her own time what had so upset her. He was prepared to wait.

Ernie and Trix were there to greet them. The smell of freshly brewed tea filled the kitchen and the aroma of home baking tantalised their nostrils. Ernie had prepared something special for her return. But after a welcome cup of tea Carrie was persuaded to dress up in her finery and give them a preview of her interview outfit.

Carrie, with all the excitement of a small child ran up the

stairs to change. She fiercely brushed her wild hair taming it into a neat roll and taking a deep breath, tilted her chin and glided down the stairs to the kitchen.

"All right, you can look now," she purred.

The two men took their hands away from their eyes and drank in the vision before them.

Admiration and pride filled John's eyes as he saw his younger sister standing proudly before him. She looked stunning. A beige pink crepe blouse with a high ruffled neck harmonised beautifully with the two piece outfit and Carrie had managed to find an exact match for the blue thread in her suit in a pretty hat, clutch bag, gloves and strapped shoes.

Ernie was the first to speak, "Like a picture you are. Good enough to go on show. Turn round."

Carrie obediently twirled before them and John agreed, "Carrie, you look beautiful."

The words were said simply and sincerely and Carrie knew she had chosen well.

"Mam's dress sense has rubbed off on you," said John.

"Do you think she'd approve?"

John nodded, his eyes glistening.

"Then I've done right. Now, what's for tea? I can see Ernie's been busy."

"Upstairs and change first, my girl," he gently scolded, "Hang those up neatly and put them away for best."

"Yes, Sir," she saluted and shaking her hair free from the constraints of her hat and unpinning the roll she ran up the stairs to do just that.

Ernie had prepared a veritable feast and although it was deliciously tempting Carrie found she couldn't eat it all. She pushed her plate away apologetically, "Sorry, Ernie I can't manage it all, tasty though it is."

"But it was prepared in your honour, Carrie fach."

"I know, it's all the excitement, I'm sorry. Besides I had the most enormous lunch at the Castle Hotel."

"You went to the Castle?" John said surprised.

Carrie nodded and went on to relate the events of her luncheon with Michael Lawrence.

"But what I can't understand is why you went to meet him in the first place?"

"Neither can I. I don't know what possessed me. I just found myself there. And him being as pleasant as anything when all he was doing was gathering information for the court case."

"That may not be true," observed Ernie. "It sounds like he was being genuine, and this solicitor fellow just happened along. Besides your idea of selling him grain was a good one. We ought to fulfil that deal."

"Not if I have anything to do with it," hissed Carrie.

"Now come on be fair," coaxed Ernie, "The profit would be good for Gelli Galed and at the same time you would ensure Hendre's stock was being looked after. It makes sense."

"You can do what you like. Make your own deals. I want nothing to do with it!"

"Ernie's right. I know you hate the thought of helping him but it would benefit us in the long run."

Carrie grudgingly accepted what they were saying, she wasn't so blinded by her dislike of Michael Lawrence not to know the correct thing to do and sighed reluctantly, "Very well, as long as I'm not forced to have any contact with him you can go ahead."

"Right. I'll follow this up on Monday," said Ernie. "Plenty of time then."

Ernie's sixth sense had also observed that in spite of Carrie's protestations that other emotions were revealing themselves, but he said nothing.

Six weeks had gone by since Carrie's encounter with Michael Lawrence. Carrie's seventeenth birthday had passed and the family were preparing for reaping. Carrie had everything arranged for the villagers' fry up. But for now, she was taking some time off from her domestic duties and doing what she loved best, which was walking on the mountainside with Trix and away from the workers.

Carrie felt at one with all around her. Her hair blew wild and free in the wind. She belonged here. No matter where she travelled or what she would do, this was the place of her roots. Here she would always return.

Maybe by accident or maybe by design, Carrie found herself walking past Hendre, and along the rutted mountain track that led to Bull Rock.

She sat on its mossy edge and looked down at the now seemingly benign waters of the Black River.

It was as if she was gazing into the mists of time as memories tumbled through her mind. Some were painful, some a delight. She scratched at some moss with her finger dislodging a clump that cascaded down the hillside taking with it a shower of small stones. Trixie, who had been lying at her side, pricked up her ears and cried softly in her throat.

"What's the matter old girl? Dreaming are you?"

But the dog stood up and listened intently. She gave a small bark and proceeded down the slippery slope towards the river.

"No Trix! Come back!" Carrie shouted. "Here Trix! Here girl!" She called again, becoming alarmed at the path her dog was taking.

Trix whined and started to yap loudly and pawed at the ground under the overhang of another smaller rock.

"Come!" she ordered but to no avail as the animal continued to yelp and dig. "You've got another thing coming if you think I'm going to stick around whilst you chase rabbits. Come on!" Carrie scrambled to her feet and pretended to move back up the mountain, but the collie ignored her and continued to scratch at the ground making excited noises in her throat.

Carrie stopped. It was unlike Trix to behave like this. The dog looked up at her and gave a succession of barks, wagging her tail challengingly the whole time. There was nothing for it but for Carrie to try and see what it was that had attracted Trixie's attention. Gingerly she edged her way down the slope. She knew that one wrong foot could send her sliding into the river with its tangling weeds.

She grabbed at a handful of fern and bracken to steady her descent until she was almost level with her dog. Just as she reached the boulder she heard what Trix's keen sense of hearing had told her earlier. There was another dog somewhere down there.

Carrie inched her way across the overhang and lowered herself underneath it, scraping her arm in the process. She landed awkwardly and gave a small cry as her ankle wrenched underneath her.

"Damn and blast!" she rasped, "This is all I need. Stuck down here with a twisted ankle and no one to know."

Trix looked at her beseechingly and licked Carrie's face.

"Stop it you mutt. You'll have me over! Now, what was it that brought you down here in the first place, eh?"

The surrounding ground was riddled with rabbit holes. It was into one of these that she had pushed her foot when she clambered down over the rock. She parted the bracken by the overhang and heard a snuffling and a whimper coming from a deep burrow on her left. Carrie grimaced as she manoeuvred herself into a more comfortable position and peered into the warren. She could just make out the tell tail markings of the black and white terrier collie-cross called Boots.

"Boots! Here boy! Come!" But Boots was wedged part way down and could move neither forward nor back. Carrie reached inside and tried to fasten a hold on the squirming dog. Trix dug away the soil at the entrance helping Carrie to gain access. Carrie managed to grab a quantity of skin and fur and tugged. Boots yelped but gained some ground scrabbling backward an inch. Carrie reached in again and succeeded in getting a firm grasp of the dog's back legs. She said a silent prayer and pulled once more, hoping that she wouldn't dislocate Boot's back legs. She was rewarded with a rush of soil that flew into her mouth and hair, plus the tiny wriggling body of Boots.

"Gotcha!" she breathed.

The little dog seemed none the worse for his ordeal and thanked her wetly and warmly with his tongue. But now Carrie had a problem. There was no way she could crawl back up the overhang and reach the comparative safety of Bull Rock without help. No one was likely to be within earshot. John and Ernie were in the fields. Come ten o' clock the villagers would be ready for their fry up while she was stuck here. If only she could make Trix understand that she needed help.

Carrie took a minute or two to think. She ripped off a length from her petticoat and strapped it around her swelling ankle that was already turning blue. She tried testing her weight on it. It was no good. On the flat she might cope but on this hillside it was an impossibility.

"Trix, get help. Find John. Go on. Find John," she ordered.

Trix gave a bark and scrambled her way back up the slope and disappeared from view. Boots sat with Carrie and made no attempt to leave her. In fact, Carrie was quite glad of the little dog's company.

A cloud passed over the sun and Carrie groaned, "That's all I need. A downpour will just about finish me off."

She knew that if indeed it did rain, then her situation could become not only precarious but also very dangerous indeed. This mountainside was deadly when wet and the fern and bracken's tenuous hold on the land could loosen and come away in her hand and send her sliding down the slope as easily as a twig is snapped from off a rotting branch. Carrie was relieved to see that it was only a passing cloud and the sun smiled down once more.

Some forty minutes later she was pleased to hear the sound of someone crashing through the undergrowth at the top of the path and Trix came tumbling down beside her. Her tail a frenzy of wagging.

"I'm down here," yelled Carrie. "I've hurt my ankle. I don't know how you're going to get me out." She pulled herself up and peered up the incline and was horrified to see the face of Michael Lawrence looking down on her.

"Hold on," he called. "I'll get a rope," and disappeared from view.

Carrie slumped back down on the ground. Of all the most embarrassing things to happen. Still, she could hardly call out and ask him to get John. She would just have to be patient and wait until she was safe and then she could remove herself as far away from him as possible.

She didn't have to wait long for his return. He tied one

end of a rope around a stout beech then secured himself and dropped the rest of the line down to Carrie.

"Tie it around you and I'll haul you up. Can you manage that?"

"I can manage," Carrie grudgingly replied. "Wait until I've got a firm grip on your dog."

"Is Boots with you?"

"Who did you think I'd got?" she said caustically. "It's his fault I'm down here."

"I can't hear you. Wait until you're at the top," Michael shouted down.

Carrie pursed her lips and tied the rope around her. She held on tightly to Boots who had started to wriggle at the sound of his master's voice. She signalled on the rope to say she was ready and Michael Lawrence began to draw her up.

It was a struggle to hold onto the dog and guide herself up the slope at the same time. She was quite exhausted when she finally reached the top.

Michael's face and arms were covered with a fine sheen of sweat from his exertions. He put his hand out and grabbed her round the waist, pulling her into him. She shoved him away roughly and winced as she tried to bear her weight. Boots scrambled out of her arms and ran off up the track back to the house.

"Here, lean on me. Let's get you back to Hendre and we'll have a look at that ankle."

"It's all right, I can manage," she said abrasively.

"It's no bother, really."

Carrie stiffened and stood her ground, "I said, I'll be all right now, thank you."

"Very well. If you're sure?"

"I'm sure," said Carrie vehemently. She waited until he had started to walk away and then hopped forward on her good leg. She succeeded in taking a couple of steps before finally tumbling to the ground. She gave a sharp cry of pain that brought Michael Lawrence back to her side. Ignoring all her protestations, he scooped her up in his arms and much to her embarrassment carried her back to Hendre.

Gelli Galed

Sixteen

"I can't stay here," Carrie protested. "I've got the fry up to do for the reapers."

"Well you're not going any place on that ankle," said Michael firmly.

"I've far too much to do. John can't cope on his own. No one knows where I am."

"Might I make a suggestion?"

"What?" Carrie snapped ungraciously.

"No arguing and no buts, just listen first without interruption," he asked.

"Go on."

"Firstly, let me see to your ankle." Immediately Michael said that Carrie started to bluster.

"I said no interruptions," he commanded. Carrie stilled her cries and attempted to listen making it apparent that it was the last thing she wanted to do.

Michael firmly reaffirmed his statement, "Firstly, your ankle."

Carrie groaned.

"Next, I will go down to the fields and appraise them of the situation. I'll talk with John and if he's willing I'll do the fry up."

"You can't do that!"

"Why not? I've cooked for large numbers before. In Africa I took my turn with the other men at camp to produce a meal. I'm not incapable."

"I wasn't implying that, it's just..." she tailed off.

"It's just what?"

"Well, for one it's not your place to do it, and two, I feel awkward about it."

"Well, for a start you're not going anywhere without help, so you might as well give in gracefully."

Carrie understood that what Michael was saying was correct but inside she fumed. Michael took her silence to mean agreement and went to fetch his medicine chest.

Carrie looked around for something to use as a crutch with which to make her escape but as there was nothing available she resigned herself to having her ankle treated. As soon as Lawrence was out of the way and her ankle strapped, she decided that would be the time to make her move.

Michael Lawrence returned carrying a tin box and a velvet covered pouffe. He ensured Carrie was comfortable in her chair and then gently lifted the bruised ankle onto the footstool. Her shoe and stocking were removed and he examined it carefully. His cool hands on her silky soft skin sent a shiver through her. He thoughtfully scrutinised her injured ankle, now puffy and blue.

"Can you move your toes?" he asked.

She acquiesced by wriggling them. He softly manipulated her foot, exerting pressure here and there ascertaining when she winced or exclaimed in pain.

"I don't think it's broken. But it is a very nasty sprain. I'll pack it in a cold compress to see if that will reduce the swelling. I'll just get some ice from the refrigerator."

Carrie mused to herself, 'A refrigerator and ice. Huh, he couldn't be doing too badly.'

Michael came back with ice wrapped in muslin, which he applied to her ankle. He placed newspaper on the seat and rested her foot on a small bowl to catch the melting drops.

"There that should do the trick for a minute. Can I get you something to drink?"

"Mr. Lawrence," she sighed. "If you will just strap my ankle, I'll be on my way, I have no wish to be here longer than necessary," she muttered.

"All in good time," he answered. "Let the ice have time to work. In the meanwhile how about some tea?"

Carrie tried desperately to hide her exasperation and rolling her eyes heavenward grumbled, "If I must."

Forced into this undignified position she decided that she had better make the best of it and so suffered his ministering in silence.

When the ice had nearly melted he dried her leg and applied tincture of flower of arnica to the bruising and strapped the ankle tightly with a crepe bandage, securing it with a safety pin.

"Now, if you'll stay put I'll go up to the fields and see your brother. I'm sure we can come to some arrangement. There's a newspaper if you're interested and a couple of books on the floor beside you. You might find something of interest there."

Carrie wanted to say that the most interesting thing she could do would be to get out of his sight, then she would feel a whole lot better. But she forced a smile and nodded, willing him to leave.

He called to Trix who happily accompanied him on his climb up to Gelli Galed and John.

Carrie waited a reasonable amount of time to give Michael Lawrence time to clear the boundaries of Hendre. She hobbled up from her seat and hopped out of the kitchen into the glasshouse and yard, hunting for some sort of stick that would help her to bear her weight. She found nothing.

Carrie spent the next ten minutes struggling painfully to the gate. She gazed at the steep climb ahead of her and knew it was a nonsense to try and reach home with her ankle in this condition so with a scream of frustration she turned back to Hendre and the comfort of the chair and stool in the kitchen, and there she waited glumly for Mr. Lawrence to return.

It was early evening by the time Michael Lawrence arrived back. Carrie had dozed off in the chair, and the evening sunlight glittered on her cloud of curls. Michael Lawrence entered almost silently. Boots rose to meet his master and as Michael stooped to ruffle the dog's fur he glanced at Carrie and was almost mesmerised by her beauty. He cleared his throat startling Carrie from her slumbers who took a minute or two to adjust to her surroundings.

"Sorry, I didn't mean to wake you. How are you feeling?"

"Oh, all right. Where's John?" she asked.

"It's all settled. Don't get in a panic. John will be busy in the fields until ten. Gwynfor has gone home to Bronallt for his sister Megan."

"Megan? Why?"

"She's going to help me cook and serve the fry up at Gelli Galed."

"What?"

"Don't get alarmed. It's all agreed. It's impossible for John or Ernie to get away, so tonight you're to stay at Hendre. I'll take you down to see Dr. Rees in the morning. After which I'll take you home. No harm done."

"No harm done?" Carrie almost shrieked, "Do you think I'm three ha'pence short of a farthing? I'll not stay here with you. Fetch me a stick. I'll make my own way home."

"It's no use getting excited. It's the best thing you'll see."

Carrie glared at Michael Lawrence, "This is all your doing. Instead of sending Gwynfor home, why didn't you bring him back here? He could have carried me home easily."

"Because I didn't think of it, Carrie and no one suggested it. Besides I don't like this anymore than you do. I don't want a grouch for company this evening. I can well do without your tantrums."

"You don't have to put up with them. Loan me your horse and I'll ride home."

"I would but he's in need of shoeing I can't risk him going lame."

"Very convenient," said Carrie sulkily.

"Look this isn't very easy for me either. We'll just have to suffer each other for one night. Not even that really. I'll get you some supper..."

"I'm not hungry," she snapped.

"Fine! I'll make some anyway, you might change your mind."

"You're wasting your time," she muttered.

Michael Lawrence ignored her and continued, "I'll make sure you're comfortable and then I'll leave you to go and help with the fry up. All right?"

"All right," she hissed, setting a downward turn of her lips. Michael allowed himself a half smile at her petulance and set about making a meal.

The aroma from the dish was tantalising and Carrie was

beginning to regret her refusal of supper. Michael spread a clean cloth on the table and laid it for two. He tucked into the cheesy bake hash he had concocted with fresh runner beans and carrots.

Carrie had forgotten how hungry she was. The sight of this food set her taste buds tingling and her mouth watering.

"Are you sure I can't help you to any of this?" he asked noticing her watchful eye on each mouthful he took.

Carrie stubbornly shook her head.

"I'll pop it in the oven to keep warm, just in case you do decide to share in my humble fare," he said with exaggerated humility. "Don't let it dry up. If you really don't want any, do me a favour and take it out. I can have the rest tomorrow then," and with that he pushed his chair under the table and sat on the window seat by the range to put on his boots. He took his plate out and with a cheery whistle left the kitchen. Carrie heard him call good-bye as he shut the glasshouse door.

She waited until sufficient time had elapsed to allow him to reach the track then she struggled out of her seat and removed the food from the oven. She looked at the amount left and dished herself a very small portion trying to make it look as if it hadn't been touched. She added some beans and carrots and tasted it. It was delicious. He had added some sort of herb that really enhanced the flavour of the meat.

Carrie relished every forkful. She was just contemplating giving herself a decent serving as she finished the last mouthful when to her horror she heard the catch on the outside door.

Michael Lawrence entered. He tried to hide his smile, when he saw Carrie's guilt ridden face with the remnants of the meal in front of her.

"Look who I found on the track. Obviously looking for you so I brought her back for company."

Trixie padded in through the door, wagging her tail.

"I'm off now. I'll leave you in peace." He looked at the casserole dish and her plate and added, "Why don't you have some more? It doesn't look as if you've touched it. Cheerio!"

And before she could answer he whistled his way out

through the kitchen again. Carrie's cheeks burned with humiliation. She picked up the spoon and hurled it at the door.
Then she saw the funny side of things and started to giggle.
She was still giggling when she filled her plate and this time
ate a proper portion.

Gelli Galed

Seventeen

"Nothing to worry about. It's a bad sprain. Just keep off it and give it plenty of rest. Otherwise you've done all you can."

"Thank you, Doctor," murmured Carrie. She leaned heavily on her father's ash walking stick that Michael had brought home with him from Gelli Galed.

She limped outside to Michael who was waiting with the horse and wagon. He jumped down nimbly to her side when he saw her emerge from the surgery. His arms lingered as they encircled her waist while he deftly lifted her up on to the passenger seat.

Carrie rapped his hand, "Thank you!" she said pointedly.

"Sorry, I was just thinking."

"Well, can you think some place else? Like when we're on the road or something," she said fiercely, her face beginning to burn under the close scrutiny of Mrs. Chappell whose net curtain was twitching whilst she studied the comings and goings at the doctor's surgery opposite.

"No offence meant," he said lightly.

"None taken," she maundered.

"Now, I suppose I'd better get you home before Gwynfor comes to rescue you and carry you off to Bronallt," said Michael mischievously.

"Gwynfor?" Carrie said surprised, "Why Gwynfor?"

"I thought you knew," exclaimed Michael watching her face closely.

"Knew what?" she questioned.

"Well, if you don't, everyone else does. Gwynfor has quite a shine for you. I think he has you singled out as the future Mrs. Thomas."

"That's ridiculous! We've been friends since we were small. He's just like a brother to me."

"Well, I don't think he wants to see it that way. Ever so

concerned, he was. It was all I could do to stop him running to Hendre and whisking you away."

"That's just your imagination. Anyway, it will be a long time before I'm ready to settle with anyone, if at all."

The conversation lulled into silence as they negotiated the bend in the road leading to the railway crossing, the old Neath Road and the track up the mountain.

Carrie lost herself in thought while she digested the information about Gwynfor. She could do worse she decided, but she was convinced Michael was wrong. Besides she intended to see something of life before tying herself down.

His voice interrupted her thoughts, "Thank you for letting John go ahead with the deal on animal feed. It is appreciated."

John runs the farm, it's up to him to decide what to do."

"You want me to believe that you have no sway?"

"I didn't say that. But there are more important things to consider. I can't let personal feelings get in the way of business. Although, you're lucky I didn't use my influence to completely block the arrangement after that little stunt you pulled."

"If you're talking about the unexpected arrival of the solicitor at our lunch I can assure you I did not know he was coming."

"No. He quite spoiled your plans didn't he?"

"I tell you I had no ulterior motive in inviting you to lunch other than to thank you for your kindness. It was not done to pump you for information as you put it. Like it or not, I owe my life to you."

"What a shocking responsibility. To think I could have saved everyone a lot of trouble if I'd just minded my own affairs."

Michael Lawrence spurred the horse on, "Well, I'll not burden you with my distasteful presence any longer than necessary."

"What do you mean by that?"

"As soon as I've dropped you off at Gelli Galed I'll not come calling. I'm even thinking of leasing the farm until this messy business is sorted out."

"Won't that just complicate the issue? Besides I don't know whether legally you'll be allowed to do that with a court case pending."

"Maybe not. But I'll instruct my solicitor to explore all the avenues before I decide. I've had enough of this Godforsaken place and its unfriendly people."

"You're looking at it with the wrong eyes. Hendre is the most beautiful place in the world. Even when the rain is sheeting down from the sky and everything is covered in a grey mist I can still see the rich majesty all around."

Michael turned his head and caught a glimpse of fire in Carrie's eyes. He heard her passion and in that moment perceived Hendre was more than a house. He almost yearned to discover its secrets, to see the land as Carrie saw it. But he knew that only one privileged to share her world would be permitted that experience.

The climb up the track was slow and no more words passed between them. They reached the gate of Gelli Galed and Michael stepped down to help her alight. He took her cool hand in his and felt electricity pulse up his arm. She gave a sharp intake of breath and her gaze lingered on his face; his eyes like forest pools, to which she was drawn, fastened onto hers and as if time was suspended his head began to move closely to hers.

There was a shout from the gate and the moment was broken by the arrival of John. "Carrie! Hello there, we've missed you. Are you all right?"

Carrie snatched back her hand and ran her fingers through her untamed tresses and smiled. "Well enough! It'll soon mend, plenty of rest and I'll be roly polying down the hill with the best of them."

"Will it be better in time for your interview?" queried John.

"Dr. Rees says it will."

"When's your interview?" asked Michael.

"Carrie's seeing the Matron of the maternity home in September. If she's successful she'll be leaving us for a while."

"It looks like all your dreams are about to come true,"

said Michael. "I wish you well." He extended his hand to her once more.

Carrie hesitated before taking it and said, "Thank you. But you're wrong, not everything, not yet. But it will do, you'll see."

"Maybe, but I don't think I'll be around to see it."

John puzzled over this interchange, which left his sister and Michael Lawrence standing awkwardly still studying each other's faces hard.

"Well, thank you, Mr. Lawrence for all you've done. I'll be in touch," and he turned his sister away almost forcibly and helped her down the path.

Michael Lawrence watched them go, a turbulence raging inside him. He swung himself up into the wagon and savagely pulled the horse's head around. With the frenzy of a soul possessed he rattled off down the mountain at far too great a speed than was safe.

As Dr. Rees had instructed, Carrie rested her ankle and in less than a fortnight she was able to remove the strapping. All trace of the injury had gone.

The time for Carrie's interview was drawing near. There were mixed emotions in the household. Carrie's anticipation and excitement mingled with John's anxiety and fear. He felt that although he couldn't stand in her way, he was losing Carrie forever.

She struggled to reassure him, "Listen, we don't know if I'll get a job; and even if I do it won't be forever. I'll come back to the valley and Hendre. I still have my dreams."

"But you'll have changed. Things won't be the same."

"I'll always be the girl whose back you tickled to get me to sleep. Nothing changes that much."

"You promise you'll hold off until Thomas arrives from Australia?"

"I'm not making any promises I can't keep. The future is a blank piece of paper. And this time I shall control the pen. I won't write or draw anything unless I want to."

Ernie offered his own words of advice, "You can trap a bird in a cage, but you can't make it sing. Better to leave it in the garden and all enjoy its song."

Ernie had more of his own philosophies for Carrie, "Do what you wish. You'll never be content till you do; only then will you see the truth in what's right under your nose."

"Oh, Ernie, whatever do you mean?"

"I'll just say this once and then no more," he shook his head fiercely so his rubicund face reddened further and his cheek jowls slapped together like piglets eating at a trough.

"For true happiness, you need look no further than your own back yard. But you'll find out for yourself. You won't need telling."

John and Ernie drove Carrie to the station. She wore a simple cotton dress and linen jacket for travelling. Her precious suit was carefully packed in her overnight bag.

"Now, remember to hang your clothes up when you get there. So all the creases drop out. Do it straight away. No dawdling around the town, right?" Ernie ordered.

"Yes, boss," said Carrie laughingly giving him a little mock salute.

"Good luck, Carrie fach, may you get what you want," said Ernie pulling off his beret sending his sparsely tufted hair wiring up.

Carrie hugged him warmly, "Thank you. I'll see you in two days. Think of me won't you?"

She pressed the side of her face against his whiskered cheek and added, "Now I know why you keep that beret glued to your head. Hair like a Brillo Pad you've got and twice as rough."

Ernie chortled and responded by firmly replacing his hat. Carrie turned to John who stood by almost shyly.

"Bye, John. Wish me well?"

"Course I do, cariad. More than anything. You have a safe journey now." He held her tightly and joked, "I've put labels in all your clothes; there's a clean pair of knickers in your handbag and you've got your pills, so you should do."

Carrie gave him a playful slap on his shoulder before opening the heavy carriage door. She pulled down the window and secured it by fastening the leather strap and leaned out to talk some more. As she looked down the platform she was surprised to see the familiar stride of Michael Lawrence heading towards them.

He quickened his pace when he saw the guard ready with his whistle and hurried to the carriage door.

"I don't mean to intrude," he explained, "But I was coming to the village this morning and I just wanted to give you this for good luck." He pressed a small box into her hand.

The guard raised his flag and blew his whistle, and the great iron engine steamed out of the station. John walked down the platform alongside the train as it chugged away. Michael Lawrence and Ernie stood and waved until the train rounded a bend and Carrie's head could be seen no more.

Elizabeth Revill

Gelli Galed

Eighteen

Carrie pushed her bag into the wire mesh luggage rack above her head and sat back in her seat with a sigh. She looked at the box in her hand and opened it. Inside was a small, white, lace butterfly on a pin and a card.

"My mother always believed butterflies brought luck. Wear this and see if her words are true, Michael."

Carrie removed the delicate brooch and examined its fragile beauty. It was a work of art. Someone had taken a lot of time and care in its making. She turned it over and could just make out some lettering on the back of the pin. It read Isobel. Carrie wondered if that was his mother's name.

Carrie watched the scenery trundle by. She took an interest in all that she saw, people on the platforms, the houses and streets that straddled the railway line. She even reverted to her childhood game of imagining what the people in her carriage did for a living, what they thought and how they spoke. It helped to pass the time.

She arrived in Aberystwyth, which was the terminus, feeling a little nervous. The furthest afield she had been was Cardiff for Netta's trial and a Sunday school trip to Porthcawl. She had never travelled this far alone.

She stepped out cautiously onto the platform, snuffing the air like a collie dog. The smell of the steam couldn't completely disguise the fresh salt air that drifted on the breeze.

A seagull circled above her mewling and calling to its mate. She loved that cry. It invoked in her a feeling of wanting to be at one with nature, a part of the sand, sea and air.

She put away such whimsical thoughts and left the sooty, station exit coming out into the street beyond, and headed for the taxi rank.

"Where to love?" inquired a bushy faced driver.

Carrie replied shyly, "I'm not sure really. I'm looking for somewhere to stay the night. I've an interview tomorrow."

259

"Where might that be?" asked the cabbie trying to be helpful.

"At the maternity home in Carradog Road."

"Let me see," he thought for a moment, "There's a fine little boarding house, not far from there. Pleasant View it's called. Mrs. Montgomery runs it. She should have room for you. You'll have no difficulty finding the unit in the morning. The other guest houses and hotels are mainly near the sea front. It's a tidy step from there."

"I'll take your advice then. Pleasant View it is."

He opened the door for her and ferried her round to Mrs. Montgomery's. The sign said, 'Vacancies' so with a cheery wave the cabbie deposited her and returned to his pitch at the station.

She checked into her room, which was clean and serviceable; and was offered a cup of tea, which she accepted with thanks. Mrs. Montgomery was a great chatterer and soon had Carrie at her ease. Before long, they were talking like old friends.

"Yes, it's easy to get to the Mat. Unit from by here. You won't need a taxi. I'll give you directions in the morning. Now, I'll leave you to freshen up, dinner is at seven-thirty sharp. There's a wireless in the lounge, you can listen when you want. Now, is there anything else?"

"No thank you, Mrs. Montgomery, you've been very kind."

"Well, you better go and unpack your clothes. If you want to borrow an iron, just give me a shout and I'll show you where the utilities are kept."

Carrie thanked her again and smiling to herself made her way back upstairs. Ernie would approve, of that she had no doubt. This Mrs. Montgomery could be his cousin for all her platitudes and sayings.

Carrie critically regarded her reflection in the mirror.

"Yes, Carrie my girl, you'll do," she murmured aloud. "There's just one thing missing," and removing her mother's cameo mourning brooch from her neck she replaced it in its box. With hesitant hands she took out Michael Lawrence's butterfly and pinned it to the neck of her blouse. At first glance it appeared to be a fine bow tie or lace jabot, closer inspection revealed the detail and work that had gone into its making. It was beautiful and it finished her costume completely.

Carrie settled her bill at Pleasant View and followed Mrs. Montgomery's directions to the letter. She entered a quiet residential area in the heart of suburbia. The road was tree lined and still in full leaf making her think wistfully of home. The road led to the steps of the National Library of Wales. Carrie didn't even know there was one. The houses were early Edwardian, built in about 1902, still modern by some standards.

She paused on the steps to the main entrance by a big hard wooden door, painted brown that had opaque stained glass panels at the top. She entered the lobby and examined her surroundings. On the right were some cupboards, which she presumed, housed the gas meters; on the left was the way to the wards. There was no sign to say where she could find the Matron's room.

"Excuse me," she asked of a scurrying body in navy uniform, "Could you tell me the way to the Matron's Office?"

"You're in the wrong building, fy merch 'i. Go out the way you came, next to the unit you'll see some almshouses; Matron's office is there in Bronglais. You can't miss it."

"Thank you," Carrie left the home feeling in awe of its size and the strangeness of it all.

She found Bronglais just as described and tentatively entered.

A secretary ushered her to a hard backed chair placed outside the office. She glanced at her watch, she was a little early. Rummaging in her handbag, she took out a small compact that had been her mother's and checked her reflection. She wanted to make a good impression.

A stubborn curl that had escaped from the brim of her hat was forcibly tucked back inside.

The door to Matron's quarters opened and one of the clerical staff emerged, clutching a pad and pencil. She smiled at Carrie, "Miss Llewellyn?"

Carrie nodded dumbly.

"Matron will see you now."

Carrie took a deep breath, rose from her seat and holding her head high walked into the office of Dr. Rees' sister, Matron Moira Hughes.

The Matron was seated behind a heavy oak desk with hand carved legs and panels. She stood up and came round to meet Carrie. Her handshake was firm and warm.

"Miss Llewellyn, please sit down." She indicated a comfortable easy chair in front of a fire where a small table had been laid with a pot of tea, and plate of digestive sweet meal biscuits. "I want to try and make the interview as informal as possible."

Carrie sat and daintily crossed her feet at the ankles as her mother had always said, 'That's the way ladies sit, Carrie. It always makes a good impression.'

"It's, Carrie, isn't it?" the Matron asked kindly. Carrie nodded again seeming unable to find her voice.

"Would you like some tea?" Matron asked graciously, lifting the silver teapot from its stand.

For an instant Carrie didn't know whether it would be more polite to accept or refuse, but decided that if the table had been laid, she was expected to take refreshment. She found her voice and replied, "Yes, please."

"Milk? Sugar?"

"Milk and no sugar thank you."

Carrie accepted the proffered cup and watched as Matron took a white linen napkin, shook it from its crisp folds and placed it across her lap. Carrie did likewise. A plate was passed to her and a biscuit taken.

There was a pause whilst the tea was sipped. Carrie's wide eyes looked around the office, its walls adorned with the photographs of previous Matrons.

Matron smiled at her. She was a vision in her hospital blue uniform, and white starched hat, black belt with enormous silver buckle and tiny fob watch pinned at her breast.

Her voice was resonant with an attractive lilt. She tried to put Carrie at her ease. "You come highly recommended, Miss Llewellyn. My brother tells me you have a natural aptitude for nursing.

"He's very kind."

"No. That's not in my or the hospital's interest," she firmly admonished. "I cannot afford just to take a chance on someone. My brother has told me of your splendid efforts," she glanced at her notes. "With your father, brother and more impressively Mr. Lawrence."

Carrie blushed.

"I'm prepared, Miss Llewellyn to offer you a position as auxiliary, providing you pass the necessary test in English and Maths that has been prepared. After your interview you will be given two one hour papers in a room set aside for that purpose, after which you may take some refreshment whilst they are being marked. Normally you would be notified by post of your success or failure, but I will make an exception in your case."

"Thank you, Matron."

"If successful, you may begin as an auxiliary and when the year is completed I recommend you apply to a teaching hospital. There are excellent facilities at Dudley Road Hospital in Birmingham."

Carrie nodded gratefully and the interview continued to progress well.

She was asked about her life on the farm, her reasons for wanting to nurse and her interest in world affairs.

"Tell me, what do you think of the current events in Europe?"

"I'm not that well up on current affairs. I do listen to the wireless and I believe there is trouble brewing. From all accounts it seems likely that Italy will mount an attack on Abyssinia. And I don't entirely trust the actions of Herr Hitler."

"In what way?"

"It appears that he is working hard to build up his economy but the inference is that he has other reasons behind those plans, a hidden agenda."

"Such as?"

"Well, my brother and I think it's a cover for something more dangerous. He's building up his arms and military might and I think he sees Europe as ripe for the taking."

"You're in agreement with our higher statesman Winston Churchill?"

"Not exactly, not politically anyway. But I do think Chancellor Hitler is a dangerous man."

And so they continued; discussing, and chatting. Matron had the distinct impression that Carrie was intelligent, single-minded and had the strength of personality for the job.

Matron smiled brightly and drew the interview to a close. Carrie felt calmer and more assured now that it was over. She was taken to a small office and there she was left to take the tests of which the Matron had spoken.

"Miss Llewellyn?" Carrie was brought out of her misty eyed reverie by the same clerical officer who had bade her go into Matron's office.

"Yes?" Carrie replied, hurriedly replacing her teacup in its saucer with a clatter.

"Come this way, Matron will see you now."

Carrie rose from the table in the canteen and followed the woman. 'They hadn't taken long,' she thought. She had puzzled and pored over her maths paper until she finally got into her stride. The English paper had been straight forward enough and she could only have been sitting in the canteen for about twenty minutes. Carrie hoped the results wouldn't be bad. She stiffened as the clerk knocked on Matron's door, recovered her composure and entered on the instruction with her head held aloft.

Gelli Galed

Nineteen

Carrie could barely contain her excitement as she left the Matron's office. She was bubbling over with delight and could not suppress the huge grin that had fixed itself on her face. She smiled brightly at everyone she passed.

"I take it you were successful?" greeted the clerical secretary from administration she had seen previously.

"Yes," breathed Carrie happily.

"Congratulations! We shall be seeing you in the next week I understand?"

"Yes, I've one or two things to tie up at home and then I shall be back to stay... Tell me do I have to arrange my own accommodation?"

"If you'd like to step into the office for a moment I'll give you all the information you need, what we provide and so on. Don't worry about accommodation we should have room for you in the Nurses' Home. Now, let me see...."

Carrie waited patiently whilst Mrs. Barrow, for that was the name on her desk, rummaged through a filing cabinet.

"Ah! Here we are," she sighed. "All you need to know and more. Take it away with you with my compliments."

"Thank you, Mrs. Barrow."

"Don't mention it. Now, is there anything else?"

"Yes please, would you mind if I telephoned for a cab? My train leaves in forty minutes. If I miss that I'll have to stay over until tomorrow and my funds won't quite stretch to that."

"Certainly. If you wait on the steps of Bronglais with your luggage I'll direct the driver to pick you up there. Just hold on while I ring the station and see if there's one available."

Mrs. Barrow rang the cab rank and nodded firmly at Carrie as she replaced the receiver.

"That's fine. There'll be one along in about ten minutes.

You should be in ample time for your train."

Carrie thanked her again and collected her case from the hospital porter and waited on the steps as directed. Before ten minutes had elapsed the familiar shape of a black cab drew up in front of the building. Carrie recognised the cheery face of the cabbie that had helped her the previous day.

"Hello there. How did you get on at Mrs. Montgomery's?"

"Fine! She was everything you said and more," said Carrie loading her case onto the board at the front.

"Good, that's nice to know. I don't want to recommend somewhere and disappoint the customer. And, more importantly, how did you get on with the job?"

Carrie flushed with pleasure, "It's mine," she said beaming.

"Well done you, now hop aboard, you've a train to catch." And with that Carrie made herself comfortable in the back and they set off for the station.

Carrie yawned and stretched. She glanced at her watch. The train was due to arrive in Crynant in ten minutes. She had just managed to get the connection from Neath with minutes to spare due to a delay on the line. She wondered if John would be there to meet her with the cart, otherwise she'd have a long hike home. But, she needn't have worried, for as the train pulled into the platform she could see him standing there, his eyes, searching the carriages, as each one trundled past.

Carrie gave him a quick wave, their eyes met, and his face lit up in a smile when he saw her. He hurried along the platform to her carriage door and wrested it open as the train came to a grinding halt.

"Carrie!" he exclaimed and lifted her off her feet as she stepped out. John gave his sister a quick hug and then retrieved her bag from the carriage, carrying it for her as they left the station for the waiting wagon.

"Well? How did you get on?" he asked anxiously.

"I got it," said Carrie with a satisfied grin.

"That's wonderful," said John. But Carrie didn't see the light leave his eyes to be replaced with a terrible sadness.

Some forty minutes later the wagon rolled into the yard. It was now quite dark. Trix was there to meet them and Ernie had a freshly brewed pot of tea waiting to be poured.

"Well then, cariad, tell us all about it," enthused Ernie in his gravelly voice, and for the second time that evening she went into detail of her visit and interview at Aberystwyth.

Carrie had barely time to pause for breath when there was a knock on the door. Carrie looked in surprise at John. It was unusual for visitors to call so late at Gelli Galed.

"I hope nothing's wrong," murmured Carrie thinking of Mam-gu, as John went to answer the door.

"It's probably that young man of yours," winked Ernie, "Wanting to know how you got on."

"What young man? I don't have a young man. Stop talking in riddles, Ernie."

"The sounds of voices drifted through the passage and presently John returned followed by Michael Lawrence.

"Mr. Lawrence?"

"Sorry to call so late but I saw the lights of the wagon go past when I was out in the barn with one of my ewes. I guessed it must be you and I had to find out how you had got on."

Once again Carrie launched into an account of her interview at Aberystwyth.

"So you see," she concluded, "You are now looking at Auxiliary Nurse Carrie Llewellyn of the Maternity Unit Carradog Road, Aberystwyth." And she giggled mischievously.

"Well done," he congratulated, "Perhaps my mother's brooch brought you luck after all." He nodded at the butterfly adorning the neck of her blouse.

Carrie blushed, "Luck had nothing to do with it, my own talent and determination won the day." She started to remove the pin from her blouse, "Here, thank you for the thought." She offered him the brooch.

"I had hoped you might want to keep it," Michael said quietly.

"Well," Carrie hesitated and John stepped forward.

"If my sister wishes to return it, Sir, then I think you should accept." John took the butterfly and pressed it into Michael's hand, "You should know my sister by now, Sir, that she means what she says."

"I would rather hear from Miss Llewellyn herself," said Michael quietly.

Ernie looked across at John and frowned, "Aren't you over reacting a little, John?"

John blustered and turned on a surprised Carrie, "I thought you wanted no truck with the man?" John hesitated fractionally and when he received no answer turned on his heel and crashed out of the kitchen.

Carrie looked after her brother in embarrassment and dismay.

Ernie said softly, "Your going has hit him harder than you know, cariad."

"I've come at an awkward time," muttered Michael apologetically. "I'll see you again." He looked at the brooch in his hand, "Will you change your mind?"

Carrie confused by the rush of emotions flooding through her shook her head, "You heard my brother, Mr. Lawrence. I never change my mind." She stared defiantly at him.

"I was mistaken," Michael volunteered, "I thought you made your own decisions, not have them foisted on you by others. It would seem you are not so much of your own woman after all. I'll see myself out." Michael turned crisply and marched down the passage from the kitchen.

For a moment Carrie was speechless, she wasn't quite sure what was happening here, but in seconds her fiery temper had returned and she shouted after him, "Next time wait until you're invited!" Her answer was the slamming of the front door.

Carrie plonked herself down in the chair as she pulled off her hat. She looked at Ernie, "I behaved badly, didn't I?" she questioned.

Ernie raised his wiry brows.

"All right," she muttered. "You don't have to answer."

Ernie continued to stare at her.

"Stop it, Ernie. You're making me feel guilty."

"So you should be my girl. He only called out of kindness and was met with a barrel of rudeness. It will be a long while before he comes calling again."

"Suits me."

"Does it? I thought you were letting bygones be bygones?"

"Yes, well..." Carrie had no real reply or excuse for her behaviour. "All right, stop looking at me like that, like I've murdered the cat or something. I'll go and see him in the morning."

"If I were you, I'd go and see your brother now," Ernie nodded sagely.

"Yes... I can't think what's got into him." And Carrie rose from her seat and went out in search of her brother. Ernie looked into the flickering flames of the fire. He had seen the look on John's face, the fierce anger and the passionate jealousy and he was worried.

Gelli Galed

Twenty

Carrie sat on her bed, deep in thought. Ernie's words were going round and round her brain, "Carrie fach, there's trouble brewing for you, trouble that's going to break hearts and minds."

She puzzled over this trying to make sense of what he'd said. She didn't think he meant Michael Lawrence, in fact she was sure he was referring to John.

A furious blush spilt over Carrie's cheeks as she remembered incidents from the past. Surely Ernie couldn't have known of the intimacies that had nearly passed between her and John and yet... She felt guilty at what his words implied.

A terrible sadness gripped her heart as she started to undress for bed. She looked around her room, memories of her childhood and life stared unblinkingly at her from the walls.

Mam's treasured silver vanity set glinted brightly and a tide of emotion washed through her. "Oh Mam," she whispered huskily to herself, "What would you do?"

The light from the oil lamp flickered round the room together with a soft breeze that rippled the hem of the curtains and a warm feeling spread from her toes throughout her body; a feeling of inexplicable calm placated and quieted her pounding heart.

Carrie knew she had to leave even if it did hurt John. She had to fulfil her own ambitions and desires. Confined forever to a life on the farm would blunt her soul and constrain her mind. She had to leave to be true to herself, to live and grow before returning to settle and fight for her rights and Hendre.

Her mother would wish it; wish for her to follow her heart and dreams and be true to herself. The stubborn pride of Miri Llewellyn coursed through her veins. Carrie knew she had to harden her heart to achieve her aims.

The face of Michael Lawrence interrupted her thoughts.

Emblazoned with passion she tried to brush his image from her mind, but obstinately it refused to go.

She talked sternly to herself, "Now, my girl, remove that young man from your mind, he's not for you," and she vigorously brushed her fiery Titian hair into a soft spangled mass of curls.

Carrie slipped between the cool cotton sheets. She lay there, her hair showering the pillow with its wild tresses. Sleep eluded her. Her mind leapt and raced as she started thinking through all the possible permutations of her situation and relationships.

The resonant tones of the grandfather clock struck two. Carrie leaned across to her bedside table and turned down the wick on the lamp. The enveloping darkness was comforting. She embedded her head in the pillow willing a peaceful slumber to come. As dawn was breaking she eventually drifted off into a fitful, restless sleep.

There was great excitement next morning after the arrival of the postman. An entertaining letter from Aunty Annie had been delivered with an enclosure from Thomas who had managed to raise his fare and was travelling back to England. The letter had taken six weeks to reach the Llewellyn's and by Carrie's reckoning cousin Thomas would be arriving in Britain in less than two weeks. This welcome news lightened Carrie's feelings of guilt. She knew now that help would be on hand to run the farm in the form of cousin Tom.

The weekend passed quickly as Carrie sorted out her belongings and packed her trunk. The spare bedroom was aired, the bed made up and the tallboy emptied of all its clutter. Before Carrie was to leave she wanted to be certain that everything would be ready for Thomas.

Thoughts of Michael Lawrence no longer hampered Carrie's thinking. She put him out of her mind completely, refusing to be drawn on any question about him from Ernie.

Carrie struggled with the lid of her trunk, trying to force it shut. She bounced up and down on it several times but couldn't quite manage to get the lock to connect.

"John! John," she clamoured from the door of her room.

"What?" came the reply from the foot of the stairs.

"Come and give me a hand, I can't get this thing to close."

John bounded up the stairs two at a time and pushed open her door. He saw the wardrobe door swing open depleted of Carrie's clothes. He looked around her room, noting the trinkets and ornaments she had removed.

"Not taking Mam's set then?"

"No, it's too precious to risk. I don't want it stolen. Besides, I have to leave something of me here so that you'll know I'll be coming back."

"And will you, Carrie? Will you be coming back?"

"Of course. In time, you'll see." And the beginnings of a blush started to grow on her cheeks. John's penetrating stare seemed to reach out and pull at her, irresistibly; bringing her closer. In fact John had taken two steps towards her. He took her by the shoulders and gazed soulfully into her eyes, those woodland pools in which he yearned to drown with desire.

Carrie tried to break the spell by sitting down firmly on the trunk with a bump. She giggled deliciously, "Come on John, lend a seat!"

John sat beside her, his proximity was disturbing. She giggled again, this time a little nervously.

"Come on, you're not trying. I've got to get it shut. On a count of three stand and bounce down, see if that will do the trick."

"It's no good, cariad. You've put too much in. You'll have to leave something behind."

"I can't. I need everything. Come on, John. Try once, just for me?"

"How can I refuse?"

They performed their routine and landed with a jolt on the trunk. Electric needles pulsed through John's arm as shoulder brushed shoulder. Carrie's laughter died away and she bit her lip as John turned his head to hers. A sigh melted on his lips and Carrie saw with alarm that he was bending to kiss her. She felt unable to pull away, unable to fight the powerful instincts that smouldered within him threatening to spark and ignite inside her. A thousand thoughts scrambled for understanding in her mind all in the fraction of a second.

When John's searching mouth was nearly upon hers a gravelly voice awoke her from her hypnotic trance and she started with a jump.

"Hello you two, need a hand? Looks more like you need another seat," greeted Ernie from the door. His interruption was most fortuitous thought Carrie and in that moment she knew that she was right to be leaving.

"Ernie!" Carrie exclaimed. "Come and help."

John moved back as if he'd been stung. Wild fury hurricaned dangerously in his eyes, which he suppressed and stilled. But Ernie noticed. Ernie saw and knew and John was ashamed.

An air of false frivolity entered the proceedings and between them they managed to close the trunk, which Carrie locked before it, had an opportunity to burst open yet again.

John left the room muttering jokingly, "I'll just check the cart. See if it will support that thing."

Ernie turned to Carrie and added gutturally, "If there was a maggot of doubt about going surely, it must be all eaten up now?"

Carrie nodded silently, her heart pounding. She too, was afraid to face her innermost feelings. She too, was afraid to look inside her soul in case what she saw was a betrayal of Miri and Bryn.

Carrie stood up from the trunk and picked up her cloche hat tossing it on the bed. She surveyed the room around her and the faces of those she held dear. Faces that she was soon only to carry in her heart.

A new chapter in her life was beginning.

Lightning Source UK Ltd.
Milton Keynes UK
UKOW041803170413

209389UK00001B/1/P